Here's what critics are saying about
Anne Marie Stoddard's books:

"*Murder at Castle Rock* is Amelia Grace's first appearance, and I hope it won't be her last."
—Cozy Mystery Book Reviews

"Murder takes center stage and demands an encore in *Murder at Castle Rock*, a fast-paced and entertaining backstage pass to mystery"
—Rochelle Staab, bestselling author of the Mind for Murder mystery series

"The book emphasizes rock 'n' roll, but not at the expense of the mystery, which is packed with surprises. There are so many layers, motives, and hidden agendas that I had a good time untangling it all."
—P.J. Morse, author of *Heavy Mental*

GH00801669

BOOKS BY ANNE MARIE STODDARD

Amelia Grace Rock 'n' Roll Mysteries:

Murder at Castle Rock

Caper at Castle Rock
(short story in the "Killer Beach Reads" collection)

Deception at Castle Rock

Sleighed at Castle Rock
(holiday short story)

DECEPTION AT CASTLE ROCK

an Amelia Grace
Rock 'n' Roll Mystery

Anne Marie Stoddard

This book is dedicated to Teri Phillips.

Acknowledgements

While the list of people I would like to thank for supporting me while I wrote this book could probably fill enough pages to be its own novel, I'd like to take a quick moment to single out a few individuals to whom I owe extreme gratitude. Thank you first and foremost to my husband, Eric, for your unwavering support, love, and understanding when I'd stay glued to my computer trying to meet my deadline. Second, to Theresa Green, thank you for your criminal justice expertise and for being the best beta reader/part-time editor/pep talk giver I could ask for. Thank you to my editors, Sally and Wendi, for giving the book the polish it needed to really shine. To my publisher, Gemma Halliday, thank you so much for believing in my writing and giving me a chance to share Amelia and her friends with the world. Last, thank you to anyone who takes the time to read this book or any other story in the Amelia Grace series. Getting to share Ame and her world with you has been a dream come true.

CHAPTER ONE

———

"Flight Five-Four-Two from Los Angeles." I squinted at the screen mounted to the nearby wall. It was a warm spring Friday in mid-June, and I was standing in the middle of Atlanta's Hartsfield-Jackson Airport. "It looks like the plane arrived twenty minutes ago," I called over the noise of the bustling baggage claim area.

My best friend, Kat Taylor, was perched on the edge of an aluminum bench a few feet away, flipping through a discarded copy of *SkyMall*. "What is it about these catalogs that makes me want the most random junk?" She scrunched her nose and held up the magazine so I could see the page she'd been reading. "Like, who knew that glow-in-the-dark toilet seats were a thing?" She giggled. "No, wait. I get it—so you don't have to blind yourself with the bathroom light if you get up in the middle of the night to pee. Why didn't I ever think of that?"

"Maybe we should get those for Castle Rock's bathrooms. They'd be perfect for the Black Light Rave Night in the Dungeon next month." I smirked. "Anyway, the guys should be walking up any minute."

Kat set the magazine on the bench and came to stand next to me. "Can you believe it's been five years?" she asked. The last time we'd seen Jack Pearson, Mickey Ward, and Chad Egan, they were just three college dropouts dreaming of recording an indie-rock album. Our pals left Georgia State senior year and moved to L.A. to try to land a record deal. Half a decade later, they were three-fifths of the mega-famous rock outfit, Royal Flush.

"Shouldn't be hard to spot 'em," Kat said, surveying the crowd. "Just look for the throng of swooning girls." Her light brown hair bounced as she dubiously shook her head. "You'd think they were freakin' One Direction the way women get their panties wet over them." She rolled her eyes. "It's kind of ridiculous."

"Be nice," I scolded, though I was smiling. "They're still the same old goofball stoners from down the hall in the dorm freshman year. Plus they hooked us up with exclusive booking rights for all of their shows in Atlanta."

Kat rested her hands on her hips. "Which would be great if they played here even once in the past five years. It's like they've been shunning ATL until now. Where's the hometown love?"

I shrugged. "Yeah, well, that's part of what made the tickets for tomorrow night sell out so fast." I patted her arm. "Come on. It'll be fun to see them—like a mini college reunion."

"Yeah." Kat nodded, her lips twisting in a goofy grin. "I can't wait to see if Chad can still throw down on some Mario Kart like the old days. My Xbox is on the top shelf in my closet, just in case."

"You bet your skinny butt I can, Taylor," called a voice from behind us. Kat and I exchanged excited looks and turned to find a lanky, red-haired man strutting toward us. "Hey there, strangers." His freckled face stretched in a wide smile as he set down his luggage and wrapped one arm around Kat.

"Chad!" Kat squealed, returning his hug.

Chad pulled me close with his other arm. "Hey, Amelia. Long time no see."

When he'd released us both, Kat stepped back and sized him up. "Dude, you haven't changed a bit."

Chad Egan arched a bushy, red eyebrow. "Not true. I didn't have these before." He pointed to the quarter-sized black discs plugging his gauged earlobes. "Or this," he added, lifting his shirt. Tattooed on his pale chest were five playing cards—the ace, king, queen, jack, and ten of hearts. The bottom half of each card was missing, and bright red-and-orange flames licked at what remained. Beneath the burning cards was a pile of black ash that spelled the letters *R* and *F* for Royal Flush. "So, what do you think?" Chad shifted his gaze back and forth from his ink to Kat and me, trying to read our reactions. "Pretty wicked, huh?"

"Very," I said, giving him a high five.

"Badass!" Kat reached out and poked at the tat with one finger and then tickled Chad's ribs.

"Cut it out, K." He laughed and grabbed her shoulders, holding her at arm's length as he looked her up and down. "*You've* definitely changed—you went and got hot while I was away." He gave an appreciative whistle.

"Please!" Kat scoffed. "I was always hot, and you know it." That was true—my best friend had looked like a Victoria's Secret model since high school. She had wavy light brown hair that tumbled down past her shoulders, eyes like blue chips of ice, full heart-shaped lips, and legs for days. Though I didn't look half-bad myself, hanging around Kat had sealed my fate as the perpetually single sidekick up until college.

"Yeah, yeah." Chad rolled his eyes. "So, about this Mario Kart face-off—"

"I hate to break up the love fest, y'all," I interrupted. "But where is the rest of the band?"

Chad aimed a sly grin my way. "Yo, slow your roll, Ame," he said, using the old nickname Kat gave me when we were kids, like *Amy* without the *y*. "I beat the rest of the guys off the plane. I know you're dying to see your old lover boy, but chill. He'll be along in a minute."

Heat rushed to my cheeks. "I wasn't just talking about Mickey," I protested. Royal Flush's drummer, Mickey Ward, was my first serious boyfriend. We'd dated for about a year and a half in college that ended in a messy breakup right before the guys skipped town. I hadn't spoken to him since. Five years was a long time to go without official closure, but I'd moved on a long time ago. That's what I kept telling myself, anyway. Still, the thought of seeing Mickey again after so long filled my stomach with butterflies—something I wasn't about to admit to Chad.

"Oh, come on." Kat eyed me pointedly. "That hot outfit you're rockin' has nothing to do with the fact that you're about to see Mickey for the first time since college—seriously?"

"What?" I glanced down at my tight-fitting, knee-length, blue wrap dress with a plunging neckline, which I'd paired with a cute pair of black leather ankle boots. It was a far cry from my normal work wear: the first thing from my laundry pile that wasn't too wrinkled and smelled clean enough. "I was just trying to look more professional." I smoothed a wrinkle in the fabric near my waistline. "We are technically working right now, after all—picking up tomorrow night's performers."

Kat wagged a finger at me. "Don't give me that, Missy. I see the way you dress on a daily basis, remember? And that includes the occasional chauffeur duty from the airport." She reached out and lightly tugged a strand of my shoulder-length auburn locks. "You don't straighten your hair and break out the mascara for just anyone. When's the last time you came to work not sporting jeans and a ponytail?" *Damn.* The downside to having a best friend who's known me since we were in diapers is that she's mastered Amelia Grace Psychology 101. I can't get anything past her.

"Busted!" Chad cried gleefully.

I shot Kat an arctic look. "Traitor," I muttered. So, I dressed a little fancier than usual today. There's no rule that says a girl can't look her best when seeing an ex again for the first time post-breakup, even if she no longer has feelings for him. "Is it a crime to try to look nice for my friends?" I asked indignantly. "And besides, I'm seeing someone—you know that, Kat." My cold expression thawed a little at the thought of Emmett, my boyfriend of the past seven months.

"Hey, good for you, Ame." Chad grinned, holding out his fist so I could bump it with my own. "Get you some!"

"Get some what?" The familiar masculine voice made my insides flutter. Keeping my breathing even, I raised my eyes toward the man walking up to meet us. "Hey," Mickey Ward said, his lips pulled wide in a brilliant smile. The noise of the busy airport fell away when we locked gazes. My mind ran through a gag-worthy montage of our college romance that was one sappy Paula Cole song away from being an episode of *Dawson's Creek:* meeting Mickey in our music management class, sharing our first kiss on the quad after a Georgia State basketball game, the look on his face when he'd spot me in the crowd at one of his gigs—and the devastation in his eyes when I handed back the engagement ring he'd just placed on my finger. *Stop that,* I chided myself. *This isn't some made-for-TV movie. Don't make things weird.* So what if I hadn't seen him since the day I'd turned down his proposal? We could still be normal around each other, right? Of course, *normal* for Mickey and me was being attached at the lips...and maybe a few other parts. *Crap.*

"Hi, stranger," I said, trying to sound casual as I looked him over. "Long time no see." The extra five years looked good on Mickey—he was tall and broad-shouldered, not quite as trim as he'd been in college, but still in great shape. His brown hair had grown down to his shoulders and was tied loosely behind his neck. Mickey's face was round with a soft jaw line, and there was still a little white scar on his chin from a shaving accident when he was seventeen. He'd never been conventionally handsome, but in all honesty, that was part of why I was attracted to him to begin with. That, and his eyes. Mickey had the sweetest eyes I'd ever seen—warm and golden brown, like two drops of wild honey. Even staring into them now made me want to melt.

"And you," Mickey began and then paused, as if not sure what to say. "Amelia, you look...wow." I glanced down at my own slightly slimmer figure, giving myself a mental high five for shaving off about ten pounds this year doing yoga. I looked back up just as Mickey's face broke into that charming boyish grin that I fell in love with in college. Despite my best effort to keep cool, my insides turned to mush. "I can't believe you're really standing in front of me right now," he said. Mickey slid his carry-on bag off his shoulder and dropped it at his feet, holding his arms open wide. "Get over here!"

I stepped forward to accept Mickey's hug. The smell of his Burberry cologne sent even more memories spiraling through me. *He still wears the same scent I bought him for Valentine's Day junior year.* I gulped, pulling away from his embrace before he seemed ready to release me. I cast a glance at Chad and Kat, who were huddled close together, staring at our interaction and whispering to each other like a pair of gossiping housewives.

Chad caught my eye and broke away from Kat to join us. He slung a casual arm around my shoulder. "Ame was just telling us about her new man," he said to Mickey, his mouth quirking at the corners. Chad really hadn't changed a bit since our Georgia State days—he always liked to stir the pot. For once I was relieved that he was a sucker for drama: he'd broken the news to Mickey so that I wouldn't have to. Still, I hated seeing the glint of pain in Mickey's eyes. Maybe I wasn't the only one looking for closure.

"Oh." Mickey quickly recovered from the look of regret that flashed across his handsome face. "Good," he said warmly. "I'm happy for you."

"Thanks." I suddenly felt self-conscious in my tight dress. I slipped out from under Chad's arm and adjusted the purse strap on my shoulder. "Hey, there's Jack!" I pointed toward the mob of women, young and old, who were crowded around our college buddy and his entourage. The Royal Flush front man was signing autographs and flashing his signature half-smile as fans shoved in front of each other to snap photos with him. Standing behind Jack and his flock of lusty ladies were two men who I recognized as the newest members of Royal Flush, Sid Malone and Zane Calloway. Sid joined the guys right before they left Atlanta, and they'd met Zane out in L.A.

A curvy woman with fiery red hair ushered Jack and the others through the throng of women, shooing more fans away with her over-sized rolling suitcase. "We've gotta go," she commanded as they reached us. "If we don't lose these broads now Jack will be signing autographs in this freakin' airport until next Easter."

"That's why we should've sprung for a private jet," Chad quipped from beside me.

The woman rolled her eyes at him. "It would've been a waste of money considering Jack's the only one the ladies are flipping out for. I don't see a flock of girls knocking over luggage carts to get to *you*, Egan."

Chad stuck out his bottom lip. "I'm incognito," he said, pulling his shades down over his eyes.

"I'd knock down a cart to meet you," Kat said, bumping him with her shoulder. Chad's cheeks turned pink.

"You must be Ginger," I said, stepping forward and extending my hand to the red-haired woman.

She shook my hand. "Yes. I'm Ginger Robbins." Her tone was professional yet polite. She squinted at me. "Amelia, right? I believe we spoke on the phone a few times."

"That's right." As both the booking agent and general manager for Castle Rock, I handled all of the paperwork and dealt with tour managers like Ginger for each concert we produced. "We've rented an Escalade so that Kat can take you and the band over to the hotel. I've also got my car parked nearby to transport luggage if needed."

"Thank you." Ginger's glossy lips parted to show perfectly white teeth. "The tour bus will be here tomorrow morning with all the gear, but the rest of our luggage should be coming down the chute any minute." She inclined her head toward Jack, who was nuzzling the neck of a short, dark-haired woman I assumed was his latest girlfriend. "Can you believe he's got a whole carry-on just for his hair products?" Ginger asked in a conspiratorial whisper. She shook her head and made a clucking sound with her tongue. "Rock stars."

I smiled. I liked this woman already.

Kat wagged her finger back and forth, counting everyone in Royal Flush's entourage. "It looks like there are too many people to fit in the Escalade," she said, turning to Ginger and me. "It seats seven, including the driver."

My eyes roved over the group in front of us. Five members of the band, plus Ginger, Kat, me, and the girl glued to Jack's side.

"Hmm." I chewed my lip. "Someone can ride with me in my Jetta."

"I'll do it," Mickey offered, a smile cresting his lips. "It'll give us a chance to catch up."

I exchanged a wide-eyed look with Kat. "Er—" I stammered, trying to think of an excuse to have anyone but Mickey ride along with me. Being alone in a car with my ex-almost-fiancé was dangerous territory.

Mickey saw my expression, and his own face fell. "Hey, I don't bite," he said, sounding hurt. "I just thought it'd be nice to talk. I wanna know what you've been up to for the past five years."

Getting over you, for starters. I forced down the lump in my throat. *Come on, we're both adults. It's just a quick ride. It's not like he's proposing marriage...again.* "Sure, that'd be great," I said evenly.

After hugging Jack and greeting the rest of the band, Kat and I helped them retrieve their luggage. Then we headed into the parking garage where Kat led the others to the Escalade while Mickey and I climbed into my little gray car. I ducked my head so he couldn't see the involuntary look of panic that crossed my face as he slid in beside me. Being trapped alone in a moving vehicle with my ex was pretty far up there on my list of awkward situations I'd like to avoid, and yet, here I was. I took a deep breath as I backed out of the parking space, silently praying he wouldn't want to talk about why things between us had gone sour.

Turning down Mickey's proposal hadn't been part of my life plan. For the longest time, I really thought we would be together forever. But when he got down on one knee and popped the question right after telling me that he and the guys were dropping out of college to move to L.A., something inside me sort of…snapped. It didn't matter how much I cared for Mickey—I wanted to stay in Atlanta and graduate. I just didn't see myself fitting into the life he wanted for himself: on the road with the band, never staying in the same city for more than a couple of days, never sleeping in his own bed.

Back then, all I wanted was to find a steady job in the music industry and work toward owning my own venue here in Atlanta. Kat and I had achieved that dream last year by taking over Castle Rock. I was happy with the path I chose, but—full disclosure—I'd be lying if I said I didn't often think about what might have happened if I'd said yes to an adventure-filled life on the road with Mickey. While I was happy the band was back in town, having him around this weekend was going to stir up all those doubts and feelings again.

Just grin and bear it, I thought as I pulled my Jetta onto I-85. *It'll all be over soon.*

* * *

To his credit, Mickey gave me a good twenty minutes of enjoyable conversation before he dredged up the topic of our failed relationship. We chatted about what life was like for him in California and how much fun it was to be on the road. He

even shared a few crazy stories from Royal Flush's world tour—
including being chased by an unruly rooster around a hotel
courtyard in China. Gradually we tested the waters of
reminiscing our college days.

"Have you talked to Dillon lately?" I asked, referring to
our old buddy Dillon Green, Royal Flush's original bass player.
Jack booted him from the band just weeks before the guys
moved out west. Being with Mickey at the time, I knew Jack's
claim that they'd had 'creative differences' was to cover up the
real reason he'd kicked the old bassist to the curb—Dill had
drunkenly made a pass at Jack's girlfriend.

"Nah." Mickey gave a dismissive wave. "We used to text
back and forth sometimes, back when Royal Flush was first
starting out in Cali. After a while, we just kind of lost touch. You
know how it is." Out of the corner of my eye, I saw him sneak a
glance at me before turning to gaze out the window.

"Yeah. To be honest, I don't even know if he's still in
town," I admitted. "Kat and I were never really close with him. I
guess with you guys gone, he didn't see the need to stay friends
with us."

"What a shame." Mickey shook his head. "He was such a
cool guy before that beef with Jack. Part of me has always felt a
little guilty that we blew up right after he left the band. That
success should've been his too."

"Oh, hey!" I reached for the volume dial on my radio.
"Speaking of your success..." Royal Flush's first big single, "The
Hand You're Dealt," emanated from the car speakers. "This one
takes me back," I said, bobbing my head up and down as we
cruised the interstate. I peeked over at Mickey. "Do you ever get
used to hearing your own music on the radio?"

He shrugged. "Yes and no. It was a lot more exciting
back when we first got our break, ya know? Flipping from
station to station, waiting for a deejay to play one of our singles,
seeing our names move up every week on the *Billboard* charts—
there's no other feeling like it." Mickey paused. When he spoke
again, his voice was softer and a little sad. "But even all of that
kind of loses its thrill when you don't have someone special to
share it with."

Here we go. I sucked in a breath and mentally braced myself. *Let's just get this over with.*

"I miss you," Mickey said quietly. In my periphery, I saw his hand move toward my knee. At the last second he pulled back, curling his fingers away from me.

"Mickey, look," I started, my voice harsh from frustration. I took a beat to collect myself and softened my tone. "I miss you too," I admitted. "A lot. But we were just kids back then." Cliché or not, it was the truth. "You've been gone five years. We're not even the same people anymore. If you had really wanted to be with me, you would've come back. But you—"

"That's not fair," he interjected, his voice bitter. His hand clenched into a fist in his lap. "You meant the world to me, but the band was going places. I couldn't just throw away everything we'd worked for—the guys were counting on me. I wanted you to come with us."

"I know." I stifled a sigh. "I don't blame you for leaving, Mickey. You've been living your dream for the past five years, and that's not something that many people can say." A sad little smile curved my lips. "I'm proud of you. Really."

"Thanks," Mickey said, but his tone was melancholy. Silence stretched between us for several long moments before he spoke again. "I just wanted you to know that I regret it," he said quietly. "Storming out like I did when you said you wouldn't marry me. Never coming back. That—that's not how things should have ended between us."

"I appreciate you saying that." I kept my left hand on the steering wheel and reached down with my right hand to touch his arm. "And I'm glad you guys found a new tour manager to replace me. Ginger seems nice."

"Yeah, she's all right," Mickey agreed. "A bit of a hard-ass sometimes, though. And no one could ever really replace you. You're still the best manager the band's ever had." He cleared his throat. "So, tell me about your new guy. He's good to you, I hope."

"He is." I couldn't help but grin as I thought about my new beau. I'd met FBI Special Agent Emmett Larson last November when an assignment brought him to Castle Rock. He and his partner were investigating an allegedly reformed Vegas mobster named Shawn Stone. As it turned out, Stone was still very active in his mob family's business. When I found myself in the middle of all the chaos, Emmett came to my rescue. Though the attraction between us was undeniable from the moment we met, it wasn't until Emmett saved my life that we acted on our feelings.

Unfortunately, when Stone caught wind that the feds were closing in, he skipped town. Emmett and his partner, Special Agent Gavin Addison, hadn't been far behind him. That was seven months ago, and since then I'd only seen Emmett in person five or six times. We talked on the phone several times a week, but the frequent calls were no substitute for up-close-and-personal affection, if you know what I mean. Of course, I wasn't going to share all of this with my ex.

The sun had set by the time we reached North Avenue, and darkness slowly curled around the cityscape. "Wow," Mickey murmured when we crested a hill and Castle Rock came into view. He gazed out the window as we drove past the large, gray building. The venue had been named for its resemblance to a gothic castle—similar to the ones you see in movies like *Dracula* or *Robin Hood*. It was a huge structure of stones, wooden doors, turrets and parapets—the whole nine yards. We even had a majestic rear tower that, well, *towered* (for lack of a better word) over the surrounding neighborhood. Two large, red flags with black guitars waved in the breeze high atop the building, like beacons that attracted music lovers from all over Atlanta and beyond. That, as well as the flashing electric red "Castle Rock" sign, made us pretty hard to miss. The venue stuck out from the surrounding condos and skyscrapers like a Marilyn Manson fan at a Taylor Swift concert.

"I can't believe we're finally playing there tomorrow night." Mickey sounded awestruck. "I used to dream about selling out a show at Castle Rock as kid. And now you freaking *own* the place!"

"Co-own," I corrected him. Kat had inherited Castle Rock from its previous owner under sudden, tragic circumstances. While I still served as Castle Rock's general manager and booking agent, Kat had graciously asked me to be her business partner. Having dreamed about owning a concert venue since high school, I'd happily accepted.

Mickey and I rode in companionable silence for several more minutes until we reached the Georgian Terrace Hotel on the corner of Peachtree and Ponce de Leon. "Are you and Kat joining us for dinner?" Mickey asked, lingering in the passenger seat as I pulled up behind Kat's rental Escalade.

I smiled apologetically. "Can't. We've got a show starting in…" I checked my watch, "…twenty minutes. How about we grab coffee tomorrow morning instead?" I'd blurted the invitation without even thinking—wanting to spend more time with Mickey just felt natural. Regret rushed in as soon as I caught the eager look on his face. Did he think it was a date?

Mickey's lips quirked. "Sure. I can't wait." He started to lean toward me, his eyes half-closed. When I pulled back slightly, he hesitated, and his face flushed an embarrassed red. "Sorry," Mickey said sheepishly. "Old habits die hard, ya know?" Without another word, he ducked out of the car and moved to unload the luggage from my trunk.

When Mickey was gone, I smacked my forehead with my palm. *He wanted to kiss me,* I thought, remembering with bittersweet clarity how it felt to press my lips against his, to close my eyes as he wound his hands in my hair. I exhaled a shaky breath. *I would've kissed him back.* That realization was dangerous—I had a boyfriend, for crying out loud! A sweet, sexy, hard-working boyfriend who, at this very moment, was hunting down a lunatic so he could keep me safe. Yet, like an idiot, I'd just asked a man who was technically my *ex-fiancé* out for coffee. Just the two of us. What had I been thinking?

That it feels good to see him again, chimed a voice in my head, a bit wistfully. I'd missed Mickey a lot more than I realized. Our banter in the car had only been a watered-down version of the deep connection we once shared, but it was enough to stir something inside me. *It's a good thing Mickey's leaving town on Sunday,* I thought guiltily as Emmett's face flashed through my mind. *Or I'd be in big trouble.*

CHAPTER TWO

───────

"How'd it go with Mickey?" Kat asked, leaning against my car. It was ten minutes later, and we had just pulled into Castle Rock's employee parking lot.

"Fine," I said quickly. I was reluctant to spill the details of our awkward good-bye at the hotel.

"Just fine? No earth-shattering confession about how he's still madly in love with you?" she asked. I looked up to find her smirking.

"Hey, don't mock me!" I laughed and playfully pushed Kat's hand off my car. In a more serious tone, I added, "We're okay now, I think. He said he misses me, but we're both better off."

"Good." Kat grinned. "For a minute there I was worried we'd all get caught up in the drama between you two this weekend."

"Us? Drama?" I deadpanned. "Never." I climbed out of the car and stood on shaky feet. Kat waited patiently while I leaned down to stretch. I'd been stabbed in the leg back in the fall, and the blade had practically torn my left calf muscle to shreds. Thankfully, the damage wasn't permanent, but it had been a rough recovery. In typical clumsy Amelia fashion, I'd also sprained my left ankle just a few weeks ago. Now that I was finally back on two feet again, I was being extra careful.

Kat's happy mood deflated as she stepped into the corridor that led to our offices. She stopped halfway down the hall, her eyes fixed on the wall to her left. I watched her gently run her hand across the small, black frame that housed the first ticket stub and dollar collected by the venue's previous owner, Parker Deering.

It had been less than a year since Parker's murder. The months following his death weren't easy for any of us, but his death was especially hard on Kat. She put on a brave face most of the time, but there were still moments when her grief bubbled to the surface.

Kat's hand hovered over the frame, and her slender fingers trembled. I stood beside her, catching her misty-eyed reflection in the glass. A sad little sigh escaped her lips. "Seven months and it still feels like it was just yesterday." She turned to face me, a glint of pain in her blue eyes. "Will it ever get better?"

"I wish I could say that it will, but I honestly don't know." I'd never lost someone as close to me as Parker was to Kat—splitting up with Mickey was rough, but it couldn't compare to something as final and dreadful as dying. I squeezed Kat's shoulder. "But I *do* know he'd want you to keep moving forward, and I'm here to help you do that. We all are."

She nodded. Her hand dropped from the frame and fell to her side. Kat took a deep breath to regain her composure then blew it out. "The show must go on, right?" she asked, a ghost of a smile forming on her lips.

"You betcha." I grabbed her arm and tugged gently, guiding her down the hall toward the Dungeon. "Speaking of, Silent Echo should be on stage right about now. Let's check 'em out."

*　*　*

"Soooo, what do you think?" Bronwyn Sinclair asked, eying us both expectantly.

My gaze swept around the downstairs showroom. "Um," I stammered, not sure what to say. The Dungeon holds roughly the same capacity as our upstairs room, High Court, but the similarities end there. Where High Court has a vaulted ceiling with a colorful mural and a large ornate chandelier, its downstairs counterpart is dark and gritty, with a low ceiling and no overhead lighting—just a few lamps bolted to the walls.

Tonight those lamps were lit with black light bulbs, thanks to Bronwyn's handiwork. We'd recently promoted Bron from intern to marketing and booking assistant. She'd proven herself when she and our assistant manager, Reese Martin, ran Castle Rock by themselves for a weekend while I recovered from my sprained ankle. Kat and I decided to let her schedule tonight's band and handle all of the details on her own—which, for Bronwyn, meant redecorating the Dungeon for the occasion. She'd booked Silent Echo, who was the antithesis of dark, angry rock, to perform in the gothic dungeon-styled showroom. The indie brother-sister duo from California mesmerized the crowd with their ethereal pop vocals and sunny melodies, and the black lights made the colors of their outfits pop like something out of a Katy Perry music video on acid. The entire scene was quirky and a bit off-kilter—just like Bronwyn.

Kat looked around the room. "Maybe we should've ordered those glow-in-the-dark toilet seats from *SkyMall* after all."

"I'm going to assume that means you like what I've done with the place." Bronwyn beamed at her and then turned her green eyes my way. "How did it go with Royal Flush? I still can't believe you used to date Mickey Freakin' Ward." She clasped her hands together. "He's a drumming god—like, better than Travis Barker, even."

"Believe it, chick," Kat said. With a teasing grin, she reached out and pulled the hood of Bronwyn's sweatshirt over the young girl's hot pink hair. "Back in the day, Ame and ol' Mick were hotter than Brad and Angelina, or whoever the current *it* couple is. I can't keep track."

Bronwyn scowled. She yanked off the hood and fussed with her hair until it was back the way she liked it, though it didn't look any less messy. She turned her attention back to me. "If you guys were so into each other, why'd you break up?"

Because he wanted me to put my entire life on hold to be with him, and it scared me shitless. I grimaced. Time for a change of subject. "Any chance you and Reese finished filing that stack of show contracts I left on his desk this afternoon?" I asked, figuring that any mention of our hot assistant manager would get her off my case. After all, Bron's new boyfriend was her favorite topic of discussion.

Bronwyn's face flamed. "Yep!" she chirped, visibly struggling to keep from grinning. I had a feeling that filing paperwork hadn't been all they'd done. After pining after him for nearly a year, Bron had finally landed her man. They were quite the odd couple—twenty-four-year-old Reese had the body of a linebacker and the face of a California surfer, with olive skin, dirty blond curls, and gentle blue-green eyes. Bronwyn, on the other hand, was twenty years old and a petite five-foot-three, with bright pink hair styled in a short pixie cut, and an emerald stud piercing her left nostril. Despite their differences, Reese and Bronwyn were great together, and they both seemed happier than I'd ever seen them. *I guess opposites really do attract.*

Tonight, Bronwyn was dressed in dark denim jeans and a neon green hoodie with black polka dots. In the black lights, her outfit, along with her pink Vans sneakers and bubblegum hair, made her look like a slice of radioactive watermelon. "Isn't Reese amazing?" She sighed dreamily.

"He's lucky to have you," Kat said with a sad little smile. "I wish I were ready to get back in the dating game myself."

"What about Chad?" I asked. "You two had a pretty cozy reunion. Seems to me that little crush you were harboring back in college never quite went away."

Bronwyn cocked her head to one side. "Chad Egan? From Royal Flush?" Her green eyes grew wide. "Ohmigod, I could *totally* see you with him! He's the red-head guitarist with the gauged ears, right?" She nodded, as if answering her own question. "Super hot! You should go for it."

Kat snorted. "Please. It's Chad Egan. The guy's a total goofball."

"You like goofballs," I reminded her. "They make you laugh."

"Yeah, well…" Kat blew out a breath and turned away to watch Silent Echo's performance as she collected her thoughts. She turned back to Bron and me a moment later, her face pinched. "We were always just too good of friends. Plus the guys are only here for a few days. And then there's the tiny little obstacle of me not being ready to jump into another relationship just yet."

I held my hands up in mock surrender. "Okay, okay—no pressure. I'm just saying that it's all right to let yourself have fun. And Chad is definitely fun. Remember the time he pulled the fire alarm at Patton Hall?" Bronwyn gave me a curious look, so I explained. "When everyone got outside, he was sitting in the parking lot with five huge buckets full of water balloons."

I chuckled, remembering Chad's feigned innocence about the gag. *"What? I just happened to be filling these up for a kid's charity balloon fight tomorrow morning. But since we're all out here now..."* He'd started a huge water fight that lasted nearly an hour. It was a miracle he didn't get expelled for the fire alarm prank, but no one could actually prove that he had pulled it.

"Fun? Yes," Kat agreed. "But also kind of insane."

Bronwyn shrugged. "He'd keep life interesting."

We watched the show in silence and then worked together to herd the crowd out of the building at closing time. When the band packed up and left, Kat and I sent the staff home. The incident in the car with Mickey had been eating at me all night, and I finally couldn't hold it in anymore. I had to tell someone. "So, remember how I said nothing happened on the ride to the hotel?" I began, my tone sheepish.

Kat arched one thin eyebrow. "Yeah?"

I swallowed. "Well, that's not entirely true. Mickey sorta...tried to kiss me."

Kat's blue eyes grew large. "He what?"

I shook my head. "I didn't let him—and I don't think I was giving him signals or anything. He just sort of leaned in as he was getting out of the car, like nothing had changed between us and he was kissing me goodnight, like always."

Kat turned to lock the back door behind us. "Old habits die hard, I guess."

"That's what he said." I grimaced. "Maybe it was kinda my fault." I chewed my lip. "Before he tried to kiss me, I invited him to get coffee with me tomorrow morning."

"Just the two of you?"

"Uh-huh."

"Oh boy," Kat muttered. "Here we go."

"What's that supposed to mean?"

She crossed her arms over her chest. "You were practically ready to marry the guy five years ago. If he'd stayed in town, you'd probably be sporting that ring on your finger and balancing Mickey Jr. on your hip." Kat paused, a thoughtful look on her face. "Ya know, maybe letting him back into your life isn't a bad thing."

"Kat, it's just coffee." My words took a slightly defensive tone. "I told you, I gave Mickey plenty of closure on the ride to the hotel. Bucket loads. If we're going to repair our friendship though, we've got to start somewhere. And I don't start anything without a grande iced black coffee." I blew out a sigh. "And besides, I'm already in a relationship," I reminded her—and myself. "What about Emmett?"

"What about him?" Kat shrugged. "You barely even know the guy, Ame. You've been dating for seven months, and I can count on one hand the number of times he's come to town to see you."

"He's got a pretty damn good excuse," I snapped, feeling my face grow hot.

Kat reared her head back as if I'd just slapped her. She exhaled a shaky breath and pulled her leather purse strap across her shoulder as she turned away from me, heading for the parking lot.

Oh, boy. Me and my big mouth. I shouldn't have over-reacted like that. "Kat, wait!" I called, feeling like Jerk of the Year as I trotted after her. I caught up with her and placed my hand on her arm. "I'm sorry. I didn't mean to—"

"No, it's okay. You're right." She didn't turn around, and her voice was trembling. "Emmett's a good man. I hope he finds that bastard, Shawn, and makes him pay for all the pain he's caused." Kat pivoted slowly, meeting my gaze with tired eyes. "I just meant that LDR's aren't easy."

My lips quirked at one corner. "It's not necessarily a long distance relationship—he could only be a few miles away right now, for all I know."

Kat gave me a wry look. "You know what I mean."

"Yeah, I do. I'm just feeling very confused," I admitted. "I thought I was prepared to face Mickey, and then I saw him at the airport…" I exhaled. "But nothing is going to happen. We'll grab a platonic cup of joe, and that'll be the end of it."

"Need me to come along and be a buffer?"

"Nah." I smiled. "It'll be fine. I should be in my office around ten. I'd like to get here in time to post info for the new shows we've booked on the website before things get too hectic." The day of a sold-out show was always super busy.

"Okay," Kat said, slipping behind the wheel of the Escalade. "Night, chick."

"See ya." I waved good-bye and climbed into my own car. A sigh slipped from me. Being so worked up over my MIA boyfriend and pining ex was no excuse to snap at my bestie. Though she'd instantly forgiven me, I still felt like the scum of the earth. Kat had a point, though—Emmett and I hadn't spent much time together, and I really didn't know him all that well. Plus I didn't have the best track record with relationships—the last guy I'd gone on a date with before Emmett had tried to murder me. Welcome to the reality show that is my life.

I clicked on the backlight of my phone screen. No new calls or texts. My heart sank. I hadn't heard a peep from Emmett in several days. *Maybe there's a break in the search for Stone.* The thought made my belly do somersaults.

I was often plagued by nightmares about the evil mobster. Sometimes I dreamed I was coming home from a late night at Castle Rock, and he was waiting for me inside my apartment. Other times, my subconscious conjured up the image of him crouching low in the backseat of my car, ready to pounce. I shuddered, casting a nervous glance into the darkness behind my driver's seat. I was alone in the car. Locking the doors to my Jetta, I dialed Emmett's cell before pulling out of the parking lot. Just hearing his voice would go a long way to ease the major case of the creeps I just gave myself—and hopefully help me forget about Mickey, too.

"Hey there, babe," Emmett Larson's deep baritone crooned from the other end of the line. "It's after one in the morning—meaning you're either just getting off work, or you're feeling frisky." He chuckled.

"Maybe both," I said coyly. "How's work?"

Emmett blew out a breath. When he spoke again, he sounded tired. "I wish I had good news for you, but we're still not making much headway. One source claims Stone's in Europe; another says he's holed up at a buddy's place somewhere deep in the woods of Montana. If we get one lead, we get a dozen—and they're always far-spread." He was silent for a moment, no doubt trying to quell some of the frustration that was building in his tone. "We're going to get him, Ame," he said finally. "I promise."

"I know," I replied, but my voice was glum. I turned off of Piedmont Road, pulling into the parking deck for my apartment. "I just wish this whole thing was behind us. I want to see you."

"I wanna see you too, babe."

I parked on the tenth level of the deck and trudged up three flights of stairs to my floor, not wanting to risk dropping the call in the elevator. "Maybe you can sneak away for the weekend," I said breathlessly when I reached the top step. "If y'all haven't found him in the past seven months, what kind of difference would a few days make?"

"I still have a job to do," Emmett reminded me. "But that does sound tempting."

My lips curved upward. "I could make it worth your while," I purred as I unlocked my door and pushed it open. I closed it behind me and turned around, stopping dead in my tracks when I saw the man inside my apartment.

CHAPTER THREE

———

"Emmett!" I squealed, nearly dropping the phone. He was seated at my dining room table, my orange calico-tabby cat, Uno, curled in his lap. At his feet were Uno's brothers, Dos and Tres. My cry of surprise spooked the kitties, and they darted away to hide under the couch.

"Hey, gorgeous." Emmett rose to greet me. He was dressed in faded gray jeans with an untucked, black button-down shirt. His dark getup and hair made his emerald eyes pop.

I flung my purse down on the table and threw myself into his arms, pressing against him for a long, steamy welcome kiss. "What are you doing here?" I asked breathlessly as I pulled away after a few delicious moments.

Emmett's eyes sparkled as he beamed down at me. "That spare key you gave me last month has been burning a hole in my pocket. I figured it was about time I used it." He winked. "I hope I didn't scare you."

"You totally did," I admitted, though I was grinning. "That was sneaky, Larson." I wagged a finger at him. "Why didn't you tell me you were coming into town?"

"I thought I'd surprise you. Plus it was sort of last-minute." Something in the way he said that last part made my stomach flip-flop.

"What about Stone?" I asked, unable to mask the sudden anxious spike in my voice.

Emmett's smile faltered, concern etched in his handsome features. "Like I said before, he's still out there somewhere." He set his jaw in a firm line. "I'm taking a few days off from the case. I don't like it, but I was told to lay low. Montana was a bust, so we're following a new lead. Shawn knows what Gavin and I look like. If we go in with the team, we might blow their cover. I can't risk that happening again." Emmett dropped his gaze to the floor, lost in thought. His mouth slowly turned up at the corners. "But on the bright side, that means I'm all yours for at least the next three days."

I bit my own lip in a coy smile. "I can think of a few ways we could pass the time."

Emmett gave me an appraising look, his gaze lingering on the plunging neckline of my dress. "All dressed up," he said, lightly touching my straightened hair. He slid his hands down to my waist. "If I didn't know any better, I'd think you knew I was coming."

My cheeks glowed as I recalled Mickey's reaction to my outfit. "It's new," I replied, as if that were reason enough for me to be wearing the dress. I pushed my ex out of my thoughts and tugged Emmett closer. "I've missed you so much," I said, my lips tickling his earlobe.

"How much?" His voice grew husky.

I grinned. "Let me show you." I grabbed his hand and pulled him into my bedroom.

*   *   *

"So, are you working on any other cases right now?" I asked an hour later, wrapping the cool bed sheet around me as I nestled into the crook of Emmett's arm.

He placed one hand behind his head and lightly traced circles on my shoulder with the other. "Mainly sifting through reports. Nothing too exciting."

"Oh." I tried not to sound disappointed. When I'd first started dating the FBI agent, my imagination had run wild with the crazy adventures he must have. I pictured myself nuzzling Emmett in bed as he described high-speed car chases, sting operations, and drug busts. Our pillow talk wasn't nearly that exciting. Aside from the occasional undercover assignment, my honey mostly did paperwork.

I snuggled closer to Emmett and laid my head on his chest. "Do you think they'll catch Stone on this next mission?" I asked softly as I listened to the steady rhythm of his heartbeat. I jerked my head, startled by his quickened pulse.

"I hope so." Emmett shifted in the bed, causing me to slide off of his chest.

I frowned. Rolling over onto my stomach, I propped myself up with my elbows and peered at him through the darkness. "Is everything okay?"

"Yeah." He sighed. "I'm just exhausted. Work has been wearing me out. I don't remember the last time I got a decent night's sleep." He leaned over to plant a tender kiss first on my lips, then my forehead. "Goodnight, babe."

"Goodnight," I whispered, settling back against my pillow. I lay awake in the dark for a long while after that, listening to Emmett's soft snoring as he slumbered next to me. Something didn't feel right, but I couldn't put my finger on it. *Maybe you're just imagining things that aren't really there,* I chided myself. *Don't create something out of nothing. He's here now, so make this time count.* I shook the funny feeling and let myself drift off to sleep.

* * *

The delectable scent of bacon mixed with something sweet lured me awake at nine the next morning. Sunlight streamed through the open shutters of my bedroom window, and I shielded my eyes from the glare with one arm as I sat up and stretched. I slipped out of bed and padded into the kitchen where Emmett was whipping up bacon and chocolate chip waffles.

"That smells awesome," I said, feeling the hungry grumbling in my stomach as I came around the counter to kiss him good morning. I gave him a sleepy smile. "And it's not every day I wake up to a sexy, shirtless chef in my kitchen. Best Saturday ever."

Emmett's green eyes twinkled. "Don't say that until you've tried my cooking," he warned. "Gav once told me they should use my waffles in the interrogation room—he said they were so bad that he could threaten to force-feed a perp into confessing."

"In that case, I'll stick to the bacon," I joked, reaching around him to snag a piece he'd just put on a plate. I glanced over to the corner of the room and saw that he already fed my cats. The furry trio huddled together, hovering over their full bowls of Kitty Chow. "You're amazing," I said, grinning.

"I know." Emmett winked. He crossed the kitchen to retrieve a mug from one of my cabinets and then filled it. "I also made this," he said, offering me the mug. "I know how important your first cup of coffee is."

Coffee...Mickey! "Crap!" I muttered, jerking back.

Emmett looked from the mug in his hand back to me, his eyebrows lifted. "Too hot? I can drop some ice in there."

"What? No," I said, feeling my face grow warm. "I just forgot that I was supposed to meet the band for coffee this morning. I told you Kat and I were buddies with Royal Flush in college, right?"

"Yeah, you mentioned that." He took a sip from the mug and set it down on the counter. "Why don't you go ahead and meet them, then? I can clean up here and head over to Castle Rock later and help get ready for the show."

I shook my head, trying to ignore the rock of guilt taking shape in my stomach. "No, it's fine. You went to all this trouble to make us breakfast. Plus they'll be getting to the venue early anyway to unload their equipment when the tour bus arrives. I'll just catch up with them then."

Emmett studied me, his eyes slightly narrowed. "Are you sure that's all that's bothering you?" He grabbed a waffle off the plate and held it up, aiming it at me like a ninja star. "Because I have ways of making you talk."

I laughed. "I'm fine, I promise. I'll just shoot them a quick text." I padded back to the bedroom to retrieve my phone and scrolled through until I found Mickey's number. Though I hadn't dialed it in years, thanks to the stalkerish world of technology, it re-synced to my contacts every time I bought a new phone. *Can't meet for coffee,* I typed. *Something came up.* I started to send another message, telling him I was sorry and that I'd make it up to him somehow, but instead I plugged the phone back into its charger and walked away. No sense in giving him more false hope.

I set the table as Emmett brought the food into the dining room. He disappeared behind the morning paper, and I poked at my bacon, wondering if Mickey had received my texts. It had been a mistake to invite him out for coffee in the first place. *Having Emmett show up last night must be the universe's way of keeping me in check.* I should have been relieved that my boyfriend was there. Having him around this weekend would allow me to keep an emotional distance from Mickey, even if I hung around with the guys before they left for the next stop on their tour. *It's for the best,* I reassured myself.

So, why didn't I feel any better?

*   *   *

Royal Flush's tour bus was already parked in the gravel in front of Castle Rock when Emmett and I arrived an hour and a half later. It had tinted windows and was painted solid black, save for the large flaming card logo on either side, like the one that Chad tattooed on his chest. "Not conspicuous at all," I remarked sarcastically as we drove past the oversized vehicle and pulled into the employee lot.

Bronwyn had been standing out front when we drove by, and Emmett and I walked arm-in-arm back toward the main entrance to meet her. She stood in the gravel, hands on her hips and a wide grin on her face as she stared up at the marquee. Two young men in jeans and black sleeveless tanks were setting up a ladder in front of the sign. Our new bouncer, Derek Hayes, held the ladder steady as Reese Martin climbed the rungs to swap out the large black letters announcing Royal Flush's sold-out show in High Court that night. We normally hosted performances outside in the rear courtyard on summer Saturdays. Having the guys back in town was a special occasion, though, and they'd requested to book our upstairs show room instead.

"Hey," Bron greeted us absently when we joined her. Her gaze was fixed on the backside of Reese's tight jeans as he reached the top of the ladder and began sliding new letters onto the sign. "That man has a perfect ass," she murmured, biting her lip. She turned and winked at me. "Have I told you lately just how much I love this job?"

I rolled my eyes. "Only every time Reese changes the marquee. Shouldn't you be working?" I teased.

"I *am* working," Bronwyn cupped her hands around her mouth like a megaphone. "A little more to the left, babe!" Reese bent to the side and stretched his muscular arms to push the first letter where Bron directed and then looked down at her for approval. "Perfect," she called, giving him a thumbs up. Bronwyn turned and grinned at Emmett and me. "See? I'm supervising."

"Yeah, yeah," I said dryly. "How about running and telling Kat that the alcohol delivery is here instead?" I nodded to the Heineken truck pulling to a stop at the corner. Bronwyn stared longingly at Reese. "But he's still got five more letters to go," she whined.

"I think he'll manage," Emmett said, ruffling Bronwyn's short, pink hair. "Good to see you, kid."

"Hey, Agent Larson," she said in a flat tone. She cast one last look at Reese and sighed. "All right, fine," she sulked, her bottom lip puffed out. Bronwyn shuffled off toward the entrance, sneaking quick glances over her shoulder at Reese's beefy body as she went. I grinned and shook my head. "Young love," I said, reaching for Emmett's hand and giving his fingers a squeeze.

"Hey, Ame." Reese had climbed down from the ladder and was making his way toward us, dusting his hands off on his jeans. Derek Hayes strode behind him with the ladder hoisted over one shoulder. Reese shifted his gaze to Emmett, and his face broke into a wide grin. "Emmett! What's up, man?" He leaned in and pounded my honey on the back in one of those macho half-hugs. "Good to see ya."

I introduced Emmett to Derek as he joined us. The tall man set the ladder on the ground and reached out to shake Emmett's hand. His ebony skin glistened as he wiped a few beads of sweat from his brow. "I know it's early, but do you think we could go in and get a drink?" he asked me. "It's hotter than a strip club on a Saturday night out here."

I smirked. Derek would know—he'd been a bouncer across town at the Pink Pony for several years before coming to Castle Rock. When Reese was promoted to Assistant Manager earlier that spring, Derek had stepped in to fill his shoes as our head doorman. Derek wanted a change of pace from the sometimes violent gig of protecting the dancers. "Less drama in the rock world, if you can believe it," he'd said. "And I won't go home every night covered in body glitter. It's a bitch trying to get that stuff off the upholstery in my car."

"Yeah, go ahead," I told Derek and Reese. "I think you two have earned a cold one."

"By the way, Ame," Reese said, hiking his thumb back toward the tour bus. "The band is here. Derek and I helped them unload their gear about half an hour ago. Kat's getting them settled in the upstairs green room."

"Thanks for the heads up." I started for the door, turning my back on Emmett and the guys. The beads of sweat on my forehead had nothing to do with the summer heat. *Time to introduce Emmett to Mickey.* Em caught up to me, slinging his arm around my shoulder as I led the others inside through Castle Rock's main entrance.

The venue's front hall boasted plush red carpet and a multi-colored crystal chandelier that cast a rainbow of refracted light against the gray stone walls. A pair of stained glass windows on either side featured winged guitars soaring over moats of fire. If Elvis had ever traded Graceland for a castle, I imagined it would've looked something like this.

We padded up a flight of stairs and down the hall toward the High Court green room, stopping in the showroom's bar so that Emmett, Derek, and Reese could each grab a beer. I reached for a Diet Coke and then thought better of it, opting for a Corona instead. I'd have preferred something even stronger to take the edge off of what would no doubt be a tense day, but I couldn't justify drinking hard liquor before noon. My gaze flicked to Emmett, and I thought about Mickey nearly kissing me the night before. *On second thought...*I reached for a small bottle of Jack Daniels, slipping it into the back pocket of my jeans. *Just in case.*

Back in the hallway, we bumped into Kat heading for the stairs. She did a double take at the sight of Emmett. "Hey there, stranger," she said, giving him a hug. She cast a questioning look at me over his shoulder. I shrugged. "I let

Bronwyn hang back in the green room," she said. "She's watching the band practice." She released Emmett and turned to Derek and Reese. "Could you guys handle the alcohol delivery?" Glancing at Emmett, she added, "I'm sure they wouldn't mind an extra hand carrying those kegs if you're up for it, Larson."

"Sure thing." Emmett grinned. "I could use the workout." He leaned down to give me a quick peck on the cheek before following Derek and Reese to the stairs. As soon as they were out of earshot, Kat rounded on me.

"Wasn't expecting to see him this morning," she said, nodding in the direction of Emmett's retreating figure. She arched her thin brow. "I know I said you barely see the guy, but I didn't think you'd call and get him to hop the first flight here."

I shook my head and held up my hands, taking a step back. "I didn't know he was coming—I swear. He surprised me last night when I got home."

Kat nodded, her gaze flitting toward the green room. "Well, at least that explains why Mickey's been moping around in there like someone killed his puppy." She gave me a sidelong glance. "I'm assuming you didn't show up for your little coffee date."

"It *wasn't* a date," I insisted, beginning to feel like a broken record. "But no, I sent Mickey a text to cancel when I woke up to Emmett making breakfast this morning. He never responded to the message." I wrapped my arms around my middle, feeling sick. "I didn't mean to hurt him."

"Meh, it's probably for the best." Kat shook her head. "The guy is totally still hung up on you. With Emmett in town, at least he'll take the hint that you've really moved on."

"I guess," I said softly. I wasn't so sure I *had* completely moved on.

"Don't stress about it." Kat gave a dismissive wave. The corners of her mouth crooked up. "So, out with it! What kind of sexpionage did you and Secret Agent Boyfriend get into last night? Did you show him your Double-O Face—"

"Hey!" I cut her off. "Enough with the bad James Bond jokes. He's FBI, not British Secret Service." I smirked. "Though he *would* look damn good in a tux, huh?"

"For sure." Kat giggled. "Anyway," she said, flipping her light brown locks over her shoulder. "Royal Flush's gear should be set up on stage by now—we should let them know they can move their rehearsal to High Court."

I cast a nervous glance toward the green room and grimaced. "Can't you go tell them without me?"

Kat shook her head firmly. "Nuh-uh. You can't hide from Mickey Ward for the rest of the weekend, honey. Woman up and get your butt in there."

"Aye aye, captain." I gave a half-hearted salute. With a weary sigh, I dragged my feet after Kat toward the High Court green room.

A sweet acoustic melody drifted through the open door, and we stepped inside to find Bronwyn sitting in the center of the room, her cheeks glowing as pink as her hair. The members of Royal Flush sat in a circle around her, serenading her as they plucked away on acoustic guitars. Mickey beat his drumsticks on a practice pad in his lap to keep the rhythm, and Zane, the keyboardist, was seated in the far corner of the room plunking out a harmony on our spare piano. The whole scene was adorable.

Mickey looked up and met my gaze. His hand slipped, throwing the rhythm temporarily off beat. He recovered quickly and turned away from me, his face stretched tight in a pained expression. My heart thumped. I dropped my own gaze to the floor as I hurried past him.

"Good morning, Amelia," Ginger Robbins called. She was perched on the plush gray sofa at the far end of the room. Ginger's red hair was pulled into a sophisticated roll at the nape of her neck, and she wore a black pantsuit and gold chunky earrings with a matching necklace. Though she didn't look more than a few years older than Kat and me, her sharp style made me feel juvenile in my jeans and faded retro Nirvana shirt.

"Hi, Ginger." I waved back and crossed the room to join her.

A petite, dark-haired woman was seated on the couch next to Ginger. I recognized her from the airport the day before—the girl who I assumed was Jack Pearson's girlfriend. "This is Suzie Omara," Ginger said, gesturing to the young woman. Suzie blinked up at Kat and me with her brown, almond-shaped eyes. She was short, probably not much taller than five-foot-four, with a waifish figure and glossy black hair that flowed down to her waist. My gaze was drawn to a long, pink scar on her cheek. The young woman didn't speak, but instead lifted her hand in a shy wave, pulling my attention to the diamond ring glittering on her finger. "Suzie is Jack's fiancée," Ginger explained.

"Hi," I said brightly, extending my hand. Suzie didn't shake it. Instead, she gave me a wan smile and then turned her attention back to Jack as he sang and strummed his guitar. I blinked at her.

Ginger rose from the couch and gently pulled at my elbow, leading me to the corner of the room. Kat followed. "Forgive her. Suzie was in a bad car accident last month while the guys were in Tokyo," Ginger said, her voice lowered. "Jack hopped the first flight back to be with her. He insisted we bring her on the road with us from here on out so that he can take care of her." She clucked her tongue and gave a little shake of her head, casting a pitying glance at Suzie. "The poor thing has been rattled ever since it happened. She barely speaks to anyone but Jack."

"How terrible," I murmured. It seemed the cut on her cheek wasn't the only scar left behind from the accident.

Royal Flush ended their private performance, and Bronwyn clapped and cheered. "That was so awesome!" she gushed. She held up her cell phone in one hand. "I can't wait to go post the video online!" Bron gave an excited squeal and practically skipped out of the room.

"Hey," Mickey said from close behind me. I whirled to face him, forcing down the pesky lump forming in my throat. Mickey's face pinched. "About this morning," he said, but I held up a hand to cut him off.

"I'm really sorry," I said, hoping we could just drop it.

Mickey's mouth pressed in a firm line. "Did something really come up? Or did you back out because I almost kissed you last night?" He rubbed his hand over his face. "Ame, I didn't mean to. It just sort of happened. A reflex, I guess."

"No, it wasn't that." I put a hand on his arm. "Look, Mickey, I have to tell you something—"

My words died in my throat as someone reached from behind me and slid their arm around my middle. I immediately let go of Mickey's arm, letting my hand fall limply to my side. "All the kegs are unloaded, babe," Emmett said, leaning down to give me a quick smooch. He looked from Mickey back to me, arching his brow. "Sorry—am I interrupting something?"

My throat tightened, and I made a little coughing noise. Mickey's gaze shifted from Emmett to me. Understanding dawned on his face. "Oh," he muttered, and I caught the pain that slid behind his eyes. Mickey recovered quickly and extended a hand toward Emmett. "I'm Mickey Ward," he said, his voice gruff.

"I know who you are." Emmett squinted at Mickey for a few long moments and studied him. I bit the inside of my lip, anxiety pulling my chest tight as I waited to see what he would do next. Finally, Emmett's face relaxed into a wide smile. "It is so great to meet you, man!" He pumped Mickey's hand up and down enthusiastically. "I must've played the whole *Double Down* album cover to cover at least a hundred times when it first came out. You've got some killer drum solos on that record." Though I was relieved they weren't pummeling each other's faces (yet, anyway), I nearly groaned. Of all people for my boyfriend to get star struck over, it had to be Mickey.

"Glad you dig it." A wicked grin played on Mickey's lips. He glanced at me. "That's the one with your song on it, Ame."

Emmett's brows shot up. "'Gamblin' Grace' is about you, babe? No way!"

"Way," I said meekly. *Bet on love but fell flat on my face/Guess that's what I get for gamblin' with Grace...* An old, familiar pain rose to the surface. Mickey wrote that song about our breakup, and then it became their second big single. As if being heartbroken wasn't bad enough, I'd had to relive it every time "Gamblin' Grace" came on the radio for months after that. It was a Billboard Top 40 slap in the face. I hated that song.

"Well, it was nice meeting you," Mickey said to Emmett before shifting his attention back to me. "I'll take a rain check on that coffee, Ame." There was an almost imperceptible bitterness in his tone, but I knew him well enough to pick up on it.

"Come on," I said, grabbing Emmett's hand. "I'll introduce you to the rest of the guys." I pulled him away from Mickey before things could get ugly.

After my honey had met Ginger, Suzie, and the other members of Royal Flush, I brought him back down to my office. For the next half-hour, Emmett typed away on his laptop while I worked on contracts at my desk. Neither one of us spoke, and the silence only worsened my feeling of shame over Mickey. I hadn't exactly told Emmett about our history yet. It wasn't so much that I was lying than I'd just sort of…failed to mention it.

Finally, I couldn't stand it anymore. "I have to tell you something," I began, pushing my chair away from my desk.

"Yeah?" Emmett looked up at me from his laptop with interest.

"Mickey and I…" My voice trailed off as I tried to find the right words.

"Used to date," Emmett finished for me.

I gaped at him. "How did you—?" I closed my mouth, a blush forming on my cheeks and neck. Of course my FBI beau would be well aware of my past romantic history. For all I knew, with a snap of his fingers, the man could probably have someone draft a full report on my Facebook relationship status changes over the past decade.

Emmett closed his laptop and set it down on my office couch. "I saw the way he looked at you," he said simply. "That was the look of a man who knows he had something good and lost it. Plus he mentioned that 'Gamblin' Grace' was about you—there's definitely a bad breakup story behind that song."

"It's kind of complicated." I dropped my gaze to the floor. This wasn't going to be a fun conversation, but I owed it to him.

"How so?"

"We were sort of almost engaged once."

"I see," Emmett said, his even tone not giving away what he thought about that little bombshell. "What happened?"

I took a deep breath and slowly let it out. "We dated for a year and a half before Royal Flush really took off. I was managing the band at the time, and the guys decided they wanted to drop out of college and focus on touring. I wanted to stay in school and get my degree." I chewed my lip for a moment. "I thought the proposal was his last-ditch effort to get me to go on the road with them. I said no. We broke up, and the guys hired Ginger. The rest is rock 'n' roll history." I looked meaningfully at Emmett. "It was a long time ago. Five years. Mickey and I are totally different people now."

Emmett grunted, a cryptic noise that could've meant pretty much anything. It wasn't the response I was hoping for. I rose from my desk chair and slid his laptop over so that I could sit beside him on the couch. "How does that make you feel?" I asked, searching his emerald eyes.

He was silent for what seemed like an eternity. With each passing second, my heart sank lower into the depths of my stomach. I fought back the urge to cry, afraid I would break down if he didn't say something soon.

Finally, Emmett shrugged. "The past is the past." He reached for my hand and squeezed it then lightly traced a line up my arm until he reached my cheek. His palm opened and cradled my face. "All that matters to me is the present." Emmett leaned forward and dipped his mouth to mine for a slow, sweet kiss. Relief flooded my chest, and my heart gave a happy thump. As far as talks about exes go, that could've been *so* much worse.

"Get a room, you two," Kat called dryly from the doorway.

I pulled away from Emmett. "We've got one. This is *my* office." Smirking, I grabbed a green throw pillow off the couch and tossed it at Kat. She ducked at the last minute, and the pillow sailed past her out into the hallway.

"Yeah, yeah." Her voice dripped sarcasm. Kat retrieved the pillow and heaved it back at me. Then she wagged a finger at Emmett and gave him a mock stern look. "Don't distract her for long, Larson," she said. "There's tons of work to be done—we've got a sold-out show tonight."

CHAPTER FOUR

———

"Thank you, Atlanta!" Jack thrashed about, his wavy hair shrouding his face as he screamed into the mic. Jack Pearson had been hailed by *Rolling Stone* as "Kurt Cobain reincarnated" and with good reason—not only did his throaty vocals resemble the style of Nirvana's lead singer, but with his long, straw-colored hair, dark brows, and piercing blue eyes, he was practically the late grunge rocker's doppelganger.

Beside him, Chad struck one last power chord on his ivory Fender Stratocaster guitar. The sound reverberated throughout the room for several long moments before Chad dropped the guitar and let it hang from his shoulder strap. "Wooooo!" he screamed, throwing up devil horns with both hands. The crowd roared back at him.

Behind the drum set, Mickey dropped his sticks, letting them crash against the cymbal. He shook his dark hair out of his face and lifted up the front of his *Pearl Jam* T-shirt to mop the sweat from his forehead, exposing a set of perfect abs. A group of girls in the front row whistled and cheered.

"Holy crap—you could grate cheese off those things!" Bronwyn's eyes bulged at the sight of Mickey's six-pack. She looked back at me in disbelief. "You really used to date him?"

"Uh-huh." I bit the inside of my lip. Mickey did have a really nice body. Seeing him in action during their set had taken me back to those nights in college when a twenty-three-year-old me would stare adoringly at him from the front row at each performance. Emmett cleared his throat behind me, jarring me from my reverie. *Whoops.* I reached back and fumbled for his hand, grasping it firmly in mine.

A collective groan of disappointment sounded from the girls in the front row when Mickey pulled his sweat-soaked shirt back down. Squinting past the bright spotlights, he waved to the crowd before rising from behind the drum kit. From the far left of the stage, Sid Malone set down his bass guitar and stepped forward, running one hand through his spiky black hair. Zane Calloway banged out a choppy melody on his keyboard before leaping over its stand like a runner clearing a hurdle. He brushed his own curly blond mop out of his eyes as he joined the four other rockers at the front of the stage. After high-fiving and hugging each other, the quintet dipped forward in a synchronized bow. Mickey and Zane waved to the crowd on their way off the stage, and Chad blew his fans several kisses.

"That was awesome!" Bronwyn gushed when the band reached the wings.

"Thanks!" Zane said brightly. He reached down into the white cooler I'd set on the floor just off stage. Wading through the ice, he pulled out two beers and handed one to Mickey. They popped the tops off and clinked their bottles together.

Sid Malone sidled up to me, a sly grin playing on his lips. "Hey, Amelia. Bet ya can't guess what song we've got planned for the encore."

I wanted to gag. *Please, not that.*

"'Gamblin' Grace,' huh?" Kat guessed. Zane and Sid rewarded her correct answer with a couple of high fives.

Mickey glanced at me, a look of smug satisfaction on his face. "Royal Flush can't make the big return to A-town without playing the song that put us on the map. Gotta give the home crowd what they want." He tilted his head back and took a large swig of his beer, heaving a refreshed sigh as he pulled it away again. He wiped his lips with the back of his hand. "It feels good to be back." Mickey checked his watch and cupped his hands around his mouth like a megaphone. "Hey, Jack!" he yelled over the roar of the crowd. "We've got twenty minutes till the meet and greet. Let's give 'em one more tune."

Jack stood off to the side, his face plastered to Suzie's. He pried his lips away from hers and considered Mickey with a lazy smile. "Let's do it," he said. He gave Suzie one more peck and strolled back on stage, causing a crescendo in the cheers from High Court.

I cringed. "That's my cue to leave," I told Emmett. Turning to Kat, I added, "I'm gonna start setting up for the fan meet and greet in the tower."

"Not staying to hear your song?" Mickey asked as I turned to leave.

"Nope," I called over my shoulder without looking back. "Break a leg," I added under my breath, feeling a bit less sorry for bailing on him this morning. *Stupid "Gamblin' Grace."* I grabbed Emmett's hand and headed for the stairs leading up to Castle Rock's rear tower.

After a lot of discussion, Kat and I decided to turn the tower's lone room into an events space for VIP experiences at the venue. It provided a unique and memorable backdrop for after-parties and fan meet and greets, allowing attendees to enjoy the breathtaking view of the Atlanta skyline from the tower's open windows.

As Emmett and I reached the top of the stairs, I spotted a familiar silver-haired man kneeling next to a PA speaker, unraveling a string of cables. My back stiffened. I'd forgotten that 95Rox's most arrogant DJ, Tim Scott, was running tonight's station-sponsored meet and greet. *We're making a ton of money off this,* I reminded myself. *And letting Tim interview the band for his show is good exposure for Castle Rock.* Tim's widely-syndicated radio talk show, *Tune Talks,* was broadcast on nearly every rock station in the Southeast and even a few on the West Coast. He'd do anything to get a juicy story for his segments, and he didn't care whom he hurt or what lines he crossed to get the scoop. Tim called it being a good journalist—I called it being a huge douchebag.

Tim looked up as we approached and flashed me a cheesy grin. "Good evening, Miss Grace."

"Hi, Tim," I said, forcing a polite tone. "You remember my boyfriend, Emmett."

Tim bristled, and a scowl melted through his plastic smile. "Of course I remember *Agent Larson*," he said dropping the pile of cables and rising to his full height. He begrudgingly stepped forward and gripped Emmett's hand. "I don't suppose you're here to block me from broadcasting even more important news?" he asked through clenched teeth.

"I hope you haven't been giving Amelia a hard time while I've been away," Emmett said, narrowing his eyes at the man. He wasn't a fan of Tim's, either.

"Wouldn't dream of it," Tim said dryly. His annoyance evaporated, and an eager look crossed his face. "That reminds me, how *is* your case going? Caught that slimy mobster yet?" Tim's lips twitched, and his eyes narrowed in challenge. "Why else would you be back here?"

"Sorry, Scott. Classified info. You know how it is." Emmett shrugged, but I saw his jaw muscle flex and felt him go rigid beside me. I got the feeling he wasn't in the mood to play twenty questions with the shady journalist.

"Need a hand with your equipment, Tim?" I cut in before he could continue to grill Emmett further.

The man shook his head. "No, thank you. I'm almost set, and my intern should be back up here any minute with the camera. We're going to get some shots to post on the 95Rox social media accounts." Tim stooped to resume his task of untangling speaker cables while Emmett and I set up a folding table and chairs for the band. We set a stack of black and white promotional photos of Royal Flush on the table, along with several gold markers.

Bronwyn bounded up the stairs then, her arms full of water bottles. "The band is ready," she called. She placed a drink on the table in front of each empty chair. "Reese is lining up the station's meet and greet contest winners in High Court." Bron tapped the microphone on her headset. "Should I radio him to bring them up now?"

"Yeah, go ahead," I said absently. My attention was fixed warily on Tim. His conniving smirk had returned at the mention of the band. *What stupid stunt does he have planned this time?* I wondered. Tim had risen to radio fame by interviewing the world's most famous musicians and reporting live from some of the biggest events in entertainment history. Now that his career was beginning to dry up, however, he was known to pull "shock and awe" publicity stunts for the sake of increasing his ratings. If he had something up his sleeve, I wanted to be ready for it. I leaned back against Emmett's chest and tilted my head up to whisper in his ear. "Keep an eye on Tim."

"You got it, babe." Emmett squeezed my shoulder.

Bronwyn reached for the walkie-talkie hooked to her jeans and mashed the button on its side. "We're good to go in the tower, Reese," she spoke into her headset. "Bring 'em up."

Static belched from the speaker. "Roger that," Reese's deep voice crackled. "On our way."

"Thanks, sexy." Bronwyn made a smooching noise into her mic and then released the radio button. She came to stand next to Emmett and me as the noisy stomping of footsteps echoed up the stairwell. A few moments later, Reese and Kat appeared at the door leading a line of ten lucky Royal Flush fans into the tower.

Tim flashed a cheesy game-show-host grin. "Welcome to 95Rox's 'Rock After Dark' with Royal Flush!" he said, going to each fan and shaking their hand. "Congratulations on winning a seat at this exclusive post-show event. The band will be up shortly for an autograph signing and photo session." He flicked his gray ponytail over his shoulder and gestured for the group to line up next to the table.

The excited winners chattered amongst themselves as they filed in. Two blonde girls that looked to be in their late teens or early twenties led the line, followed by a couple in their thirties, two middle-aged men, two college-aged men and a woman wearing Georgia State T-shirts, and a man with an Atlanta Braves baseball cap pulled down low over his eyes. Something about the last fan seemed oddly familiar. I squinted at him, trying to get a better look at his face.

Applause erupted from the group of fans as Royal Flush entered the tower room. Chad and Zane walked in first, followed by Sid, Mickey, and finally Jack. The two blonde girls squealed with delight as Jack appeared. Suzie and Ginger entered right behind him. The two women and Kat joined Bronwyn, Emmett, and me off to the side as the musicians took their seats behind the autograph table.

Emmett leaned down and put his lips close to my ear. "Gotta use the john," he said. "I'll be right back." He planted a kiss on the top of my head before heading toward the stairwell. I couldn't help but notice that Mickey gave him the stink eye as he passed.

Reese ushered the fans into a line starting at the left end of the table where Sid Malone was seated. One by one, each winner handed their black-and-white Royal Flush photograph to Sid. He signed the pictures before passing them assembly-line style to Mickey, Chad, Zane, and finally Jack, who was seated at the other end of the table. Each rocker chatted with the fans as they reached him. Chad bumped fists with the two younger men in the Georgia State tees. The blonde girls walked around to the back of the table and leaned down on either side of Mickey. He placed his arms around them as they posed for a picture.

"I've gotta tell you," one young man said to Jack. "I have this crazy theory about the meaning of your song 'House of Cards'."

"Oh yeah?" Jack grinned. "Hit me. What's your theory?"

The young man's face lit up with excitement. "So, check this out," he began, gesturing with his hands. The rest of the band turned to watch him with interest. "You know how you've got that one line that goes, 'We're all just livin' in a house of cards, and it's bound to come tumblin' down'? Well, I think you wrote that as your way of saying that our nation's government is so weak and corrupt that the next big political scandal could unravel the whole thing." The fan looked at Jack hopefully. "Am I right?"

"Whoa. That's deep," Jack said with a chuckle. He shook his head. "I'm afraid it's not nearly as profound as that."

The young man's face fell. "What's it about then?"

Chad held up a hand. "I can answer that one." He flashed the kid a toothy grin. "Sorry to burst your bubble, dude—but one time in college, we got really stoned and decided to build a fort out of playing cards. It took us nearly fifty decks and some tape, but Mickey and I finally constructed four flimsy walls and a roof."

Mickey gave a hearty laugh. "I remember that. Then Jack came in and went all Big Bad Wolf on us. He literally blew our house down."

"Oh." The fan said, deflated. "Er, well, thanks for listening to my theory, anyway."

"It's a good one," Jack said, winking at the kid. "Hold on to that. The song can mean whatever you want it to. That's the great thing about art."

A loud thud pulled my attention to the other end of the table where Sid Malone was seated. "What the hell's your problem, bro?" he snapped at the man in the Braves cap. Sid pounded his fist so hard that he rattled the whole table. He pushed his chair back and stood up, his chest puffed out as he glowered at the fan.

"You stole my shot at fame," the man replied nastily. His voice sent a bolt of recognition through me...*Dillon?*

The man pulled off his Braves cap and flipped it around so that the bill faced backward before setting it back on his head. Though it had only been five years since I'd seen Dillon Green, he looked to have aged twice that. He was slightly thinner than I remembered, and a thick layer of scruff covered his cheeks and chin as if he hadn't shaved in a week. His disheveled appearance, combined with his almost palpable anger, made our former friend seem deranged.

I glanced at Kat. Her eyebrows were raised, her lips parted in surprise. She'd no doubt reached the same conclusion. Kat met my gaze and moved closer to me. "You've gotta be kidding me," she whispered, gripping my arm. "I *thought* he seemed familiar, but I didn't get a good look at him before."

The other fans had taken a few steps back from Dillon and were glancing around the room nervously. Tim Scott stood on the opposite end of the room, wicked glee written all over his face. He rubbed his hands together and eagerly bit his lip as he fumbled for the microphone. "A hundred bucks says Tim arranged this as a publicity stunt," I muttered to Kat.

She looked over at the conniving deejay and then gave me a sidelong glance. "One hundred? How about a thousand?" Kat ground her teeth. "I really want to clock that jerk right in the face."

"Get in line," I said dryly.

Sid scowled at Dillon and crossed his arms defiantly over his chest. "If you had any talent, you'd probably still be with the group," he spat. "Why don't you crawl back into your has-been hidey hole and leave us *real* rockers alone?" He flicked a glance toward his bandmates, looking for them to back him up.

Chad, Mickey, and Jack gaped at Dillon as if they were seeing a ghost. Zane eyed him warily and then leaned over in his seat. "So this is that Dillon guy who Jack kicked outta the band?" he asked Chad.

"Not now, man," Chad muttered, poking him in the ribs with his elbow.

"Dude," Mickey said to Dillon. "What are you doing here?"

Dill glared at him. "What's the matter, Mick? Not happy to see an old friend?"

Mickey held up his hands in a placating manner. "No, man. I'm just surprised is all. I thought about calling you while we were in town, actually."

"You're not welcome here," Jack said, his tone gruff. His handsome face puckered, and he squinted daggers at his former band mate.

"Like hell I'm not!" Dillon held up his 95Rox VIP badge, his expression smug. "I'm a contest winner. You guys owe me a meet and greet." He stepped forward, turning in a circle with his arms stretched wide. "So here I am. Greet me, jerks," he challenged.

"Don't mind if I do." Sid stomped around the table, his jaw clenched. His arm shot out, connecting his fist with Dillon's jaw with near lightning speed. Then chaos erupted. The two men collided in a tangle of swinging arms and thrashing legs. Excited cries echoed around the tower as the other fans scrambled away from the brawling pair. Dillon punched Sid in the neck, and the wiry bass player returned the favor with a knee to the stomach. Dillon staggered backward but recovered in time to block another one of Sid's jabs. There was a sick crunching sound as he slammed his fist into Sid's nose.

"No!" Ginger cried, breaking my state of horrified paralysis.

"Stop," I called, rushing forward with my arms outstretched. Chairs scraped the stone floor as the rest of the band pushed back from the table to help break up the fight.

I reached Sid and Dillon first and attempted to wrench my arms between them. "Amelia, look out!" I heard Kat yell over the racket. I jerked my head toward her just as something smashed into the right side of my face with an explosion of pain. The lights went out as I dropped to the floor.

CHAPTER FIVE

———

"Amelia?" A voice floated through my consciousness, and I felt a gentle tap on my cheek. I cracked open an eyelid and found Mickey peering down at me—at least, I thought it was Mickey. It was hard to see through all the stars clouding my vision. "Ow," I groaned.

"Are you all right?" he asked. I opened my mouth to answer but closed it again as the pain in my head swelled. I squeezed my eyes shut and pushed out a breath, trying to stop my world from spinning. The air moved beside me as Mickey sat down. I felt his hands slide gently underneath me and lift. When I opened my eyes again, he was cradling me in his lap.

Kat stooped beside us. "Shit, Ame! You were out for nearly a full minute." She peered at the side of my face, lightly touching the spot where a flying fist had smashed into my right temple. "That's gonna leave a bruise. Bronwyn, ice!" she called, and I winced at the loudness of her voice.

Through my blurred sight, Bronwyn's pink hair looked like a puff of cotton candy bobbing toward the autograph table. She brought a cold water bottle over and gently pressed it against my temple. "Thanks," I mumbled weakly. I blinked a few times until her face came into focus.

Bronwyn mashed the button on her radio and spoke into her mouthpiece. "Yo, Derek, we've got a code…" She paused and looked at Kat, her eyebrows drawn up in question. "What's the code for 'Ame got her lights punched out by some arrogant douche canoe'?"

Kat huffed and snatched the headset from around Bron's neck. "Derek, if everyone's cleared out downstairs, we could really use your help up here," she said, her voice tense.

"On my way," came the reply through the small speaker.

"What the hell is going on here?" Footsteps thundered toward us, and suddenly Emmett was on the ground next to me. He looked from Mickey to me, the muscles in his face tightening. "I can take her," Emmett said, and I felt Mickey's body tense as Emmett pulled me out of his arms and slowly helped me to my feet.

"Ow," I moaned again. I leaned heavily on Emmett.

He pulled me closer and brushed the hair out of my eyes. "What happened?" he asked softly.

"Sid and Dill got into it," Mickey said, rising from the floor. "And Sid punched her when she tried to break up the fight."

"It was an accident!" Sid cried, sounding both startled and angry. "The bitch got in the way. It's not my fault."

"Don't you call her that," Mickey warned, his voice a low growl. There was a grunt, and I turned my head in time to see him shove Sid hard in the chest. The spiky-haired bass player staggered backward and bumped into Dillon, who immediately brought his fists up again.

"No," Mickey warned, his own hands clenching at his side. "This is over—now."

Emmett motioned to Kat, who came over and wrapped her arm around my middle to support me. Emmett released his grip on me and walked over to stand next to Mickey. They nodded to each other, a silent understanding passing between them, and then they turned to Sid with twin expressions of anger. "You need to cool off," Emmett said through clenched teeth. He grabbed the bass guitarist by the shoulders and walked him toward the stairs.

"Sid couldn't go *one* night without causing trouble," Ginger muttered. "I'm so over this." The irritated band manager raked her manicured nails through her hair and blew out a breath. She cast a weary glance at Kat and me. "The meet and greet is over." She turned and scurried after Sid and Emmett.

Dillon stood with his arms folded across his chest, his expression smug. "At least I know better than to hit a lady," he grumbled. He caught my pained expression and his cheeks flushed. "Sorry, Amelia. I didn't mean for you to get in the middle of this."

My anger boiled over like hot lava. "What are you even doing here, Dillon?" I snapped. "Get out."

Reese stepped forward and wrestled the disgruntled former band member's arms behind his back. "He was just leaving." Reese gave Dillon a menacing look. "Weren't you?"

"Get your hands off me!" Dillon protested. He struggled against Reese's iron grip. Derek appeared in the tower and joined Reese in subduing the jilted rocker. "I could press charges," he threatened as they led him away.

"Hey, um," stammered a voice near the autograph table. All eyes turned to one of the contest winners, a middle-aged man in black jeans and a gray Royal Flush T-shirt. "What about our group photo?" he asked timidly.

Are you freaking kidding me? I glared at the man and gingerly rubbed my temple. "I think I'm gonna be sick," I told Kat, my voice tight with pain.

Kat nudged Bronwyn. "Get her downstairs. I'll handle this mess." She inserted her pointer finger and thumb between her lips. I flinched as she blew a shrill whistle, silencing the chatter among the anxious fans. "Sorry folks," she said.

While Kat took care of things in the tower, Bronwyn ushered me slowly into the stairwell. A grunt escaped Bron as she supported my weight down the first step. "I think I can make it on my own," I insisted.

Bronwyn snorted. "With your track record? Let's not take any chances, Amelia Graceless."

I scowled. My old rival, Stacy, used to call me that. "Let's just get to my office," I muttered. We took each step one at a time, carefully making our way down to Castle Rock's ground floor. When we had finally reached the employee hallway, I slipped my arm from around Bronwyn's shoulders. "I can handle it from here," I said, taking the last few wobbly steps to my office. I eased into my desk chair and opened the top drawer, rooting around for my bottle of aspirin. I popped two pills and chased them with the bottle of water Bron had fetched from the signing table. Opening the small compact mirror next to my keyboard, I held it up to inspect my face. A sigh slipped from me as I took in the large mark just below my temple that was already darkening to a purplish hue. "That's gonna be one hell of a bruise," I groaned.

"Could've been worse," Bronwyn said, backing toward the hallway. "Can I get you anything?"

"Nah," I waved her away. "Go on and find Reese. If everything's shut down for the night, you two can head out." I paused for a moment. "Actually," I amended, "have Derek and Reese escort Tim Scott out before you leave." If I had to see that jerk's face again tonight I really was going to be sick.

When Bronwyn was gone, I forced myself out of my chair and trudged back down the hall, intent on finding Emmett. I retraced my steps to the second floor and headed for the High Court green room, thinking that must be where he'd taken Sid after the fight broke out. Angry shouting reached my ears through the room's open door, and I froze before reaching the threshold.

"What in the hell is your problem, Sid?" Jack snarled. "I thought we agreed you'd dial back the drama on this tour."

"Yeah," Zane chimed in. "We can't even make it through one show without you pulling some kind of bullshit stunt."

"Don't pin this on me!" Sid shot back. "That jerk started it. He came here to pick a fight—I thought you guys would have my back."

"You're outta control, Malone," Mickey said, the rage apparent in his tone. He swore loudly. "If Amelia is seriously hurt, you're going to wish you'd never been born."

"Oooh. Big words coming from a whipped loser like you," Sid jeered. "Why are you so hung up on that chick? Does she spout bourbon from her tits? Got a scotch-flavored crotch?" He snorted. "She's not even that pretty, man."

My face flamed. *Don't let him get to you*, I thought, but hot tears threatened to spill down my cheeks. His words were unnecessary and cruel. Apparently, Mickey thought so too. There was a loud growl and the sound of shattering glass. A woman shrieked—whether it was Ginger or Suzie, I couldn't tell—and the sounds of another scuffle followed.

Oh, for crying out loud. I wiped my eyes and took another step toward the green room, my jaw tight with anger.

Before I reached the door, Sid stomped out into the hall, his hands thrown up in exasperation. "That's it!" he shouted. "I quit!" He turned back toward the door and spit. "You're all going to regret this," he added before hurrying toward the stairs. He didn't even look at me as he passed. A vindicated smirk curled my lips as I noted the blood trickling from his left nostril. *Serves him right.*

"Sid, come back!" Ginger called, hurrying through the doorway. She shot an angry glare over her shoulder. "Real nice, guys," she said, her tone caustic. "I'm getting really tired of always having to fix things." She brushed past me, her heels clicking a staccato rhythm down the hall. She nearly bumped into Emmett as she reached the stairs. Muttering under her breath, she stomped down toward the ground floor. Emmett watched her go before looking up and spotting me.

"There you are." His emerald eyes lit up, and he rushed forward to wrap his arms around me. I yelped when Emmett's bicep brushed against my wounded temple. "Oh, babe. I'm sorry." He released me at once and leaned down to inspect the wound. "I should've been there to protect you," he said, his tone bitter.

"It's okay," I said, though I flinched when he lightly ran a finger over the bump. "It'll be gone in a day or two. I'm not really in much pain—more than anything, I'm exhausted."

Emmett reached down and squeezed my hand. "Then why don't we go back to your place? I saw a bag of blueberries in your freezer that we can use to stop the swelling." With a twitch of his lips, his concerned expression melted into a sly, suggestive look. "We can open that bottle of merlot I brought and draw a bubble bath."

"That's sweet," I said. "But I can't leave until the band is gone." My resolve was fading even as I spoke. The thought of Emmett all soapy and naked in my bathtub made my whole body hum with renewed, primal energy. "Tell you what—" I fished into my pocket and retrieved my keys, which I handed to him. "I'll wrap things up here and have Derek drop me off. I should be there within the hour."

Emmett looked at me with smoldering eyes. "Perfect. I can't wait."

"Me neither." I bit my lip and leaned into him, inhaling the rich scent of his aftershave. Standing on tiptoes, I pressed my lips to his. Emmett kissed me back, wrapping one arm around me while his other hand wound through my hair, careful not to graze the bump on my temple again.

A cough sounded behind us, and I pried myself away from Emmett to find Mickey standing in the doorway of the green room. Pain flickered behind his brown eyes as he watched us.

I cringed, glancing back and forth from Emmett to Mickey. Emmett took the hint. "I'll see you at home, babe," he said, dipping down to give me one last peck before heading for the stairs. My heart swelled as I watched him go, grateful that he understood my need to settle things with Mickey—and that he trusted me.

I turned back to find Mickey staring at me, his expression one of disbelief. "'See you at home?'" he repeated, his tone questioning. "So, what—he, like, lives with you now?"

"Of course not." I shook my head. "He's just visiting for the weekend."

Mickey crossed his arms over his chest. "Awfully convenient for him to pop by for a visit at the same time that I'm back in town."

I narrowed my eyes at him. "What's that supposed to mean?"

Mickey took a step toward me. "I still know you better than anyone, Ame. I know that you still have feelings for me—you're just scared to admit it. Hiding behind Tall, Dark, and Douche doesn't change the fact that deep down you still care about me."

I scowled. "Emmett's not a douche—he's sweet." I threw my hands up in frustration. "Let's not rehash this fight again, all right?" I swallowed and forced out a few calming breaths. I didn't have the energy to argue. "I actually wanted to thank you," I said, suddenly feeling sheepish. "You know, for, er, defending my honor in there." I gestured toward the green room.

Mickey's face turned pink. "You heard all that?" he asked, his expression pinched.

"Unfortunately."

Mickey's jaw clenched. "I owed him that uppercut to the jaw just for what he said about you. But seeing him lay a hand on you earlier..." The veins in his neck thrummed visibly, and he tightened his hands into fists. "I should've killed him for that."

"Hey." I put a soothing hand on Mickey's shoulder. "I'm okay. It was an accident. I got in the way."

"Maybe you're right," Mickey said, but his face remained stormy. "That's still no excuse for the way Sid acted. He's been a first-class A-hole for a while now. We'll be better off without him." He pulled his phone from his pocket and checked the time. "It's late," he said, turning back toward the green room.

"Wait." A frown creased my brow. "How are you going to tour without a bass player?"

Mickey lifted one shoulder and let it fall. "We'll find a way. All I know is I hope I never see Sid Malone again."

* * *

I was humming to myself as I got dressed and put on my makeup the next morning. I stepped out of the bathroom and tiptoed past my bed, pausing to admire Emmett as he slept, half-covered by my bed sheets. With a smile, I slipped out of the bedroom and carefully closed the door behind me. He'd earned a little extra sleep after the previous night. I'd come home to scented candles, a bottle of merlot, and a hot bubble bath—and, more importantly, a hot, naked boyfriend—awaiting me. Needless to say, I was feeling much more relaxed.

I opened the refrigerator and surveyed its contents in search of something I could fix us for breakfast. Aside from two eggs, three slices of bacon, and a questionable-smelling block of cheese, I came up nil. *There's always chocolate raspberry scones from Java Joy.* I closed the refrigerator and grabbed my purse. Java Joy was the new coffee shop down the road from Castle Rock that Bronwyn was always raving about. Kat and I had been salivating for days over their delicious scones that Bron brought in the week before.

And it's only a two-minute drive from Castle Rock, I reminded myself. We were closed on Sundays, and while I originally planned to hang with Royal Flush before they left for

Orlando, I'd decided to spend the day with Emmett instead. Still, I needed to stop by my office and fax over a contract to one of our upcoming acts. I could go pick up some coffee and pastries, drop by Castle Rock, and be back to my apartment within half an hour, probably before Emmett even woke up.

"Keep an eye on him, boys," I said as I bent down to fill the food bowls for my three furry amigos. I stroked Uno and Dos behind the ears and ran my hand over Tres's soft back. "I'll be home soon," I promised, and then I slipped out the front door. I resumed my happy humming as I strolled down the hall and out to the parking deck.

My mood soured as soon as I turned on the car. "It was a battle of the bass players last night in the VIP room of Castle Rock." Tim Scott's voice filled my speakers. "During our 95Rox meet and greet with Royal Flush, original bass guitarist Dillon Green made an unexpected appearance and confronted his replacement, Sid Malone—and I had a front row seat to watch them trade blows."

"Unexpected my ass," I muttered. Tim had planned the little stunt to drum up some drama for his show—I just knew it. I didn't care if letting him broadcast for *Tune Talks* got Castle Rock exposure. I was going to talk to Kat about banning him from the venue. Every time he showed up, bad things happened.

"Their heated exchange escalated when Malone struck Green across the face. As the pair began to brawl, Sid mistakenly hit Castle Rock co-owner Amelia Grace," Tim continued.

My cheeks burned at the mention of my own name. With an angry growl, I jammed my thumb down on one of the radio preset buttons. A peppy dance song thrummed through the speakers. I tried singing along for a few bars, but the happy beat and catchy lyrics couldn't distract me from thinking about the fight between Sid and Dillon the night before. I lightly touched my fingertips to the bruise on my temple, remembering how Mickey had nearly lost control when he came to my defense. Had Sid really quit the band? And if so, what were the guys going to do without their bass guitarist for the rest of the tour?

Not your problem, I reminded myself. This wasn't college. I wasn't Mickey's girlfriend or the band's manager anymore—it wasn't my job to smooth things over at the first hint of a brewing argument. They were grown men, and they could resolve their own conflicts. If that didn't work, it was up to Ginger to mediate. I turned up the radio, letting the heavy bass drown out any thoughts about Royal Flush and their backstage drama.

After making a quick run through the drive-thru at Java Joy, I sped over to Castle Rock and parked in the gravel along the side of the building, closest to the back entrance. Grabbing one of the chocolate raspberry scones from the bag, I nibbled the pastry as I made my way toward the back door.

To reach the rear entrance of the venue, I had to walk around Royal Flush's black tour bus, which was now parked behind Castle Rock. Kat and I agreed to let the band keep the over-sized vehicle out back until they left on Sunday for their next tour stop. As I rounded the bus, I stopped short, frowning at the passenger's side door. *Why is the bus open?* When I'd left Castle Rock the night before, Kat was about to shuttle the guys, Ginger, and Suzie back to their hotel. Maybe they forgot to close up the bus after loading their equipment. *No way,* I thought, shaking my head. The guys wouldn't leave their instruments in an unlocked vehicle overnight.

A sense of unease crept over me as I approached the open door. What if a bum had wandered aboard? Or a thief? *Don't be ridiculous.* I shook it off and stepped up onto the small set of stairs that led inside the tour bus.

I was immediately overwhelmed by a cloying, coppery odor. "What is that?" I asked aloud, wrinkling my nose. The inside of the bus was dark. I squinted, waiting for my eyes to adjust. "Hello?" I called. Either my imagination was playing some horror movie-style tricks on me, or someone—or some *thing*—responded with a muffled groan. Fear pricked at the hairs on my arms and neck. The noise had come from the back of the bus. Was someone back there?

There was a fleeting moment where I almost turned and bolted, figuring it would be safer to wait and inspect the bus when someone else had arrived, like Emmett. Or Reese. Or maybe a SWAT team. Then the low moaning noise sounded again, and I sucked in a breath. Something about it sounded oddly familiar. Curiosity got the better of me, and I began to move deeper into the bus's interior.

I quietly inched my way past the black leather benches that lined the walls of the vehicle, and I sidestepped around the table that stuck out from the little breakfast nook. Digging into my purse, I produced a small can of pepper spray and a key chain that held a mini-flashlight. One finger hovered over the trigger of the can ready to unleash a cloud of pepper spray on anything that moved.

Before I could turn on the flashlight, my foot connected with something solid in the middle of the floor. With a startled cry, I dropped the can and the keychain as I toppled down, landing on something cold and sticky. The coppery smell grew stronger, and a feeling of nausea rolled over me. I fumbled around on the floor for my flashlight, but instead my fingers closed over something hard and smooth. I ran my hand around the object, trying to identify it. *A shoe?*

My pinky grazed against the cold metal of the mini-flashlight, and I reached for it. I clicked it on, illuminating the space in front of me. A shock wave of horror slammed through me. I screamed and scrambled to my feet, backing quickly toward the bus's entrance. The hard object I'd felt before was a boot, all right—and it was still on the foot of Sid Malone's corpse.

CHAPTER SIX

————

It took several brutal minutes for the shock to wear off. When I could breathe normally again, I called the police. After hanging up with the emergency dispatch, I reluctantly inched closer to Sid's body to retrieve my fallen pepper spray can. A morbid curiosity took hold of me as my gaze traveled slowly over the bass guitarist's corpse. *How did he die?*

Sid was sprawled on his stomach across the floor of the tour bus, his already pallid complexion even more ashen than usual. His arms and legs were tangled underneath his slumped form, as if he were unconscious—or maybe already dead, even—when he fell to the floor. I stared with horrified fascination at the dark stain that spread across the back of his shirt, turning it from light blue to a sinister purplish black. My gaze lit on a rip in the fabric near what seemed to be the source of the blood. Shining my flashlight on the spot, I caught sight of Sid's torn flesh. The gorge rose in my throat, and I regretted eating that chocolate raspberry scone. I turned away, placing a hand over my mouth.

It's a stab wound, I thought without glancing back at the body. Goosebumps sprouted down my arms, and an involuntary shudder worked its way down my spine. Sid had been murdered. He may have been a chauvinistic uber-jerk, but he didn't deserve to be stabbed to death. What was I going to tell the guys? *Mickey...* Fingers numb, I fumbled through my purse to retrieve my phone again. I couldn't let Mickey, Chad, and the others find out about Sid from some random APD detective. I punched the call button next to Mickey's name on my contact list and bit my trembling lip as I waited for him to answer. A moment later, a loud buzzing from the back of the bus nearly made me drop my phone in startled surprise.

I froze in place, my gaze darting wildly about as I surveyed the bus. Nothing moved. The buzzing continued for several more seconds. A sinking feeling pulled through me as my call to Mickey went to voice mail, and the vibrating noise stopped. *It can't be,* I thought, pressing redial. My throat went dry when the buzzing started again just moments after I pressed *send.* I ended the call, and again the noise stopped. Mickey's phone was somewhere on the bus.

My mind called forth the image of Mickey holding his iPhone the night before. He'd had it when I last saw him. That meant he'd been on the tour bus sometime last night after I left. He could've jumped aboard for a few minutes before heading back to the hotel—and the phone could've fallen out of his pocket. *Or maybe he's back there, and he's hurt. Or worse.* Fresh horror coursed through me, and I cast a frightened look toward the back of the dark bus.

I took a few calming breaths, working up my last remaining nerve before creeping past Sid's body. Another soft moan sounded, closer this time. I froze, terror rooting me to the spot. *Come on, Amelia. You can do this.* With a gulp, I forced myself to move deeper into the bus. The beam of my small flashlight illuminated the floor in front of me, one circular patch at a time. I had almost reached the bunk beds in the back of the vehicle when my light panned over a head of tangled brown hair.

"Mickey!" I inhaled a sharp breath and nearly dropped the flashlight again. I crouched beside him. Mickey was sprawled across the ground, his arms and torso in the aisle and his legs spread-eagle over the threshold of the tour bus's bathroom. I placed a hand on his cheek and sagged with relief. His body was still warm to the touch, and his gentle breathing tickled my fingers. *Thank God he's alive.*

I gently shook Mickey's shoulder, trying to rouse him awake. His eyelids fluttered but didn't open. He grunted, and his head lolled to the side. The strong scent of bourbon burned my nostrils. *Is he...drunk?*

I huffed, my relief giving way to frustration. What was Mickey doing here, passed out mere feet away from Sid's dead body? How could he have been so sloshed that he could sleep through a murder? A morbid question pinged through me, bringing fear back into the mix. *If Mickey was here when Sid was killed, why hadn't he been harmed too?*

"Wake up!" I slapped Mickey's cheek. Though his eyes remained shut, his nostrils flared, and his lips curled in a pained grimace. I slapped him again. "Mickey! Can you hear me? You have to wake up." No response.

The third time was the charm. As I smacked him one last time, Mickey's head jerked. He cracked open his eyelids, his golden brown eyes rolling around in their sockets. Mickey's expression was strained, as if he was struggling to focus. "Wha—?" he croaked. He shook his head a few times and placed his palms on the floor, pushing up slowly into a seated position. "What the hell happened?" Mickey blinked rapidly a few times and then squinted at me. "Amelia? Is that you?"

"I'm here," I whispered.

"What's going on?"

I closed my eyes and pushed out a deep breath before opening them again. "We have to get out of here," I said, my voice trembling despite my best effort to keep an even tone. "Something horrible has happened."

Mickey's face became pinched. "What's wrong?"

I slowly swiveled my flashlight back down the bus aisle until the beam of light rolled over Sid's body. Mickey stared unblinking at the body for several moments, not seeming to understand. Then the blood slowly drained from his face.

"Sid?" He looked from his band mate back to me, panic making his eyes go wide. "Is he...?"

I nodded.

"Sid!" Mickey cried. He struggled to his feet, but his legs buckled, and he went crashing back to the floor. He brought me down with him. Mickey landed on top of me, taking my breath away—not in a romantic way. For several seconds, I really couldn't breathe.

I fought to suck air back into my lungs as Mickey's weight pinned me to the floor. Limbs tangled, we both struggled to free ourselves. Mickey rolled off me and onto his back, and sweet oxygen returned. "Ow," I gasped as I lay there, panting.

"Sorry," Mickey said, equally breathless. He pushed himself to his feet and then offered me his hand. We huddled together, staring down at Sid's lifeless form. Mickey's hand slid into mine and gripped it tightly. "What happened to him?" he asked sounding hoarse.

"I was hoping you could tell me," I said softly. I looked up at him, my expression serious. "The police are on the way, Mickey. Do you remember anything about last night? Why were the two of you here instead of back at the hotel with the others?"

Mickey knit his brows together, and his eyes squeezed shut. "I…I can't remember." His voice was thick with unshed tears. "He hit you, and I was mad. So mad I wanted to hurt him."

I sucked in a breath. *"Seeing him lay a hand on you earlier…I should've killed him for that."* I recalled the dark, angry look in Mickey's eyes when he'd spoken those words the night before. *"I should've killed him…"*

I blinked at Mickey, a cold fear snaking through my chest. It wound its way down my arms, leaving me feeling paralyzed. *I have to get out of here.* With a halted breath, I broke out of my frightened trance and withdrew my hand from Mickey's grip.

He cocked his head to the side and stared at me, confused. His jaw tightened, and he reached out to grab my hand again, pulling me back to him. "Wait!" His dark eyes bore into me. "I didn't kill Sid," he insisted. "You know that, right?"

I gulped down the golf ball-sized lump in my throat and glanced at the floor where my flashlight lay. Its light shone directly at Mickey's gray and white Vans sneakers. The rubber on the front of both shoes was smeared with dark, dried blood.

"Tell me you believe me," Mickey demanded, his voice jumping in pitch. He tightened his grip on my fingers.

Terror ballooned in my chest, pushing its way up into my mind until I could barely think straight. *Get out! Get out!* chanted the voice in my head. Trembling, I reached my free hand behind me, feeling for the small can of pepper spray tucked into my back pocket.

Mickey released me and staggered back a step, his gaze darting from me back down to his hand. I held up my own newly free hand, noting that my fingers were several shades lighter where he'd cut off the circulation when he squeezed. "I'm sorry," Mickey said in a small voice. "I didn't mean to hurt you. But, Ame, you have to believe me. I don't know *what* happened, but I know I didn't kill Sid."

He opened his mouth to say something else, but I didn't wait to hear the rest. I whirled and bolted toward the front of the bus, leaping over Sid's corpse like a hurdle. There was a crashing sound, followed by the thud of heavy footsteps as Mickey chased after me, calling out my name.

I scrambled down the bus steps, one finger still firmly planted above the trigger of the pepper spray can in my right hand. My eyes struggled to adjust to the blinding brightness of the morning sun after spending nearly fifteen minutes on the dark tour bus. As I paused, squinting, movement brought my attention to the left. Shock reverberated through me as the muzzle of a handgun protruded from around the front corner of the bus. A familiar tidal wave of terror washed away all thoughts of Sid and Mickey, carrying me back to the last time I'd found myself staring down the barrel of a loaded gun.

No! my mind screamed, and my fight-or-flight instincts kicked in. I jerked my hand out in front of me and mashed the trigger of the pepper spray.

A cry of surprise and anguish erupted from my assailant as he walked into my line of fire. The man dropped to his knees, and his gun slipped free of his grasp and skidded across the gravel. The cloud of terror fogging my brain slowly dissipated. Heart still hammering, I stared down at the dark-haired stranger as he writhed on the ground, clawing at his face. My gaze settled on the *City of Atlanta Police* patch sewn into the arm of his navy blue uniform, and my stomach knotted. This man wasn't some criminal or murderer, trying to attack me—he was a cop.

"Amelia!" Mickey cried, pulling my attention back to the tour bus's side door. He staggered down the steps, looking from me to the policeman with wide eyes. "Shit! What did you do?"

"I didn't know he was a cop," I said, my voice shaking. Mickey stepped toward me, and I backed away, aiming my pepper spray can in his direction. "Stay away from me," I warned. I flicked a glance back to the man on the ground and cringed. The skin around his eyes was swollen and red, and he was groaning and fumbling for his radio. The officer wouldn't be able to protect me if Mickey really was a psycho killer—and it was all my fault.

"Drop your weapon!" barked a woman's voice behind me, and my heart skipped a beat. "Put your hands where I can see them—both of you."

Panic seized me again, and I froze, dropping the spray can. It clattered to the ground and rolled several feet before stopping against Mickey's bloody sneaker. I looked up and saw that the color had drained from his face. He looked like a pale, frightened child, his eyes darting nervously from me to the figure behind me. He slowly raised his hands in surrender, and I followed suit. "Get on the ground," the voice commanded. Mickey and I eased down onto the gravel.

A pair of black boots stomped down next to my face, and I instinctively jerked my head away. "I said don't move," the woman warned. Hands came down and wrenched my arms behind me, securing my wrists with some kind of extra-strength zip tie. I tilted my face to peer at the nervous-looking blonde policewoman glaring down at me. "You're under arrest," she said.

CHAPTER SEVEN

———

I gaped up at the female officer as she recited my rights. "Wait!" I protested. My heart thrumming in my chest was so deafening that I could barely hear myself speak. My gaze flew to the plastic nametag clipped to the policewoman's uniform. "Officer Watts, this is a mistake. He startled me—"

"You assaulted an officer of the law," Watts said curtly. Her blue eyes narrowed as she tightened the tie that bound my wrists together. "Stay put," she instructed, and then she moved over to Mickey to secure his arms behind his back.

A low moan pulled my attention to the other officer, still writhing on the ground a few yards away. His round face was splotchy and pinched with agony, and his eyes were growing puffier by the minute.

"You all right, Thompson?" Officer Watts called to him. Thompson opened his mouth to speak, but all that came out was a gurgling, choking sound.

"It was an accident," I pleaded again. "I would never intentionally assault a cop."

The female officer ignored me and reached for her radio. "Dispatch, this is Watts requesting backup at my 20," she said. "We've got an officer down. Thompson needs medical assistance." She flicked a glance from me to Mickey. "I've got a Caucasian female, approximately five-foot-five, mid-twenties, auburn hair, and a Caucasian male, approximately five-foot-eleven, mid-twenties, brown hair. As soon as backup arrives I can verify the report about the body."

"Roger that," a nasal male voice responded over the crackle of the radio.

With any threat of immediate danger now gone, the fog of fear and panic lifted, and I went limp on the ground. Going through the emotional wringer over the past hour had squeezed every ounce of energy from me. All that was left was frustration over my current predicament. "This is just flippin' fantastic," I muttered under my breath. All I'd wanted to do that morning was surprise Emmett with breakfast in bed, but instead I'd stumbled onto the scene of a murder my ex could've possibly committed—*and* I was under arrest for assaulting a cop. When he woke up, Emmett was going to be surprised, all right.

"I'm sorry, Ame," Mickey whispered.

I swiveled my head to glare at him. "What for?" I snapped. "Passing out in a drunken stupor next to your bandmate's corpse? Or killing him?"

"You know I didn't do it." He sounded hurt.

"Shut up," Officer Watts ordered, laying her hand on her gun holster. "Not another word outta either of you, got it?" She stood over us until her backup arrived. Mickey and I were separated and ushered into separate squad cars. I ducked my head as a pudgy, gray-haired policeman guided me into the backseat of his cruiser and then slammed the door behind me.

What really happened last night? I wondered, watching Mickey disappear into the back of the other vehicle. I truly didn't know what to think. Mickey had seemed so confused when I shined my flashlight beam to show him Sid's body. My ex-honey had never been able to lie to me when we were together, and there was nothing in his reaction to seeing his dead bandmate that suggested he was being less than honest. *Still...*a thin line of doubt traced its way through my thoughts. Mickey *had* been angry with Sid the night before, angrier than I'd ever seen him. I frowned. For the most part, he still seemed like the same sweet, funny guy I fell in love with years ago—but was there something darker hiding beneath the surface? Was the ex-love of my life really capable of cold-blooded murder?

* * *

An hour later I was cowering in a cinder block cell downtown. Thanks to an influx of DUIs and drunk and disorderly charges from Saturday night, I'd been ushered straight to holding and was still waiting to be processed. My purse and cell phone were confiscated, but at least I could enjoy the comfort of my shorts and halter top for just a bit longer before having to trade them in for an ugly jumpsuit. Of course, behind-bars fashion was the least of my worries. What a Sunday this was shaping up to be—I had discovered a dead body, been arrested, and was now facing felony charges, all before my morning coffee.

"What're you in for?" drawled a woman sitting near me on the concrete bench. She was younger, probably in her early twenties, with a narrow chin and high cheekbones. A thick layer of last night's sparkly makeup was smeared above her hazel eyes. Her hair was dyed a golden tint so shiny that it couldn't be natural. In fact, in the harsh lighting of our shared cell, I could see her real hair color—a dark, blackish brown—beginning to creep back through her scalp. *Root rot. That's what Kat would call it.* I grimaced at the thought of my bestie, who would probably be finding out about Sid's murder and Mickey's and my arrests any minute now. I hadn't been granted a phone call yet, so hopefully Kat would reach out to Emmett—knowing I was in jail instead of dead in the gutter might ease his worry by at least a fraction.

"You dumb or somethin'?" Goldilocks asked, jarring me from my thoughts. She squinted at me. "Or deaf?" The young woman held up her hands and made several exaggerated gestures that I assumed were a poor attempt at sign language. "Whaaaat aaaare yooooou iiiiiin fooooooooor?" she practically yelled, stretching out each syllable.

I winced. "Assault."

"Assault?" Goldie's gaze traveled to the bruise on my temple, and her face pinched with concern. She lowered her voice. "Honey, was your man beatin' on you? Bless your heart!"

I held up my hands. "No, no—nothing like that. I, er, sort of attacked a police officer." My cheeks colored.

Goldie's eyebrows shot up. "You fought a pig?" She grinned. "That's badass!" She leaned toward me, offering her hand for a high five. I declined with a tiny shake of my head, but it didn't dampen her enthusiasm any. She sat cross-legged and leaned forward, her thin face cradled in her hands and her elbows propped on her knees. "Tell me all about it," Goldie said, her eyes dancing with excitement. "Did ya sock him good? What kind of weapon did ya use? A bat? A pipe? Or did ya clobber the sucker with your bare hands?" She caught the shocked look on my face and shrugged her shoulders. "What? A girl's gotta know how to defend herself."

"It was pepper spray," I admitted, my tone sheepish. "And it was an accident." I watched as the young woman's face fell in disappointment. "What about you?" I asked to change the subject. Judging from her skin-tight leather skirt and barely-there tank top, I had a pretty good idea why she was here.

Goldie blew out a breath. "Prostitution," she said, making air quotes with her fingers. She rolled her eyes. "It's a load of bull, though—I ain't no hooker. I get that a lot, probably because of my job."

I arched a brow. "So you're…a stripper?"

"Uh-huh," she said brightly. "Well, actually I prefer 'exotic dancer.' I work down at the Saucy Minx, near Little Five Points." She stuck out her hand and pumped mine up and down.

"Ah. Explains the outfit," I blurted.

The girl's smile faded. "These ain't my stage clothes," she said coolly.

Whoops. "Sorry." I bit my lip. "I didn't mean to offend you." It was my turn to sigh. "It's just been a really long morning."

Goldie shook her mane of shiny hair and grinned at me. "It's cool. Name's Jenny, by the way—but everyone calls me Coral. That's my stage name—I dress like a mermaid and sing dirty sailor songs for my routine. And I wear coral-colored nail polish and matching pasties on my nipples." She waggled her fingers in front of me so I could see the pinkish color of her fingernails. Her hazel eyes lit up. "Hey, wanna hear one of my songs?" She didn't wait for me to respond. Luckily, as she began to belt some tune about, er, sea men, there was a buzzing sound and the cell door slid open. A tall, muscled guard filled the threshold and stood glaring at us, his arms folded over his chest.

"You," he barked, aiming his hard gaze my way. "Come with me."

I gulped. *Time to get processed. This is it. I'm officially a criminal.* Fighting back tears, I rose from the cell bench on wobbly legs and shot my cellmate a helpless look. "Nice meeting you, Jenny," I said quietly.

"Call me Coral," she said. "Good luck, Pepper Spray Girl. When you get out, you should drop by the Saucy Minx sometime." Her lips curled up at the corners. "First lap dance is on me!"

"Thanks," I mumbled, my face flushing. I waved good-bye and then turned toward the guard, raising my arms in front of me so he could slap handcuffs on my wrists. To my surprise, he turned and stepped back into the hall without cuffing me. I followed him in stunned silence, wondering if this was some kind of trick—or maybe he was trying to win over my trust so I'd cooperate when they were ready to question me about Sid and Mickey.

After being buzzed through several more secure doorways, we reached the drab-looking lobby of the Atlanta City Detention Center. Instead of being handed a stack of paperwork, the clerk handed over my purse and phone. "What's going on?" I asked, eyebrows scrunched together.

"You're free to go," said the cop behind the counter.

My heartbeat fluttered. "I don't understand." I sent a questioning look over my shoulder at my escort.

"Officer Thompson dropped the charges," the man said. I waited for him to go on, but instead he flagged down a passing officer. "Take her to APD," he said to the short, sandy-haired cop. "Dixon's waiting for her in the bullpen."

Dixon. My ears perked at the familiar name. Detective Ben Dixon investigated the murders at Castle Rock last fall. We hadn't always seen eye-to-eye—especially when he'd listed my best friend as his top suspect—but we had a mutual respect for one another. If Detective Dixon was assigned to solve Sid's murder, then I'd do my best to cooperate.

Still dubious (yet seriously grateful!) over my sudden release, I followed the officer out to the ACDC parking lot where he ushered me into an unmarked car. The beige-colored Atlanta Police Department building was a short, two-minute drive away on Pryor Street. As I followed my escort down the catwalk that led to the double-door entrance, I retrieved my phone from my purse. There were two missed calls, two voice mails, and seven texts. I swiped open my text inbox.

Three of the messages were from Bronwyn, which wasn't surprising, given that her father was an APD police sergeant. She'd probably heard news of Sid's murder and my arrest on his home police scanner.

HOLY CRAP, AME! said Bron's first message, in all caps. I opened the second. *Just talked to Dad. They're dropping the charges. Hang tight!* The third was simply a picture of a "Get Out of Jail Free" card from the board game, Monopoly. I shook my head, a little smile curling my lips for the first time in hours.

The three messages from Kat were short, also in all caps. Based on the time stamps, she'd sent them in a rapid-fire succession:

OMG! Are you ok??
What happened?
On my way!

She'd sent the last message only fifteen minutes before I opened it. Bless her—my best friend hadn't even waited for my phone call. She was already on her way to bail me out. *I'm fine— charges dropped* I texted back. *Headed to APD. Wait for me in the lobby.*

The final message was from Emmett, also saying he was on his way downtown. My heart swelled in my chest, and my eyes grew misty again. It meant a lot that my friends and boyfriend would drop everything to come to my rescue. I wondered if the remaining members of Royal Flush were doing the same for Mickey right then.

"Excuse me," I said to the sandy-haired cop just before we reached the entrance. He turned and eyed me warily. "Do you know if the man I was with has been released too?" I asked.

The cop grunted and shrugged his shoulders. "No clue," he said.

My chest tightened, and unease settled back in my stomach. *Stay calm,* I reassured myself as I followed the officer into the building. *Maybe Dixon will have some answers.*

We passed through the lobby and entered a familiar hallway. I glanced up as I was escorted past one of the doors along the right wall, Sergeant Eddie Sinclair's office. I'd visited Bronwyn's father there once last November when, much to the Sarge's dismay, I'd taken it upon myself to try to help his men solve the murders of two of my close friends.

Based on the texts I'd received from Bron, it seemed I owed Sergeant Sinclair a *huge* debt of gratitude for getting me out of my near-felony. I'd find a way to thank him later—maybe by having his favorite pizza delivered for lunch every day for the next month. My stomach growled at the thought. I sneaked another glance at my phone and found it was a quarter till noon. All I'd eaten that day was half a scone, but this was the first time I'd felt even the slightest hunger pang. Nothing like finding a dead body to kill your appetite.

The bullpen was located at the end of the hall. At least ten desks filled the large room, each with papers and files scattered across their surfaces. Plain-clothes detectives sat behind them answering the loudly ringing phones, click-clacking away on keyboards, and interviewing witnesses for various minor crimes. My police escort led me to the desk in the far left corner of the room. The man seated there looked up from his computer monitor as we approached. He was stocky with short red hair, a matching beard, and sharp green eyes. "Good afternoon, Miss Grace," he said.

"Hello, Detective Dixon," I said politely. The officer who brought me in nodded to the detective and then took his leave. Dixon motioned to a plastic chair against the wall in front of his desk. I pulled it forward and took a seat facing him.

"I hear you've had quite the morning," he began. "Assault on a uniformed law enforcement officer—I never pegged you for a felon, Amelia." He made a *tsk tsk* sound with his tongue.

I opened my mouth to insist my innocence, but his eyes crinkled at the corners, and I realized he was teasing me. "Do you know why the charges were dropped?" I asked instead.

Detective Dixon grinned. "Somebody up there likes you. The Sarge went to see Thompson at the hospital. As soon as the poor guy was able to utter something other than words that'd make a sailor blush, he told Sinclair he wasn't going to press charges. Thompson said he saw you were being chased and knows you acted on instinct—he figured you wouldn't have pulled the trigger on that pepper spray if you'd known you were up against a cop."

I nodded, dropping my gaze to the floor. "I didn't know what was happening until it was too late," I said, my tone remorseful. "I saw his gun, and suddenly I was facing Shawn Stone's hitman all over again."

Dixon clasped his hands and rested them on the desk. He gave a nod of understanding. "Sounds kinda like PTSD." He met my gaze. "Have you sought therapy after everything that happened last year?" he asked.

"Just physical therapy for my leg," I replied, clenching my jaw. I wasn't in the mood for another dark trip down memory lane. "I'm assuming you had me brought down here to talk about Sid Malone," I added, changing the subject.

The detective studied me for a moment, and then he nodded. "Nothing gets by you, does it?" He winked as he straightened in his seat and placed his hands on his keyboard. "I'd like you to walk me through what happened this morning when you discovered the body."

"This is like déjà vu." I gave him a rueful smile.

"Tell me everything."

I gave Dixon the play-by-play of my morning, from arriving at Castle Rock and seeing the tour bus door open, to tripping over Sid's boot in the dark and shining my flashlight beam down into his lifeless face. When I reached the part where I found Mickey unconscious in the back of the bus, I paused. Was what I was about to say going to incriminate the former love of my life?

Dixon read the reluctance in my body language. "It's okay," he said, his tone reassuring. "I know you're worried about your friend, but holding something back won't do him any favors." A steely look flickered across his face. "And that wouldn't end well for you either," he reminded me.

I nodded. "I know," I said quietly. "Does that mean you're still holding Mickey?"

My heart sank to my stomach as the Detective nodded. He gave me a look of apology. "I'm sorry, Amelia, but we have to. He's the only lead we've got right now."

I slumped in my seat. "How long can you hold him if there's no solid proof?"

Dixon's brow creased. He glanced around to make sure no one was paying us any attention. Seeming satisfied that we had privacy, he leaned forward and lowered his voice. "You know I'm not supposed to be telling you all of this—especially with such a high profile case—but in light of what you went through to help us last year, consider this my way of saying thank you." He darted another gaze around the room before continuing. "We can only hold Mr. Ward for the next few days while we look for more evidence. Given Malone's and his celebrity status, we're already getting all kinds of pressure to crack this as soon as possible. If we don't find anything, Ward will walk, but if we do..." Detective Dixon's words trailed off, letting the implication sink in. I shuddered. *Mickey will go down for Sid's murder.*

The detective met my gaze. "If you want to help your friend, Miss Grace, then you'll tell me everything you know."

"All right." I took a steadying breath and continued with my statement. "Mickey was out cold, so I slapped his cheek a few times until I was able to wake him up. He swears he doesn't remember what happened when he returned to the tour bus last night..."

"Yet there was blood all over his shoes," Dixon finished for me.

"Right," I agreed, trying to keep my tone even. I fixed the detective with a thoughtful look. "But I'm not sure he had anything to do with Sid's death."

"Then why'd you run from him?"

I held out my hands, fingers splayed. "For the same reason that I hit Officer Thompson with the pepper spray," I replied. "I was scared." The detective studied me for several moments without speaking, so I kept going. "I found Mickey near the body with his shoes covered in blood, and I panicked. Now that I've had some time to calm down and think it through, something doesn't quite add up. Where was the weapon? And why would Mickey hang around after committing the crime?"

Dixon glanced down at his notes. "You told Officer Grimm down at ACDC that you smelled alcohol on Mr. Ward's breath," he said, ignoring my first question. "Maybe he killed Sid Malone in a drunken rage."

"Or maybe he was so hammered that he stumbled over Sid's body without even realizing it was there," I challenged. I leaned forward, placing my hands on the desk. "Look, Detective. I've known Mickey Ward for years, and I'm just not sure he's capable of killing someone."

"He might be where you're concerned—especially after Malone gave you that shiner." He gestured to the bruise on my temple.

I flinched. "You know about that?"

The detective didn't respond right away. Instead, he swiveled in his chair and began plunking on his keyboard. After a few taps and clicks, he placed his hands on either side of his computer. "The whole internet knows," he said finally, turning the monitor so that I could see the screen. I felt my stomach clench at the sight of the *Tune Talks* logo in the header of the website Dixon pulled up. Whatever he wanted to show me, I knew I wasn't going to like it.

Dixon clicked his mouse several more times until he located Tim Scott's blog. The title of today's post read *Royal Flush Bass Guitarists Battle and You Won't Believe What Happens Next!* A video was embedded in the post, and as the detective pressed play, I could plainly see Sid and Dillon glaring at each other from across the autograph table in Castle Rock's tower. The gritty, low-quality video clip appeared to have been taken on a cell phone, probably from one of the fans at the meet and greet. There was no sound, but it was obvious by the body language of the two men that they were arguing. Several seconds into the footage, Sid ran around the table and began to beat his fists on Dillon.

As I looked on in horror, my own face appeared on the screen. The video version of me rushed forward, arms out as I tried to break up the fight between the two bass guitarists. Suddenly, Sid's fist shot out and connected with the right side of my face. Video Ame went completely rigid and then dropped to the floor. The clip froze there and rewound on its own, repeating Sid's knockout punch to my temple over and over again while the theme song from the *Rocky* movies played in the background.

I was still gaping at the footage when Detective Dixon turned his computer monitor back around. "That must have made you pretty mad, huh?" he remarked. He clasped his hands in front of him and gave me a predatory smile. "I'd like to ask a few more questions now. For starters, where were *you* last night after this incident occurred?"

CHAPTER EIGHT

———

"I'm going to kill Tim Scott!" I thundered, slamming my fist down on the table so hard that the plates and silverware rattled. Some of my whiskey sour sloshed over the side of its glass, the splash narrowly missing my half-eaten slice of Camila's chicken pesto pizza. I ground my teeth and pushed my plate away, seething.

"Calm down, babe," Emmett said in a soothing tone. He slid his arm around my shoulders and began rubbing my back with one hand. "It's going to be all right."

"Easy for you to say," I grumbled. "A video of you getting your lights punched out didn't just go viral. The YouTube clip already has thirteen thousand views!" I slurped down more booze. It didn't matter that it was before five p.m. on a Sunday—I'd earned a stiff drink.

"Then you should be happy," Bronwyn said, her lips curled in a smirk. "That makes you an online celebrity. You're insta-famous!"

"And an insta-suspect." I blew out a breath. "I should've known when Dixon started feeding me details on what he knew about Mickey that he was just softening me up for my own interrogation."

After showing me the video on Tim's blog, the detective had turned his suspicion on me, saying the pain and embarrassment from Sid's right hook to my face could give me possible motive—and, according to him, it was "awfully convenient" that I found and reported the body. It was by the grace of a higher power (or "by the Grace of Amelia," Kat had teased, poking fun at my name) that I alibied out of the timeline they'd worked out for Sid's murder. Our bouncer, Derek, was able to confirm that he drove me straight home from Castle Rock the night before, and Emmett vouched that I was at my apartment with him all night, er, *recuperating*. Still, though I was in the clear, the viral video and temporary murder suspect status were just two more slices of stink on my crap sandwich of a day. *Ugh.*

"Relax," Emmett murmured, kissing my hair. "It was nothing personal. Dixon's gotta follow up on any and all possible leads—especially with a case like this that's going to get major media attention. Until he gets results back from the crime lab, the suspect pool is pretty wide."

"Well, hand me a towel, 'cause I'm tired of swimming," I said sulkily. I sipped my drink again. "I swear, the next time I see Tim Scott, I'm going to knee him right in the balls. He turned me into click bait!" I gave a disgusted growl.

"Sheesh," Kat said from across the booth. "Prison changed you, Ame." She playfully stuck her tongue out at me when I aimed a sour expression her way.

"Yeah, what was jail like, anyway?" Bronwyn asked, a look of wicked fascination on her face. She pulled a mushroom off her slice of Camila's veggie pizza and popped it into her mouth then chased it down with her Coke. "Did a butch chick named Bertha try to make you her bitch? Did you have to shank anyone?"

I rolled my eyes. "You've been watching too much *Orange Is the New Black*. I wasn't in prison, just a holding cell at the detention center." I gave Bron a sardonic smile. "And I think the word you're looking for is *shiv*, not shank."

"Nah, either works—check Urban Dictionary," Bronwyn joked. "They both describe something used to stab someone—" Her words caught in her throat, and a mortified expression spread across her pale face. The laughter at the table died out as quickly as if someone had just doused us with a bucket of ice-cold water. The four of us sat in somber silence, the gravity of the situation crashing back into focus. "Oh man," Bron said finally, her voice above a whisper. "I'm sorry. I shouldn't have joked about it, I just—it's so surreal, ya know?"

I nodded. "It's okay. You were just trying to cheer me up. I think we're all just trying to find a way to deal right now."

"I talked to Chad and Jack this morning." Kat shook her head sadly. "They were stunned. Sid's a total jerk-off, but he didn't deserve to die." She chewed her lip and gave me a troubled look. "Is Castle Rock cursed? I feel like every time I turn around we're getting shut down as part of a crime scene." While I was in jail, Kat had spoken with Sergeant Eddie Sinclair, who requested that Castle Rock close for a day or two while the investigation was underway. We were ordered not to enter the building in case the crime techs found anything on the tour bus that led their search into the venue.

I blew out a sigh. "Well, at least it's not like the Bobby Glitter fiasco," I said. "Our biggest show of the weekend happened last night, and we're closed from Sunday to Tuesday anyway." If ever there was a time we could afford to be shut down for another murder investigation, this was it—not that there is ever a good time for that sort of thing.

"Some freaking silver lining," Kat muttered. Her gaze shifted to something above my head, and the color drained from her pretty face. "Sharon!" she called to our waitress as the plump woman passed by our booth balancing a tray with a calzone and two pints of beer. "Can you turn up the TV?"

"Sure thing, hon," the middle-aged waitress said with a nod. She set the tray down in front of the patrons at the booth behind ours and started toward the bar counter, her red beehive hairstyle—part of her 50's style Camila's uniform—bobbing up and down as she went.

Emmett and I swiveled around in our seats to see what had caught Kat's attention. My jaw dropped. "Crap," I moaned, staring at the photograph of Mickey's face that filled the television. "The media frenzy has started."

Sharon turned up the volume, and the news reporter's voice grew louder. "…was brought in just this morning on charges of suspected murder," the blonde woman in a red skirt and blazer set was saying. "Ward is accused of killing this man—his Royal Flush bandmate, Sidney Jacob Malone." The screen cut to a close-up of Sid playing his bass guitar on stage at last night's show. "Malone was found stabbed to death on the band's tour bus. Our sources say Mickey Ward was present when the body was discovered."

"If local news has picked it up, the national media will be all over this in a matter of hours," Kat said, her voice tight with worry. She flicked a quick glance at me. "I should check on Chad and the guys. Chad said the tour's been postponed, and they'll probably be holed up in their hotel rooms to avoid the reporters and paparazzi."

I nodded. "Good idea. Give them all a hug for me. I'll call you later." I waved good-bye to Kat as she slid out of the booth. She placed a twenty-dollar bill next to her plate and headed for the door.

"You think Mickey really did it?" Bronwyn asked.

I shook my head. "I don't know what to believe," I said honestly. "He was there when I found the body, but..." I paused, looking from Emmett to Bron. "You guys should've seen him." My forehead wrinkled. "He seemed so genuinely shocked when he saw Sid's body."

"It could've been an act," Emmett suggested, running his fingers through his short, black hair. "Of course he'd want you to believe he was innocent."

I tilted my head to face him. "But what if Mickey really is telling the truth?" I asked.

Emmett let one shoulder rise and fall. "That's for the detectives to determine."

"I'll bet it was that Dillon guy who showed up last night," Bronwyn piped up, "the one who used to be in the band." She met my gaze, a look of excitement dancing across her young face. "Let's bust the sucker, Ame! Just like old times."

Our shared near-death experience back in November had left Bron more fascinated than terrified. Ever since, she'd been chomping at the bit to do more amateur detective work. Last month, she'd even managed to track down a thief who was stealing instruments from several Atlanta concert venues, including Castle Rock.

"That's a terrible idea," Emmett said. He shot Bronwyn a stern look that made her flinch. "This isn't some Nancy Drew novel or cutesy sleuth movie on the Hallmark Channel." His face reddened, and his voice grew louder. "This is real life! Your actions have real consequences. Didn't you learn anything from what happened last year? You two were nearly killed!" He was practically shouting now.

"Sorry," Bronwyn said, her voice subdued. Her cheeks glowed nearly as pink as her hair.

"Whoa, easy there, tiger." I put a hand on Emmett's arm. While everything he said was true, I was taken aback by the sudden outburst. People from other booths were even staring.

Emmett huffed, and I felt some of the tension ease out of his body as he rested against me. "Catching criminals and solving murders is dangerous," he said, clasping my hand in his. "And after this morning, it's probably best that you don't do anything that could earn you more attention from the police— that includes snooping around, looking for ways to prove your ex-boyfriend didn't kill his bandmate."

I wasn't thrilled about Emmett's *ex-boyfriend* comment, but his use of the word *snooping* was what really got my panties in a twist. "I wasn't *snooping*," I said in a clipped tone. "And what happened this morning was an accident." I hadn't told him all of the details leading up to my mistaken assault on Officer Thompson, but now didn't seem like a good time to mention that I'd been running from Mickey since it'd only support his side of the argument. "And besides, Detective Dixon told me to let him know if I came across anything that might help with the case. I don't want to see my *friend* sit in jail if he's innocent." I put extra emphasis on the word friend.

"But that doesn't give you license to launch your own investigation, babe." Emmett's jaw tightened.

"I never said I was going to," I shot back. I took a gulp of my whiskey sour, but the burning in my gut was more from anger than the alcohol. Emmett and I glared at each other in silence, the tension between us thick enough to cut with Sharon's pizza slicer.

"Um, you guys," Bronwyn said from across the booth. "I, er, just remembered I have to be somewhere else. Gotta fold laundry or file my taxes or something…" Just as Kat had done earlier, Bron slapped some money on the table and hopped out of the booth, making a beeline for the front door. I couldn't blame her. I didn't want to stick around for the fight brewing between Emmett and me either.

"What is going on with you?" I asked him when Bronwyn was gone.

"Me?" Emmett's dark brows lifted. "What about you, Amelia?" He scowled. "It's like you go looking for trouble."

"That's not fair," I said stiffly. "I didn't ask to find a freaking dead body *again*. All I wanted to do was surprise you with breakfast, but I had to stop by the office on the way home. I was just trying to do something nice, and then—" My lip began to quiver, and a lone tear slid down my right cheek.

Emmett saw the pain on my face, and his own expression softened. "I'm sorry." He sighed. "I'm just a little worked up. The job has been wearing me down lately, and then this morning when I got up, you were just gone. No note, no text—nothing. The next thing I know, Kat is calling to tell me you've been arrested." Emmett lifted his hand from the table, tightening it into a fist. He relaxed his grip a few seconds later and met my gaze. "I was really worried about you."

"I'm sorry too," I murmured. "I should've called as soon as I found Sid's body, to let you know what happened and that I was all right." I squeezed his hand. "I don't want to fight." My voice was soft, barely above a whisper.

"Me neither." Emmett leaned over to plant a light kiss on my lips. When he pulled away, his mouth stretched in a wide grin. "So, I guess I'll take a rain check on that surprise breakfast," he said, his emerald eyes twinkling.

I chuckled. "It's still in my car, if you want it—that is, if you like stale chocolate raspberry scones and—" I checked my watch—"six-hour-old coffee."

Emmett snorted. "I think I'll pass."

"Speaking of my car." I uncrossed my legs under the booth and reached for my purse. "It's still parked at Castle Rock. I should go get it before the media storm hits our block."

Emmett gently grabbed my wrist as I retrieved a few bills from my wallet. "Lunch is on me," he said. "And I'll drive you to your car."

"I think I'd like to walk there, if you don't mind." I gave him an apologetic smile. "It's only a couple of blocks away, and I need to walk off that whiskey sour before I get behind the wheel."

"Then let me drive you home. We can get your car later."

I bit my lip. "Actually, if it's all the same to you, I'd rather just go ahead and do it now. I could use a little alone time to process everything that happened today."

"Oh." Emmett's smile faded. "Sure." He nodded as if he understood, but I could tell my request for some space had wounded him a little.

I rose from the booth and leaned down to kiss his forehead. "I'll be fine. I'll meet you back at the apartment. We can take it easy tonight and go see the band tomorrow at the hotel. I imagine they're going to want a little privacy while they process the news about Sid and Mickey and sort out the next several tour dates." With Kat already on her way over to see the guys, I didn't want to crowd them.

"Great." Emmett avoided my gaze. "Hey," he said, his voice growing softer. "Are we okay?"

His words tugged at my heartstrings. "Better than okay." I gave him another kiss and flashed my best *Everything is fine!* smile. "We're great, I promise. In fact," I added shyly, feeling my cheeks grow warm, "I was sort of wondering if there was any way that you could stay in Atlanta a little longer. Just for a few more days, until the worst of this blows over." I gave him a meaningful look. "I need you."

Emmett reached up and stroked my hair. "Of course. I'll call Gavin and let the Bureau know I'm extending my leave."

Though it was exactly what I'd just asked him to do, a feeling of unease prickled my skin. "Will that be all right?" I asked, unable to mask my concern. "With the search for Stone still underway?"

"I'll handle it." Emmett gave me a reassuring smile. "Besides, you'll be safer with me here to protect you."

My face relaxed. "Thanks, babe," I said warmly.

"My pleasure." He beamed up at me. "Anything for the woman I love."

* * *

What the hell is wrong with me? I wiped the sweat from my brow and trudged onward up North Avenue on the two-block walk to Castle Rock, sifting through my tangled mess of thoughts. My charming, gorgeous, gainfully-employed boyfriend had just dropped the L word for the first time, and like the true freak of nature that I was, I'd all but bolted out of the restaurant.

I chewed my lip, picturing the look of thinly-veiled disappointment that had flickered behind Emmett's eyes at my lack of response. He put his life on hold to come down to Atlanta and see me—and I'd just asked him to stay even longer. I told him I needed him—why couldn't I also tell him I loved him?

Because I'm not sure if I do. The thought made me queasy. We'd been together for more than half a year—by this point, I should know the full scope of my feelings for him, in theory. The problem was, we'd only gotten real face time (the video calls on our smart phones didn't count) on half a dozen occasions at most. My romantic side wanted to believe that was enough time with Emmett to know in my heart if he was *the one*, but the realist in me begged for more time to make up my mind. Rather than be honest with him about my relationship bipolarity, I'd hauled ass out of the restaurant.

"He could've had better timing," I muttered under my breath, as if blaming him for sharing his feelings was a perfectly rational thing to do. After all, in less than twenty-four hours, I'd been punched in the face, found a dead body, was arrested and released from jail, was briefly suspected of murder, became an internet sensation, and was told by my adorable man that he was in love with me. Not to mention that my first love had returned to town and was, at that very moment, sitting in jail on suspected murder charges. It was enough to make a girl's head spin and not in a good way. All aboard the Amelia Grace Emotional Rollercoaster—must be *this screwed up* to ride.

I kicked a rock up the sidewalk as my thoughts shifted back to Mickey and his current predicament. Despite Emmett's warning about butting in on the investigation, I couldn't help but wonder who else might want Sid Malone dead. Speculation certainly wouldn't get me arrested again, so long as I didn't act on it. Plus the puzzle was a welcome distraction from my guilt over leaving Emmett hanging back at Camila's. I promised myself I'd sit down and talk things through with him later and then forced him out of my mind, shifting my focus toward making a mental list of people who might have wanted Sid dead.

Bronwyn had been right—Dillon Green was an obvious choice. Kat and I were somewhat close with Dillon before he was booted from the band. He'd always been a nice, down-to-earth guy before. Missing out on his shot at fame had clearly changed him, judging from his behavior the previous night. Dillon came to Castle Rock to pick a fight—but would his beef with Sid drive him to murder? And if not, who else might have it out for the arrogant bass guitarist?

Chad would know, I thought. Given his gossipy nature, Chad was sure to know if there was bad blood between Sid and anyone else on the tour. Maybe he'd mouthed off at a roadie one too many times. I decided that I would pull Chad aside tomorrow and see if he had any insight on a motive for Sid's untimely demise.

Sweat poured down my back as I began my trek up the steepest slope of North Avenue. My limbs felt heavy and stiff, and I was bone-tired from the day's stress. I pushed on, trudging underneath the overpass of the East Atlanta Belt Line and finally cresting the large hill. My relief at finally reaching Castle Rock evaporated when the entrance came into view. The whole area was already teeming with activity. Three news vans were parked in the gravel below the marquee, and several reporters stood in front, using the venue as a backdrop for their broadcasts. A dozen or more people were gathered on the street corner beside the building, some dressed all in black and others wearing Royal Flush T-shirts and hats. They huddled together, solemn-faced and grasping candles, flowers, and magazine covers with Sid's image. I blinked at the fans, surprised. *They're holding a vigil.* That this might happen hadn't even occurred to me.

A black cargo van rolled up to the building, blocking the mourning Royal Flush fans from view as it came to a stop in front of the venue. A flash of rage burned through me at the sight of the familiar red and black 95Rox station logo on the side panel. Tim Scott climbed out of the driver's side, dressed in jeans and a baseball T-shirt bearing the same logo. *Oh, hell no.* I gritted my teeth. My hands balled into fists at my sides, and I quickened my pace. I wanted to march up to Tim and kick him in the crotch for setting Sid up to fight with Dillon for the sake of entertaining his dim-witted listeners.

Rational thought caught up with me after a few steps, halting me in my tracks. *What am I doing?* Even though he'd probably orchestrated Dillon's and Sid's showdown and had immortalized my knockout punch on the internet, I didn't have the energy to pick a fight with Tim right now. Plus there were news cameras everywhere and a crowd. I'd have to confront the jerk another day.

Of course, no sooner had I changed my mind than Tim started to turn in my direction. *Shit!* I panicked, not wanting to be spotted, and dove into the bushes at the edge of the overpass. "Ow!" I yelped as I tumbled to the ground. Branches raked at my face and arms along the way, and I twisted around, landing squarely on my butt. I ignored the sharp pain that shot through my tail bone and froze, listening intently. A couple of cars rolled by on North Avenue, and the chatter in front of Castle Rock continued, but no footsteps approached. No one seemed to have noticed me or my quick disappearing act. Still, there was no way I could get back out of the bushes—much less to my car, behind the venue—without attracting attention. I was stuck.

Just when I thought this day couldn't get any worse. I blew my tangled, leaf-and-twig-filled hair out of my face and chewed my lower lip. By now I regretted the decision to walk back to Castle Rock rather than catch a ride with Emmett. I could try to wait for the news crews and crowds to disperse, but that could take hours. Plus it would be dark soon, and I'd heard some pretty sketchy stories about things that went on under the overpass late at night. I scanned the dirt around me and wrinkled my nose. A used condom lay a foot or so to my left. Next to it were a hypodermic needle and a little baggie caked with white residue. *Great, I'm trapped in a crackhead's love nest.* I shuddered and scooted away from the pile of paraphernalia.

My hand grazed something plastic in the dirt, and I jerked back, stifling a disgusted squeal. I peered down at the clear cocktail cup I'd nearly crushed. The letters *R* and *F* were etched into the plastic. *This cup came from the tour bus!* I realized, my pulse quickening. I leaned down to get a closer look. The cup was speckled with dark, reddish brown spots. *Wine?* I frowned, wondering why a drink from Royal Flush's bus would be all the way over here in the bushes. Maybe a bum had wandered onto the tour bus last night after all and helped himself to the minibar. *Or a call girl,* I thought, taking in the bright pink lipstick that stained the rim in several places. Could Sid have brought a groupie or an escort on board?

I reached down to pick up the drink for a better look but froze as my gaze settled on another item in the bushes. The silver handle of a pocketknife stuck out of the ground a few inches away from the cup. Its blade was half-buried in the dirt. Looking from the knife back to the cup, I noted the matching rust-colored stains. Despite the Georgia summer heat, a shiver worked its way down my spine and arms. *It's not wine...it's blood.* I recalled how Detective Dixon had ignored my question when I'd asked if the murder weapon had been found. *Could this be it?*

Riffling through my purse, I produced a package of Kleenex and grabbed one of the tissues. *Don't do it*, a voice in my head pleaded, sounding a lot like Emmett. I paused, my tissue-filled hand hovering just above the knife handle.

"It's not like I'm actually going to touch it," I muttered under my breath. Even I knew better than to get my prints on the knife. Pinching the tissue between my fingers, I slid it around the hilt and pulled the blade out of the dirt, lifting it to get a better look. A sick feeling ran through me as I inspected the silver handle with the familiar lightning bolt etched on the side. It looked eerily similar to one I'd given Mickey on our one-year anniversary. *Please be a coincidence,* I thought, afraid to turn it over.

With a shaky breath, I flipped the knife around to see the other side and promptly dropped it to the ground as if it had burned me. Two letters were engraved on the handle.

M.W.
Mickey Ward.

CHAPTER NINE

———

After waiting nearly an hour for the news crews and mourning fans to disperse, I was finally able to come out of my hiding spot in the bushes. I'd let Emmett know that I would be a little late coming home, texting him that I needed to wait longer to sober up before driving. I don't think he bought it—especially when I walked through my apartment door that evening looking visibly shaken and with a few leaves and twigs still stuck in my hair.

"Are you all right?" he'd demanded, leaping from the couch to inspect me for injuries. Emmett gripped my shoulders and held me at arm's length as he looked me over, concern etched on his handsome face.

I gently pulled myself out of his grip. "I'm fine," I said, avoiding his gaze. The truth was, I wasn't fine—I'd just found what I believed to be Mickey's bloody pocketknife in the bushes near the crime scene. A knife that *I* had given him. I felt nauseous at the thought that I'd unwittingly played a part in this by gifting Mickey the potential murder weapon.

Torn between turning it over to the police and keeping it in the apartment where Emmett might see, I'd finally decided to leave both the knife and the stained cup right where I'd found them. For now, at least. I'd snapped a few pictures of both pieces of evidence on my cell phone and then used the Kleenex to move them deeper into the bushes. I would return for them when I had a plan—and a better idea of who had left lipstick stains on the rim of the cup.

"You don't look fine." Emmett pulled a leaf from my hair and held it up, his brow creased. "What happened?"

"I tripped," I lied, trying to ignore the sour feeling of guilt that pooled in my belly. "On my way up the hill, by the overpass. I fell into one of the bushes." I tucked my chin and dropped my gaze to the floor, trying to look appropriately embarrassed. It *did* sound like something I'd do. *Good ol' Amelia Graceless.*

Emmett's green eyes went dark as he squinted at me. "So, that's it? Nothing else you want to tell me?" The shift in his tone made my blood run cold. It reminded me of the way Detective Dixon sounded when he was pumping me for an alibi. This must be the side of Special Agent Emmett Larson that most people only encountered across the table in an interrogation room.

"Nope," I squeaked, feeling tiny beads of sweat form along my forehead. *He knows I'm lying. He's going to torture me until I tell him everything.* I frowned—I couldn't help it. Fear was an odd reaction to have toward a man who'd just told me he loved me a couple of hours ago. *Quit being ridiculous. He's just worried about me is all.*

"Okay, fine," I said with a sigh, deciding that telling him most of the truth would get him off my back. I'd just leave out the part about discovering potential evidence. "I *might* have hidden in the bushes for a bit to avoid confronting Tim Scott." My cheeks felt hot. "As much as I'd have liked to tear that jerk a new one, I wasn't ready to star in another viral video clip. There were three other news crews there and a bunch of Royal Flush fans."

"Too many witnesses," Emmett remarked. His stony expression cracked, and his mouth quirked up at the corners. "You know, you could've just called me to come pick you up rather than playing hide-and-seek for an hour."

"Thanks, Captain Hindsight," I deadpanned. I reached out and touched his arm, my mood softening. "About before, at Camila's," I began, but Emmett shook his head.

"It's okay. Don't worry about it." His cheeks colored. "Like you said, you've had a hell of a day. I shouldn't have dropped even more heavy stuff on you." He grimaced. "I've never had the best timing with this sort of thing."

"Please don't say that." I stepped closer and leaned against his chest, tilting my head to gaze up at him. "You know I care about you."

"You just need to be able to say it back on your own time," he finished for me. "I get it." Emmett wrapped his arms around me and squeezed. "I can be patient."

A sweet, cool wave of relief washed through me. "Thank you," I whispered. I stood on tiptoe to press my lips against his. Just as our kiss began to deepen, he pulled away.

"I do have some bad news," he said, his expression turning guilty.

"I don't think I can handle any more bad news today," I muttered. I blew out a breath and mentally prepared myself. "What's up?"

"Well, I know I promised I could stay around a bit longer," he began, and my heart thumped. "But I got a call an hour ago. The Bureau needs me back in the Las Vegas office tomorrow. Just for a couple of days—I can be in Atlanta again by Friday, if not sooner."

"When do you leave?" I tried not to sound disappointed.

"Six forty-five tomorrow morning, bright and early."

Yuck. I grimaced. Glancing at the clock on the kitchen stove, I saw it was barely eight in the evening. As far as I was concerned, it might as well be past midnight. "You couldn't pay me to be up that early for a flight."

"Good thing I've got my rental car." He grinned. "I'll let myself out so you can get your beauty sleep."

I let out a long yawn and blinked up at Emmett. "Would you hate me if I started that beauty sleep now? I'm exhausted."

Emmett chuckled and placed his arms behind my back and knees, scooping me off the ground. "Come on," he said, turning to carry me to my room. "Let's put you to bed. Just promise me something," he added, his expression turning serious. "Don't get yourself into any more trouble while I'm gone, okay?"

"I won't," I mumbled drowsily. I was out before my head hit the pillow.

* * *

Emmett was already gone when I awoke around nine on Monday morning. While part of me was sad to see the empty space next to me in the bed, I was also relieved that he'd be away for at least a few days. That would give me time to do some digging into Sid's murder without causing any more tension between us. I quickly showered and got dressed and was happy to see that the bruise on my temple was nearly gone. After feeding my three little pals their morning bowl of Kitty Chow, I dropped by a nearby donut shop to pick up breakfast for the band on my way to the Georgian Terrace Hotel.

Ginger Robbins greeted me at the door to suite 207 a half hour later. I had to bite back a small gasp of surprise at the sight of her. Her long red hair wasn't in its usual flawlessly coiffed style. It hung limp around her shoulders and looked like it hadn't been brushed since she'd taken it down Saturday night. Dark circles rimmed Ginger's eyes, and I noted the smudge of day-old eyeliner and mascara in the corners. It was quite a transformation from the perfectly put-together woman she'd been a couple of days ago.

"We had to unplug the room phone from the wall," the harried band manager said, stepping back to let me in. "It's been ringing off the hook. Someone must've told the media where we're staying." She sighed wearily. "The guys can't even go downstairs without getting mobbed by reporters and paparazzi. Even the pizza delivery boy last night had a camera."

"Well, I brought breakfast," I said holding up the box of fresh pastries from Sublime Donuts. I lifted the cardboard drink carrier in my other hand. "And coffee."

Ginger's tired eyes lit up. "Ohmigod, you're a lifesaver!" She threw her arms around me, nearly knocking the drink carrier out of my hand. "I don't know how much more of this I can handle," she said in a shrill whisper, pulling back to stare at me with wide, desperate eyes. "The band's publicist quit this morning. I've been managing artists for almost ten years, and I've never had to deal with damage control for anything like this. We've had to cancel all of the band's tour dates through Thursday so far, and we don't even know the date for Sid's funeral. Plus who knows when—or even *if*—Mickey will be out of jail to make up the postponed performances." I flinched as she gripped my arm, digging her nails into my skin. "We may have to cancel the whole tour!" she practically hissed.

I weaseled out of Ginger's grasp and rubbed my arm where her nails almost broke the skin. *Ow.* "If they can't find enough evidence to pin Mickey for the murder, he should be out by Wednesday," I told her. "So for now, let's just focus on getting through the next couple of days. Castle Rock is closed until then too, so I'm here to help. Anything you need."

Ginger gave me another grateful squeeze and then led me further into the hotel suite. Zane, Jack, and Suzie were in the common room area gathered in front of the TV. Zane absently twiddled his thumbs as he sat cross-legged on the floor. Behind him, Suzie was curled around Jack on the couch, holding his head to her chest and stroking his straw-colored hair. She looked up as we entered the room and gave a tiny nod of greeting then shyly tucked her chin. Zane gave a half-hearted wave before dropping his forlorn gaze back to the blue and gray carpet. Jack continued staring at the television as if we weren't there.

"Amelia brought donuts," Ginger said in a cheery tone that sounded forced. She took the box of pastries from me and set it down on the coffee table in front of the somber trio.

"Thanks." Zane smiled weakly and leaned forward to open the box, grabbing an Oreo-crumb-covered donut. He picked cookie pieces off the top as he resumed watching the news. I flicked a glance to the TV and saw that *Hollywood Today* was airing a segment on Mickey's arrest. I grimaced when Mickey's mug shot appeared on the screen. Even in the black-and-white photo, he appeared paler, his eyes sunken. My heart ached at the sight of him.

"This is bullshit!" Jack growled. Suzie let out a startled cry as he pushed out of her lap and flung the remote at the TV. It slammed into the screen with a loud *smack* and then clattered to the floor.

"Jack, no!" Ginger yelled, rushing toward the television to inspect the damage. Thankfully, it didn't seem the remote had left any cracks or scratches.

"I'm sorry," Jack said gruffly. "But Mickey wouldn't do something like this. The whole thing is insane." He flopped back down on the couch and hung his head in his hands.

I sat down next to Jack and Suzie and helped myself to an orange-cream-filled donut. "You're right," I said. "Mickey didn't do it, and I'm going to find out who did."

"See? It's going to be okay, Jackie," Suzie said softly, squeezing his hand. It was the first time I'd heard her speak.

"Do you have any leads?" Ginger asked.

I debated telling them about the knife and thought better of it, shaking my head. "Nothing yet, but I'm hopeful. Did Mickey and Sid come back to the hotel with you guys Saturday night?"

Jack shook his head. "We never saw Sid again after he stormed out of the green room. Knowing him, he probably posted up at the nearest titty bar and downed enough Jim Beam to kill an elephant." He gave a bitter laugh. "The way that idiot drank, I wouldn't be surprised if they cut him open and find a flask of bourbon where his liver used to be."

"He carried one with him twenty-four seven," Zane agreed. "A flask, I mean," he added when I gave him a confused look. I'd momentarily pictured Sid with a spare liver in his pocket. *Ick.*

"So, Sid never came back," I summarized. "What about Mickey?"

"Kat dropped him off with us," Ginger replied. "But after that, we're not sure what happened. He and Chad are sharing the suite next door. Chad said that Mickey was there when he went to bed—but the next morning, he was gone."

A frown creased my face. "Where's Chad now?"

"In the other suite," Jack answered. He met my gaze, his blue eyes sad. "Mickey's his best friend," he said. "They're as close as you and Kat. Chad's taking this whole thing harder than anyone."

I swallowed the lump in my throat. I knew how desperately Chad must want to help free Mickey—I felt the same way. "Maybe I should go talk to him," I said, squeezing Jack's shoulder and rising from the sofa. I grabbed two more donuts and one of the to-go coffee cups. "I'll take him some food."

I made my way back into the hall and knocked on the door to suite 208. Several moments passed with no response. Frowning, I knocked again. "Chad? Are you in there? It's Ame."

I leaned forward and pressed my ear to the door, listening. There was a rustling noise, followed by whispered voices, though I couldn't make out what was being said. Soft footsteps padded toward me from the other side, and I pulled my ear back from the door just before it opened. Kat blinked sleepily at me. "Mornin'," she said with a yawn.

"Um, good morning to you too," I said slowly. I looked from her bleary-eyed, makeup-smeared face down to the daisy yellow sundress I could've sworn she'd been wearing the day before at Camila's. Had Kat spent the night with Chad? A smirk curled my lips. *Well, well, well. Good for her!* "I'd have brought an extra coffee if I'd known Chad had company," I said, my voice teasing.

My comment seemed to wake Kat up better than caffeine could. Her eyes went wide, and her cheeks colored. "This is *so* not what it looks like!"

I nodded, still grinning. "Uh-huh. Whatever you say, K." I winked.

Kat's face burned an even deeper shade of red. "Cut it out!" she said in a shrill whisper. "He'll hear you." She cast a furtive glance over her shoulder.

"Who cares?" I replied in the same hushed tone. "This is great, really. I kinda always hoped you two crazy kids would end up together."

Kat rolled her eyes. "Chad just needed someone to talk to, Ame. And besides, this is a horrible time to start something with him..." She blew out a frustrated breath, and then her expression softened. "Just cool it, okay?"

I held up two fingers. "Scout's honor—but you owe me some details later."

"You were never a Girl Scout." Kat arched a brow. She gave an exasperated shake of her head as she stepped aside to let me into the suite.

"How're you holding up, buddy?" I asked Chad, who was sitting with his eyes closed in much the same position that Jack had been on the couch in the other suite. Nostalgia pinged through me as I took in his red-white-and-blue plaid shorts and faded navy blue Atlanta Braves T-shirt. Chad and Mickey had each bought that shirt at the first game we'd attended together the summer Mickey and I started dating. I booked Royal Flush a pre-game gig performing on the brick pavers at Turner Field before first pitch, and we'd all stayed after their set to watch the Braves play the Padres. I couldn't remember who won, but I'd never forget how adorable Mickey looked with his brown hair curling up from under his backwards, wide-brim baseball cap. He'd bought me the same shirt Chad was wearing now, except it was red instead of blue. I still had it tucked away in my closet.

Chad blew out a breath. "Oh, you know," he said, sounding two parts exhausted and one part his normal, sarcastic self. "About as good as I can be, considering I'm holed up, hiding from the news hounds while my best bud is probably trying not to drop the soap in the prison shower." He opened one eye and fixed it on me then opened the other and quickly sat up, his expression turning from tired to hungry. "Ooh, are those Sublime Donuts? I haven't had those in years!" He snatched one out of my grasp and took a huge bite. "Mmmmrph," he said through a mouthful of pastry. I handed him the coffee, and he took a swig to wash down the donut. "Maple cheddar bacon—Ame, you're a goddess," he said dreamily.

"You're welcome." I sat down on the opposite end of the couch, and Kat perched between us. I turned my head to hide a grin when Chad offered Kat his coffee. I handed her the last donut—fresh strawberries and cream, which happened to be her favorite—and the three of us sat in silence for several minutes. "I want to ask you a few questions, if that's all right," I said finally, fixing Chad with an apologetic look. I knew he probably didn't want to talk about Sid or Mickey, but I needed to find out if he knew anything that could point me in the direction of another possible suspect for Sid's murder. If it meant clearing Mickey's name, I knew he'd cooperate.

"Fire when ready," Chad said, though he avoided my gaze.

I'd start with the lipstick-stained cup I'd found next to Mickey's knife. It could've been coincidence, but I wasn't going to rule anything out just yet. "Did Sid like to bring girls on board the tour bus?"

"Sure," Chad said, nodding. "We all did." He shot a glance at Kat, and his ears turned red. "To, er, play poker and stuff."

Kat rolled her eyes. "Right. Probably strip poker." She playfully punched Chad in the arm.

"How did Sid treat the girls he brought around?" I continued, trying to keep the annoyed edge out of my tone. *Now isn't the time for flirting, y'all.*

Chad frowned. "About like you'd expect. I mean, he wouldn't hurt them—" he tilted his head, gesturing to my bruise "—that was an accident, Ame. Really."

"I know," I said. "Keep going."

"All right. You know—he'd use 'em then lose 'em. If a chick managed to stick around for more than ten minutes after Sid was done with her, he'd get security to boot her from the bus. The dude was kind of a dick."

I chewed my lip. So, with the exception of my shiner, Sid wasn't violent toward women. That probably ruled out self-defense. On the other hand, it sounded like he'd left a trail of angry groupies in every state between here and California over the years. It was possible he'd scorned the wrong woman—but how did Mickey's knife come into play? Someone would have to know where he kept it—someone who'd been around longer than one of Sid's disposable girls. "Did Sid have a beef with anyone in the band's camp? A roadie, maybe?"

Chad shoved the second half of his donut in his mouth all at once, staring thoughtfully down at his hands as he chewed. "Not anyone in particular," he said when he'd swallowed. "But I didn't really pay him much attention." His freckled nose crinkled. "To be honest, Sid didn't really get along with anyone especially well. We all kind of thought he was a giant douche."

"Then why didn't you guys kick him out of Royal Flush?" I asked.

"He played a mean bass." Chad shrugged. "He was an arrogant alcoholic in need of a personality transplant—and probably a new liver, too—but he gelled with us onstage. As long as we were making good music, the rest of us just tolerated him."

Okay, so they weren't exactly running a We Love Sid Malone fan club, but that doesn't mean any one member of Royal Flush wanted him dead. Not current members, anyway. "What about Dillon?" I asked.

Chad snorted. "Dillon Green," he said, his tone bitter. "Dill's a street stain. I mean, did you see him? Looked like he'd been living in a cardboard box down on Boulevard for the past five years."

"Chad!" Kat gasped, raising her brows at him.

"What?" he asked indignantly. "You saw how he acted the other night. Sid may have been a total tool, but Dillon's no prize either. I don't care what happened between Jack and him—it was half a decade ago. He had no business showing up and ruining that meet and greet."

"I'm not so sure that little guest appearance was entirely Dill's idea," I said, thinking of Tim Scott. "Didn't you guys used to be close before the split? You didn't keep in touch?"

"Nah." Chad shrugged and dropped his gaze to the floor, his big ears burning. "I mean, yeah, we were buddies back then. But it was hard to stay friends after Jack kicked him out of the band. He was just so bitter. Mickey's the only one who tried reaching out to him." Chad rubbed his face and let out a low groan. "This is so messed up!" he huffed. "We gotta get Mick outta jail."

"I'm trying," I said. "But we need proof that he couldn't have killed Sid. An alibi, or another plausible suspect." That sick feeling returned to the pit of my stomach as I pictured Mickey's bloody pocketknife still hidden in the bushes. Could Dillon have snatched it when Mickey helped break up the scuffle? "I wish I could talk to Mickey about all this," I said aloud.

"Maybe you can." Kat leaned forward on the sofa, her ice-blue eyes practically glowing in the dim hotel lighting.

"How?" I furrowed my brow at her. "You have to give at least twenty-four hours' notice to schedule a visitation with a prisoner at the ACDC—and I'm not even sure if Mickey's been arraigned yet. They might not allow him any visitors for several days."

Kat turned to face me, and her lips quirked. "True," she admitted. "But we may have an in. Whom do we know who has an APD Police Sergeant wrapped around her finger?"

My eyes widened. "Duh! Bronwyn. Why didn't I think of that?" I smacked my forehead with my palm.

"You'd have gotten there eventually," Kat said, patting my shoulder.

Chad leaned over and wrapped his arms around Kat in a bear hug. "Woman, you're brilliant!" I couldn't help but notice that he briefly rested his forehead against hers as he spoke and that Kat went from cool and collected to blushing fiercely in zero to sixty. *D'aww.*

I rose from the couch and stepped into the little hallway to give them some privacy. Pulling my phone out of my purse, I hit Bronwyn's number on speed dial. "Hey, Bron," I said when she answered. "I need a favor."

CHAPTER TEN

———

"I really appreciate this, Sergeant," I said, shaking Eddie Sinclair's hand. It was just after noon, and we were standing in the lobby of the Atlanta City Detention Center on Peachtree Street. It felt strange to be back here less than twenty-four hours after my own brief stay in one of the cinder block cells.

"You're welcome, Amelia." He peered down at me with dark blue eyes. "I hope this makes us even for now," he added, his tone suggesting that I'd better not ask him to pull any more strings for a while.

"Oh, lighten up, Sarge," Bronwyn chimed in, giving her father a playful punch on the arm—something no one else in their right mind would do to the giant hulk of a police sergeant. Eddie was a large man, tall and broad shouldered with a head as bald and shiny as a cue ball. Think Mr. Clean with a badge. He was also Bronwyn's father, and my snarky, pink-haired assistant had him wound around her finger tighter than piano wire. He'd also been best friends with my late boss, Parker. Between helping bring Parker's killer to justice and saving Bron's life, I was currently in Sinclair's good graces. Still, that didn't mean he liked handing out favors any more than he had do.

"Thank you, sir," I said, my cheeks coloring. "And, er, thanks for talking to Thompson about the whole pepper spray thing, too."

"Like I said, we're even," Sinclair said gruffly. He looked down at his daughter, and his stern expression thawed a little. "Stay out of trouble, okay, pumpkin? I can only take so much stress."

Bronwyn rolled her eyes. "I don't go looking for trouble, Dad."

"Doesn't mean you don't usually find it," the sergeant said, leaning down and giving her a peck on the cheek. When he straightened, he met my gaze. "You're cleared for visitation at the front desk. Just stop by and give them your IDs, and Gladys will give you both a visitor's badge. Then Edmonds will escort you down to see Mr. Ward."

Bronwyn and I thanked the sergeant and made our way toward the front counter. "This is so cool!" she exclaimed in a hushed whisper as she walked beside me. "Damn, it feels good to be back on a case."

"You wanna say that a little louder?" I shot her a dark look. "I don't think they heard you down at Turner Field."

"Whatever." Bronwyn shrugged, but her glossy lips spread wide. "Admit it, Ame," she said, nudging my arm with her elbow. "We make a good crime-solving team. Like Sherlock and Watson, except way hotter."

Bron had been happy to pull some strings with her father on the condition that she got to come with me. Chad and Kat opted to remain back at the suite so that Chad could avoid any run-ins with the throng of reporters camped out in the hotel lobby. Judging by the sudden shift in the air around them, I got the feeling they might have had more romantic ulterior motives for staying behind. It made me happy that my BFF seemed to be taking my advice about opening up and giving our old college buddy a chance. They would make a really great couple.

After signing in, we were patted down and searched for potential weapons before receiving our visitor badges. Then Officer Edmonds came to escort us to Visitation. He turned out to be the same sandy-haired cop that took me to meet with Dixon the day before. "Back so soon?" he asked, flashing me a toothy grin. "On the right side of the law this time, at least."

"The day's not over yet," Bronwyn said, smirking.

I didn't smile. I guess they'd forgotten to return my funny bone with my other belongings.

Bron and I sat in two aluminum chairs that faced one of the visitation stalls. Atlanta was behind the times as far as the new video-conferencing technology was concerned, so instead we would be communicating with Mickey via telephone, separated from him by a thick Plexiglas window.

A loud buzzer sounded soon after we were seated, and I turned my gaze eagerly toward the door that led to the cells. It slid open, and I gasped audibly as Mickey was led into the room. He wore an orange jumpsuit that practically swallowed him whole, which was bizarre given his broad frame. His brown hair lacked its usual luster, hanging in limp, greasy tangles around his face. Mickey's hands were cuffed in front of him, and there were several long scratches marring his arms and neck. He was also sporting a horrific-looking black eye.

"Jeez," Bronwyn murmured from beside me. "Didn't take long for him to get his ass kicked." I nodded, turning my head away as I tried to regain my composure. My heart hurt to look at him like this.

Two officers pulled Mickey along toward the chair on the opposite side of the Plexiglas in our visitor's stall. He sat down and held up his hands as if waiting to have his handcuffs unlocked. The officer to his right shook his head, and Mickey heaved a resigned sigh. He slowly raised his gaze to mine, and there was such pain and fear in his brown eyes that I almost had to look away again.

"What happened to you?" Bronwyn blurted from beside me, and I scowled at her. Bron's nothing if not blunt.

I picked up the phone attached to our side of the stall, thankful Mickey hadn't been able to hear her. Mickey raised his cuffed hands and lifted the corresponding phone to his ear. "Are you all right?" I asked.

"Been better," he mumbled. He looked down at the scratches on his arms, and his pale cheeks colored. "Had a run-in with a guy who wasn't a Royal Flush fan. Said we were just Incubus-wannabes." A faint smile curled his lips. "In hindsight, I probably shouldn't have made that quip about his mother being one of our groupies."

"Always gotta have the last word." My own lips twitched upward before settling back into a frown. "Look, I'm sorry about before. Running from you, I mean. I was scared."

Mickey shrugged. "It's okay—I don't blame you. The whole scene must have made me look pretty guilty. I just wish I knew what really happened." He licked his lips.

"Tell me everything you remember about Saturday night." I gestured to Bronwyn, who leaned toward the phone's receiver so she could hear as well. "We want to help, but we need to know everything that happened."

Mickey's eyes misted. "That means a lot," he said, meeting my gaze. "I knew I could count on you."

Don't thank me yet, I thought, picturing Mickey's bloody pocketknife. "Tell us everything you can remember."

Mickey leaned back in his chair, the phone pinned between his ear and shoulder. "I left the hotel with the rest of the band," he began. He squinted toward the ceiling as he called forth his memory of the night before. "Sid wasn't with us. The last time anyone saw him before Sunday morning was when he stormed out after the meet and greet. Ginger chased him, but she said he was already pulling away in a cab by the time she caught up to him." He blew out a breath, and his face pinched in concentration. "We were all pretty beat after the show, so Chad and I called it a night relatively early, around one-thirty in the morning. I was just about to fall asleep when my phone dinged. It was a text from Sid, saying that he wanted to meet up. He said he wanted to apologize for earlier but wasn't ready to face the rest of the band yet. He asked if I knew somewhere private we could meet. Most of the bars would be closing soon, so I suggested the tour bus."

I arched a brow, and my mouth twisted. "So, Sid's the one who lured you away from the hotel."

Mickey nodded. "Maybe he really did want to clear the air—or maybe someone else had his phone and wanted to set me up. At the time, I assumed he was going to apologize for hitting you and ask to be let back into the band. I replied that I was on my way, got dressed, and then called a cab."

"Why do you think someone other than Sid might have sent the text?" Bronwyn asked. "He could have really wanted to meet with you, and then someone else showed up and killed him," she guessed.

Mickey grimaced. "This is where it gets really weird. When I insisted they check my phone for the text from Sid, it was gone. Someone must have taken my phone while I was unconscious on the bus and deleted his part of the conversation.

All they found was a message from me, asking Sid to meet me on the bus."

"So it looks like you lured him there," Bronwyn said.

I drummed my nails on the counter as I processed this news. I wanted to believe him, but the knife…

"I've got to ask you something," I said, sitting up in my seat and leaning toward the Plexiglas. I lowered my voice and fixed Mickey with a serious gaze. "Do you remember the present I gave you for our one-year anniversary?" I asked. Mickey opened his mouth to reply but I held up a hand. "Don't," I mouthed quickly, afraid the police might be listening or recording our conversation. I screwed my eyes upward as I racked my brain for another word to replace knife. "The pocket *watch.*" I put emphasis on the word watch and gave Mickey a pointed look. "Do you still have that pocket *watch*?"

Mickey studied my expression for a moment then nodded, his own features pinched. "Uh, yeah. Of course I do. I've kept every gift you ever gave me. They're all I have left of us." He dropped his gaze to the floor. "Why do you ask?"

"Well," I began, feeling heartsick again for a different reason. "Would anyone know where to find that watch without you knowing they'd taken it?" I swallowed. "I think it may have been used to…er…tell Sid that time was up."

Mickey stared at me. His eyes widened, and his jaw went slack. "Son of a bitch," he murmured. He sat up straight again. "Someone stole my pocket—" he saw the panicked look on my face and caught himself. "—*watch?"* He groaned. "No wonder I'm stuck in here. Of course they think I did it. That thing's got my prints—and my name—all over it." Mickey slumped down in his chair again.

I blew out a shaky breath. "So, you had it on you that night?"

"Of course I did," he said unhappily. "I took it everywhere. It would've been in the back right pocket of my jeans. I didn't check them when I left the hotel to meet Sid, but I'd pulled on the same pair I wore to the show, so it would've still been there."

Unless someone slipped it out without him noticing. I opened my mouth to continue my questioning but was interrupted by the sound of a buzzer. The door behind Mickey slid open again, and the guards that had escorted him in reappeared. "Time's up, Ward," called the shorter of the two, a stern-looking man with graying brown hair.

"You've got to believe me, Ame," Mickey said in an urgent whisper. "I know it looks bad, but I'm being set up." His desperate brown eyes burned into mine.

"Do you trust me?" I whispered back.

Mickey nodded, his face softening. "Always."

"Then hang in there. I'll do what I can to find out what really happened."

A ghost of Mickey's old boyish grin flickered across his face. "I knew you wouldn't give up on me," he said. The two officers stepped forward then, one grabbing the phone from Mickey's hand and hanging it up while the other gripped his shoulders and pulled him to his feet. Mickey cast one last glance at me over his shoulder as he disappeared through the doorway leading back to his cell.

I slumped in the uncomfortable aluminum chair, the phone still in my hand. My palm felt sweaty from gripping the receiver so tightly, and my head swam with muddled thoughts. "Let's get out of here," I said glumly. I placed the phone back on its hook.

* * *

"That was a waste of time," I muttered as I pulled the car onto I-75.

Bronwyn gave me a sidelong glance from the passenger seat. "How so?"

I inhaled slowly and pushed it out then reached down to fiddle with the AC. "Nothing Mickey told us proves beyond a shadow of a doubt that he didn't kill Sid," I said. "He claims Sid texted him first to lure him out, but that conversation is missing from his phone. He thinks someone could've stolen his, er, pocket watch without him realizing it, but there's no proof that he's not the one who—"

"All right, cut the pocket watch crap," Bronwyn cut in. "We're not at the station anymore. You can tell me what you really meant to say." I arched a brow at her, and she added, "Come on, I'm your snarky sidekick, remember? We don't keep secrets." Her lips parted, and she flashed me a toothy grin.

I turned my attention back to the lunch rush-hour traffic that crawled down the interstate in front of me. *I know I can trust her,* I thought, weighing my options. *But she* is *the Sarge's daughter.* "This doesn't leave this car, okay?" I briefly met her gaze. "I mean it. Don't tell Reese, Kat—anyone. The fewer people involved, the better."

"Cross my heart," Bron said, tracing an X over her chest with her index finger. She turned in her seat to face me, her green eyes bright. "So, spill! What awesome clue did you find?"

I rolled my eyes. "It's not awesome," I said. "In fact, it could potentially keep Mickey behind bars." As we pulled to a stop in the stand-still traffic, I turned down the radio and looked at her. "Okay, here goes. Full disclosure—I think I found the murder weapon."

Bronwyn's eyebrows shot up. "What was it?"

I gulped. "It was Mickey's pocketknife—I gave it to him as an anniversary gift in college. Has his initials engraved on it and everything."

Bron's lips formed a surprised-looking *O*. "That's not good," she agreed, slumping in her seat. "Where did you find it?"

"Near Castle Rock, in the bushes under the overpass."

"What were you doing in the bushes?" Bronwyn furrowed her brow.

"Don't ask. Anyway, if I tell the cops where it is, they'll find Mickey's prints all over it."

"True," Bronwyn agreed. "But what if they also find a separate set of prints? That would mean that the killer stole the knife from Mickey and then hid it after he used it to stab Sid."

"Yeah, but…" I let out a shaky breath just before my real worries came tumbling out of my mouth. "What if they *don't* find someone else's prints on the knife? What if Mickey did kill Sid and then hid the weapon?"

"Do you really believe that's what happened?"

"No—I don't know. I guess I'm afraid to find out that a man I almost married could be capable of cold-blooded murder."

"You still really care about him," Bronwyn said, her tone matter-of-fact.

I nodded. "Yeah, I guess I really do. More than I realized."

"Then we need to turn in that knife," she said. "If Mickey did kill Sid, then there must be something wrong with him to drive him to that kind of violence. He needs help. And if he *didn't* do it, the other prints on that knife could be his ticket to freedom."

I nodded. "You're wise beyond your years, kid." I reached over and gave her shoulder a light squeeze.

"Don't I know it?" she replied, grinning. "So, where is the knife now?"

"Right where I found it. I didn't want to move it in case I got up the nerve to call Detective Dixon. The last thing I need is for him to throw me back in jail for tampering with evidence or something."

"Well." Bron glanced up at the sky. "If we don't go grab it now, there may not be evidence to tamper with."

I followed her gaze, and my heart sank. Dark storm clouds were gathering high above the city skyline. Sudden thunder rumbled in warning, making us both jump in our seats. If the rain hit before we reached Castle Rock, it would wash off the dried blood and prints on Mickey's knife—along with any chance of proving his innocence. I glanced anxiously from the rain clouds back to the snarled traffic in front of us. I-75 looked more like a parking lot than a road. "We've gotta get off the highway," I said feeling anxiety pull my chest tight.

"Hop into the carpool lane," Bronwyn suggested. "It's moving kinda slow, but it'll get us past the worst of the traffic, and then we can take the next exit onto 10th Street."

I put on my blinker and crept my car over into the next lane, angering the driver of the red Volvo that I cut off in the process. Ten minutes and two more pissed-off drivers later, I'd managed to navigate my Jetta through the sea of brake lights and into the carpool lane. We inched forward at a marginally faster pace, my heart thumping loudly with each second that passed as the storm rolled closer. The first few drops of rain splattered against my windshield just as we reached the 10th Street exit ramp. I turned onto 10th and gunned the Jetta's gas pedal, weaving my way around other cars and rocketing through Midtown as fast as the speed limit and traffic lights would allow.

"I wish I had my dad's extra dome light," Bron said, eagerly leaning forward in her seat as we squealed onto North Avenue. I hit the brakes when we caught a red light, and she bounced in her seat, nearly bumping her head on the ceiling.

"We may be too late," I said, feeling sick. The rain was falling steadily now. Why hadn't I grabbed the stupid knife when I found it? If the evidence washed away and Mickey was wrongly convicted, it would be my fault. I couldn't let that happen. Clenching my jaw, I floored the gas as soon as the traffic light turned green. My Jetta sprang forward and hit a slick patch of pavement, causing the car to skid. Bron and I both shrieked as the back of the vehicle fishtailed. I regained control within a few seconds, and we continued up the hill toward Castle Rock.

"We won't be able to help Mickey if we die in a fiery car crash," Bronwyn muttered. "Jeez, Ame. You drive worse than I do."

I shot her a dark look and continued up the hill. Castle Rock came into view, and the overpass soon after. Pulling onto the gravel in front of the venue, I threw the car into park, and Bronwyn and I tumbled out. We sprinted down the sidewalk through the rain, sidestepping the waterlogged flowers and candles that fans had placed there as tributes to Sid. "Wait," I panted, coming to a halt as we reached the Belt Line overpass.

Bronwyn blinked at me, her own chest heaving. "What?" she asked breathlessly.

"If I move the knife now, it's still tampering with evidence." And what do we say to Dixon? He'll want to know why we were traipsing around in the bushes in the first place."

Bronwyn leaned down, placing her hands on her knees as she caught her breath. "I've got it," she said finally. She reached up and removed one of her silver skull-and-cross-bones earrings. "You and I were out for a walk when all of a sudden— oops!" She flung her earring into the bushes and grinned at me. "It looks like my earring rolled into the bushes. Better go find it."

"Genius." I smiled back at her. Bronwyn stalked into the shrubbery and stooped down, disappearing in a pile of leaves and branches. "A little farther left," I called when she popped her head above the shrubs. I pointed to the spot where I'd crouched to hide from Tim Scott and the other reporters.

"I don't see anything," she called, and my stomach did a flip-flop.

"Are you sure?" I waded into the brush after her. I got down on my hands and knees and moved the branches aside, my eyes scanning the damp dirt. The used condom and the hypodermic needle were still there—this had to be the right spot. There was no sign of Mickey's knife or the plastic Royal Flush drink cup. A slow chill went through me. "Bron," I said, my voice hoarse. "It's gone. The knife is gone."

CHAPTER ELEVEN

———

"You think the killer came back and took it?" Bronwyn asked. We were sitting on the sidewalk, our knees pulled to our chests as we leaned against the cement wall of the overpass. The storm had progressed to a torrential downpour, trapping us there until the rain eased up. "Ugh!" Bron cried when a passing car sent street water spraying over us. Her lips pulled down in a scowl. "Jerk!" she called after the disappearing taillights. She shivered. Despite the heat of the June day, our soaked clothes left us both cold. "You owe me a coffee," Bronwyn griped through chattering teeth. "And a new pair of earrings."

"Deal." I cast a glance back to the bushes. "If someone removed the knife, that makes Mickey seem a lot less guilty." My heart felt a little lighter at the thought, but we weren't any closer to solving Sid's murder. "We've got to find out who took it."

"Did you tell anyone else about it?"

"Nope."

"Not even Emmett?"

My frustration bubbled over. "I said I didn't tell anyone," I groused.

"Whoa. Didn't mean to hit a nerve there," Bron said. "I'm just trying to narrow down who else might have gone on urban safari to retrieve the murder weapon."

"I know." I blew out a breath. "Sorry," I said quietly. "But Emmett didn't know. Besides, he's gone. He left early this morning."

"Oh," Bronwyn murmured, her tone sympathetic. She scooted a little closer to me. "Was it because of the fight y'all had yesterday at Camila's?"

I shook my head. "The Bureau called him back to Vegas to keep working on the Stone case. He promised he'd return by the end of the week."

"You don't sound too thrilled about that." Bron furrowed her brow. "Everything okay between you two? Do you *want* him to come back?"

"Yes. No. Maybe?" I shrugged, and my face became pinched. "I don't really know," I admitted. "I mean, we *should* be great—he even dropped the *L* word yesterday."

"Lasagna?" Bron asked. I looked at her like she'd grown a third eye. She smirked. "I'm just kidding. That's great, though! You should be happy—unless you don't feel the same way." She raised one eyebrow in question.

"I don't know if I, er, *lasagna* him just yet. We need to spend more than two days at a time together before I can make up my mind about how I feel, ya know?"

"Totally," Bronwyn agreed. She cleared her throat. "I'm just surprised he left you all alone when a certain drummer is back in town—even if he is currently behind bars."

I frowned. "You think Emmett doesn't trust me around Mickey?"

"Do *you* trust you around Mickey?" she countered, crossing her arms over her chest. "I was there with you at the jail, remember? That Plexiglas couldn't block the major vibes between you two."

I gawked at her. "I was questioning him about Sid's murder. There was no vibage whatsoever."

"If you say so." Bronwyn didn't look convinced. "All I'm saying is there are definitely still some sparks between you and Mickey. It was obvious the minute Royal Flush walked into Castle Rock, and it's still obvious now, even if you did think for a minute that he might be a psycho."

"Can we change the subject please?" I asked, trying to keep the irritation out of my tone. I knew Bronwyn meant well, but now wasn't the time to start obsessing over my feelings again. The loud sound of pelting rain eased up, and I glanced toward the sidewalk. "We could try to make a run for the car now," I suggested. "Maybe some dry clothes and coffee will clear our heads. Then we can make a list of other potential suspects."

"Sounds good to me." Bronwyn rose to her feet and grabbed the front of her black Paramore T-shirt, twisting it to wring out the rain water. I did the same with my own purple and cream-striped top. We'd just turned to make our way back down the sidewalk when a figure leaped out from behind the cement wall of the overpass. Bronwyn and I both shrieked and scrambled backward, Bron clinging to me like a scared toddler.

"Trolls!" Boomed the scraggly man standing in our way. He stared at us with bulging, blood-shot eyes. "Stupid trolls. This is my bridge." He was skeleton-thin and covered in leaves and dirt, with ratty blond dreadlocks down to his shoulders.

"Trolls?" Bronwyn hissed, still gripping my arm. "He'd better mean those cute ones from the nineties with the rhinestone belly buttons." She reached up a hand and fluffed her hot pink pixie cut. "I've got the hair for it," she added.

"I think he means the hairy-toed, goat-eating, fairy-tale variety," I whispered back.

"Seriously? Us? He must be tripping balls—*he's* the one who smells like he crawled out of the sewer," Bronwyn huffed. She let go of me and sniffed the air. "And Jäger. Maybe he's just wasted."

I glanced at the red marks in his scrawny arms and thought of the needle I'd seen in the bushes. I was willing to bet it was his. "I think he lives here," I said. "We didn't mean to trespass under *your* bridge," I told the drug-addled homeless man. "We were just leaving."

The man stomped his foot and waved his arms, his eyes still wide. "Get out, both of you!" he ranted. "And tell your friend not to come back either. The bridge and bushes are my kingdom."

Our friend? Could this crazy person have seen whoever retrieved the cup and Mickey's knife? "Er, pardon us, your highness," I said, giving a curtsy. Bronwyn stared at me like I'd lost my mind. "Just do it," I mouthed. She rolled her eyes but bent low, bowing her soggy pink head.

I reached into my pocket, pulling out the few bills I'd gotten as change during my trip to the donut shop that morning.

"Here." I stepped forward and held out the money to the squirrelly man. "A toll for passing under your bridge," I offered.

The bum eyed me but seemed pacified. "Thank you, troll," he muttered, snatching the money from my grasp before I could change my mind.

"Can I ask you a question before we go?" I asked.

The man nodded absently, his focus on counting the five one-dollar bills I'd just given him.

I stepped closer to the man and spoke softly so that I wouldn't scare him off. "The friend you mentioned," I began, waiting to continue until I had his full attention. "Was it a man or a woman?"

"Not sure," he admitted, sounding more lucid. Maybe the crazy drug addict routine was an act. He eyed my pockets. "More money for booze might help my memory." *Yep, definitely an act.*

Aside from my car keys, my pockets were empty, and my purse was still on the front floorboard of my Jetta. I looked at Bronwyn. "Fine," she said, scowling. She pulled five dollars out of her pocket and handed it to me. I offered it to the man, who grabbed it and then took a step back.

"I think it was a woman," the bum said, wadding up the cash and stuffing it into his pocket. "Hard to tell. It was dark— late last night when I saw her—and she was wearing a hoodie. Walked right into my bedroom," he said, gesturing to the bushes. "Claimed to be looking for a missing earring." That comment won a surprised look from both Bronwyn and me. Apparently the old *I lost my earring in the bushes* excuse was more common than we'd realized.

"Anyway," the man continued, "she rifled around in my shrubs for a bit and then took off. Didn't see her again after that."

"Could you tell what she looked like?" I asked. "How tall? What color was her hair?"

"Jeez, lady," the man cut me off. "If I'd have known you were gonna be this chatty, I'd have stayed put in my hidey hole. I said I didn't get a good look at her." He scratched his arm and looked at me, his expression impatient. "What else you wanna know? Her bra size?"

"No, that's all." I struggled to keep a polite tone.

"Then be gone, troll women!" the man cried, waving his arms at us and reverting back to crazy mode. "Go back from whence ye came!" He growled at us as we skittered past him and sprinted through the still-drizzling rain.

"That was insane," I said breathlessly as we climbed into the Jetta. I quickly locked the doors behind us.

"No kidding," Bronwyn agreed. She turned to look at me and let out a whooping laugh.

"What?" I blinked at her.

"You *do* look like a bridge troll," she said, snickering.

I pulled down the sun visor above my seat and peered at my reflection in the mirror, cringing at my soggy hair and runny makeup. "Oh yeah?" I chuckled. "You're not exactly winning any beauty contests, either. You look like something that crawled out of one of Tim Burton's nightmares."

Bronwyn checked her own reflection, taking in her twig-filled pink hair, bleeding mascara and eyeliner, and the one skull earring dangling from her right earlobe. "Good point." She did her best impression of a witch's cackle. "I'm melting! Melting!" she cried. We both dissolved into a fit of giggles.

When our laughing died down, Bronwyn turned in her seat to look at me. "What now?" she asked.

A yawned escaped my throat. "Well," I said, rubbing my eyes. "I'm soaking wet, freezing, and exhausted, which means I'm pretty much useless until I've had a shower and a nap." I turned my key in the ignition and backed my Jetta out onto North Avenue. "Why don't we take it easy tonight and start fresh tomorrow?"

Bron nodded. "I'm overdue for a little one-on-one time with Reese," she admitted. We were silent for the short drive to my apartment where her new lime green Ford Fiesta was parked in the visitor's garage. "I'll call you tomorrow," she said before hopping into her car and taking off.

As soon as I was back in my apartment, I stripped off my wet clothes and threw on a pair of sweats. A shower would have to wait; I was scraping at the bottom of my energy reserves just to keep my eyes open. Instead, I curled up on the couch with my favorite purple throw and snuggled with Dos, listening to the rumble of his purrs as I drifted off to sleep.

* * *

Bronwyn didn't call until nearly one in the afternoon on Tuesday, but she had big news. "They're going to release Mickey today!" she blurted as soon as I picked up.

"What?" My face went slack. They were letting Mickey go? Had Dixon found the mysterious woman who'd taken his pocketknife? I worked my jaw up and down and swallowed a few times, trying to get my mouth working again. "What?" I repeated, as it seemed to be the only word left in my vocabulary at the moment.

"I, er, *overheard* Dad on the phone this morning after breakfast," Bronwyn said. *Overheard...eavesdropped.* To Bron, they pretty much meant the same thing. "They could technically hold him until tomorrow, but with the media knocking down their door twenty-four seven trying to get a scoop, poor Daddy wants this off his plate as soon as possible. So, Mickey's getting out a little early."

"That's great," I said, trying to keep my voice even. "But why do I get the feeling there's a catch?" I wanted to be excited that Mickey was going to be a free man by happy hour, but something in Bronwyn's tone told me that he wasn't out of the woods just yet.

"There is, sort of. It's kind of a lot to explain—mind if I come over now? I also found something you'll want to see."

Okay. Color me intrigued. "Yeah, sure," I said, rising from the couch and stretching. I glanced down at my laptop, which had several contract files open in different tabs on the screen. Just because Castle Rock couldn't open for business again until tomorrow didn't mean there wasn't work that needed to be done in the meantime. I'd spent the bulk of the morning mainlining a pot of coffee and cranking through a month's worth of agreements for shows between now and September. "I'm almost at a stopping point on paperwork," I said. "Why don't you drop by in an hour and fill me in?" That'd give me time to take that long overdue shower.

"Sure thing, boss lady," Bron chirped. "See ya soon!"

I quickly reviewed the contract I'd been working on for next month's performance from Panda Coven (a Chinese Wiccan Metal band—another one of Bronwyn's eclectic booking choices) and saved the file before closing my laptop. After plugging my phone into its dock to charge the ever-draining battery, I shuffled into my bedroom to pick out some clean clothes. I eyed the pair of faded jeans and Jimmy Eat World T-shirt lying on the top of my dresser. *Should I wear something nicer today? After all, Mickey is getting out of jail, which totally counts as a special occasion.* I cast a quick glance toward my open closet door, my gaze landing on a purple-and-white halter-top dress. *Remember your boyfriend?* asked the tiny voice that was lodged in the back of my mind like a splinter. My eyes snapped guiltily back to the jeans and tee. Whatever. When it came down to it, I'd rather be comfortable than cute anyway. I snatched up the outfit from my dresser and carried it into the bathroom, once again feeling bothered that seeing my ex had any influence over my wardrobe choices.

I was still towel drying my hair when Bronwyn knocked on my apartment door twenty minutes later. "You're early," I said as I let her in.

"I was already in the neighborhood. I stayed at Reese's last night." She blushed. "Though, if the Sarge asks, I crashed with you."

I smirked. "Fine, but if he pulls me into an interrogation room, I'm blowing your cover," I teased.

Bronwyn rolled her eyes and stepped past me into the living room. I wrapped my towel in a turban around my wet hair and then grabbed two cans of Diet Coke from the refrigerator before joining her on the couch. "All right," I said, handing her a soda. "Spill."

Bron cocked an eyebrow. "You sure?" she asked with a wry grin, opening her can and tilting it slightly toward the floor. "Because it's gonna be hard to get this outta your carpet."

"I meant about Mickey." I cut her an impatient look. "Give me the full scoop."

"Okay." Bron squared her shoulders and took a deep breath then launched into her report. "From what I could hear of

Daddy's end of the conversation, the toxicology reports came back, and it looks like Mickey was drugged. Rohypnol."

I gaped at her. "The date rape drug? Someone *roofied* him?" No wonder he couldn't remember what happened on the bus.

"Seems like." Bronwyn nodded. "And it gets weirder. The same drug was in Sid's bloodstream. So, either Mickey or Sid dosed the other and accidentally drugged himself in the process or—"

"Or someone else slipped it to them both," I finished for her, thinking of the plastic Royal Flush cup with the lipstick stains. "So the woman who the homeless man saw could have rendered them both unconscious and then taken Mickey's knife to stab Sid…" I swallowed. "He really could have been framed." I pictured my ex and the soon-to-be-dead bass guitarist passing Sid's flask of bourbon back and forth until they both slumped over. The mystery woman had probably watched, sipping her own untainted drink and biding her time until she could carry out her sinister plan. But why? What reason could one of Sid's scorned groupies have for dragging Mickey into the mix?

"You said there was more to the story," I reminded her. "If Detective Dixon knows that Mickey was drugged, what's the catch?"

"The Sarge said that's not enough to completely clear all suspicion of Mickey's involvement. For one, he was caught red-sneakered at the scene of the crime. The blood on his shoes is pretty hard to ignore." Bron took a sip of her soda and leaned down to stroke Uno behind the ears as he slunk past the couch. "He said that dosing himself could have been part of Mickey's cover—that he could've killed Sid and gulped down enough of the drugged drink to have it show up in his screening, making him also look like a victim of foul play. Still, there's not enough to pin Mickey to the murder yet, so they have to cut him loose for now. He's not allowed to leave town until the investigation is complete." She looked up at me. "So it sounds like he'll be in Atlanta for a while. Silver lining for you, right?"

I frowned at her. "Uh, remember Emmett?"

She shrugged. "Yeah, I know. But I'm still on Team Mickey."

"Well, how I feel—or *don't* feel—about him romantically isn't important right now," I said, crossing my arms. "What was the other thing you wanted to show me?"

"Oh!" Bronwyn's green eyes lit up. She set her drink on my coffee table and picked up my laptop. "I think I found a potential suspect," she said, opening the internet browser. The homepage for ATL Night Beat filled the screen. The popular local gossip blog reported the latest in celebrity scandals and sightings around Atlanta. Bronwyn clicked on the site's most recent photo gallery and tapped her finger to one of the small thumbnail-sized images in the photo grid. "Look who it is."

I followed her finger with my gaze and felt my pulse quicken. "Sid!" I cried, staring down at the bass player's pale face on the screen. "Open the full image." Bronwyn clicked on the little square, and the full image popped up on the computer monitor. My blood iced in my veins.

The caption above the photo read:

Ordering a lap dance to go? Royal Flush rocker, Sid Malone, takes the talent home with him from the Saucy Minx on Saturday night.

The image itself showed Sid dressed in the same dark pants and light blue shirt he'd been wearing the night he died. He had one hand raised in a half-hearted attempt to block his face from the camera, but his wolfish grin told me he really loved the attention. What made my blood run cold was the person in the photo with Sid. His other hand was firmly gripping the wrist of a familiar woman with shiny golden hair. Her heavily made-up face was twisted in an ugly expression, and her hazel eyes squinted daggers at the back of Sid's head as he pulled her along behind him.

"Oh my God," I breathed.

"What?" Bronwyn demanded, turning from the screen to look at me.

"I know Sid's killer. I shared a jail cell with her."

CHAPTER TWELVE

"Hold up." Bronwyn held her hand in front of her. "You shared a jail cell with a stripper, and you're just now telling me this?" An amused smile twitched her lips. "Seriously, Ame— when someone asks you if anything interesting happened while you were behind bars, that's the kind of thing you lead with."

"I'll remember that next time," I said dryly.

Bronwyn giggled. "Hmm. There's got to be a good pole-dancing joke I can use here." She screwed her eyes upward and tapped at her chin then snapped her fingers. "Something about a cage dancer, maybe?"

"*So* not the point right now," I said, giving her a sharp look. I touched my finger to the image of Sid and—what was her name? I forgot. "This is a big deal, Bron. That picture might clear Mickey's name."

"You're welcome." Bronwyn grinned. "Does this mean we'll be doing a strip club stakeout?"

"I don't know what it means just yet." I frowned. "She was still in jail when I last saw her." I paused for a moment, trying to recall her stage name. "Coral," I said after a moment. "That's what she called herself."

Bronwyn snickered. "Like the sea animal? Or that icky salmon color?"

"You're one to be bashing shades of pink," I said sarcastically, eying her bubblegum hair. I turned my attention back to the photo. "Anyway, Coral told me she'd been picked up for alleged prostitution," I said. "So maybe she killed Sid and then went looking for some post-crime company." I studied the skinny young woman, wishing I could know what was going on behind her angry hazel eyes. It was clear from her expression of hatred and Sid's roughness why the dancer might want to hurt him—but what did Mickey have to do with any of it? "The cops haven't ruled Mickey out as a suspect, and there's been no mention of a female person of interest on the news. Either they're keeping her under wraps, or they aren't investigating her for the murder. She may already be back on the streets."

"Which we could find out for sure by dropping by the Saucy Minx to see if she's working," Bron said. She glanced back down at the image on the screen, and her smirk evaporated. "Whoa. I didn't notice this before." She leaned toward the computer, squinting. "Look who's stalking. Isn't that Royal Flush's old bass player in the background?"

I jerked my head toward the laptop. I'd been so fixated on Sid and the stripper that I hadn't paid much attention to the rest of the image. "Holy crap." Sure enough, a tall, skinny man stood several feet behind the pair. Though the left half of his face was cut off from the image, I instantly recognized his narrow chin and gray-and-brown-streaked hair. Dillon's jaw was clenched, and the one dark eye visible in the picture was staring intently at Sid.

"Looks like we can't cross him off the suspect list just yet," Bron murmured. Her mouth twisted in a thoughtful expression. "Think they were working together?"

"I don't know what to think," I said honestly.

"Tell you what." Bronwyn's lips curled in a mischievous little smile. "Why don't you see if you can track down Dillon and leave finding Little Miss Strip n' Stab to me? I have a plan." Her eyes crinkled around the corners, sparkling with that devilish look that meant I probably wasn't going to like whatever she was thinking.

"Do I even want to know?" I asked, eying her warily.

"Probably not." Bronwyn rose from the couch and snatched up her purse. "But you'll find out soon enough." She winked then turned and skipped across my living room, whistling to herself as she disappeared through my apartment door.

I heaved a tired sigh and turned my attention back to my laptop. After saving the image of Sid and Coral and sending it to my phone, I dialed Kat's number. I was startled by shouting voices on the other end of the line. "Kat?" I called into the phone, alarm tightening my chest. Kat's tinkling laughter cut through the noise, and my tension eased.

"Hey," she breathed into the phone between giggles. "I was going to call you. Good news—the band is staying at my place now." Kat had recently moved into the three-bedroom bungalow in west Midtown that she'd inherited from Parker. "There's more privacy here. No more reporters and news crews circling the lobby beneath the hotel suite like a pit of sharks. The guys can come and go from here as they please. Plus I brought out my old gaming console. Right now I'm totally owning Chad and Zane at Mario Kart."

"Like hell you are!" Zane called from somewhere in the background. There was a crashing sound—I assumed it came from the video game—followed by a chorus of male chuckles.

"Take that, Taylor!" Chad yelled.

"That's not fair! I'm on the phone," Kat argued back. "Ame, hold on. Let me pause this really quickly." There were shouts of protest from the guys as the game's music abruptly cut off. "Okay, I'm back," Kat said a few seconds later. "What's up?"

"I've got some news for you too." I pinned the phone between my shoulder and ear and lifted my computer into my lap. "I hope you've got room for one more at your place. Bron pulled her little Harriet the Spy routine on her dad this morning and found out they're releasing Mickey today."

"What?" Kat cried, and I heard Zane and Chad pressing her for explanation. "Mickey's getting out," she told them.

"Holy shit! Really?" Chad sputtered. "This is great! That means the tour's back on, right? I've gotta go tell Jack and Suzie. Hey, Jack!" The guitarist's voice faded away, and I pictured him sprinting out of Kat's living room in search of Jack and his fiancée.

Crap. "Better reel him in before he gets everyone excited," I warned. "Mickey can't leave town yet." I waited for Kat to call Chad back into the room and give him the not-so-good news. No use in getting Ginger worked up only to pull the rug out from under her again. The poor woman seemed harried enough the first time she had to call around postponing tour dates.

While Kat filled Chad and Zane in on the caveat to Mickey's release from jail, I closed the ATL Night Beat page on my computer and brought up Facebook. I typed Dillon Green's name into the search bar at the top and located his profile. Though we weren't friends on the social media site, his page was viewable to the public—which meant I was able to see all of his recent activity, including several posts he'd made promoting his new band. I clicked on a link to the Dillon Green Band's page then scrolled through their list of tour dates. Apparently, Dill had been playing gigs at bars all over town for the past several months.

Running my finger down the screen, I scanned for today's date to see if the band was booked for a performance. As it turned out, they were. Sometimes the universe has impeccable timing.

"So, it sucks that the tour's still on hold," Kat said, pulling my attention back to the phone. "But we should still celebrate Mickey being free—er, well, no longer behind bars, anyway. And I'm sure he's probably hurting for a stiff drink and something other than bland jail food. I'll have Ginger call his lawyer so we can arrange to pick him up, and then we can all go to dinner."

"Uh-huh," I said, tapping my finger on my laptop screen. The Dillon Green Band was scheduled to play at 7 p.m. that night at Taco Heaven. *Perfect.* "Dinner sounds great, Kat. How do the guys feel about tacos?"

* * *

Bronwyn insisted on joining us for dinner, and she brought Reese along too. They picked me up in Bron's little green Ford Fiesta later that evening. "You guys had better enjoy my designated driving while it lasts," she griped as I slid into the backseat. "Because as soon as I'm twenty-one, it's someone else's turn to play chauffeur."

"Fair enough," I said.

"She's not really mad." Reese turned in the front passenger seat and flashed me a dimpled grin. "If you don't have your car, it'll be harder for you to escape the post-dinner activities she has planned."

"Babe, *shut up!*" Bronwyn shushed him and then locked eyes with me through her rear view mirror. She must have seen the panic that flashed across my face, because suddenly the automatic lock on my door snapped down. "Don't even think about bolting," she said, winking. I gulped. *Gee, that wasn't alarming at all.*

Taco Heaven was located in East Atlanta about fifteen minutes from my apartment. I was silent for most of the drive, lost in my own thoughts as Bronwyn and Reese chattered away up front. My mind wandered back to my conversation with Kat that afternoon with a twinge of jealousy. While she was hanging out with Chad, Zane, Jack, and their entourage, playing video games in her living room like a bunch of college kids, I was out risking my neck to clear Mickey's name. *Stop it,* my conscience scolded me. *Being on the road for a tour is hard enough without one of your bandmates getting murdered and another thrown in jail. Think of everything the guys have been through this week— and everything Kat's been through this* year. *They all deserve to blow off a little steam every now and then.*

I chewed my lip. That annoying voice in the back of my head had a point. When I'd spoken to her on the phone before, Kat sounded genuinely happy for the first time in months. She was healing—and as her best friend, I couldn't deny her a chance to finally chase away the cloud of grief that had been following her around over the past few months. Plus I knew Chad would treat her well. He was a sweet, funny guy, and he'd be really good for her.

We arrived at the restaurant at a quarter until seven and found Kat, Ginger, Suzie, and the guys waiting for us out front. My pals in Royal Flush were decked out in various hats and sunglasses to mask their famous faces. Mickey was with them, looking tired but still much better than when I'd seen him during visitation the previous afternoon. He'd traded his orange jumpsuit for dark jeans and a red-and-gray flannel shirt. The bruise under his eye had faded from light purple to a jaundiced yellow and was mostly hidden behind his aviator shades. His face had lost the jailhouse pallor as well, with a little color returning to his cheeks. A gray beanie was pulled down over his head, and his brown hair stuck out from underneath at different angles. Mickey hadn't yet shaved the two-day beard that grew like a shadow on the lower half of his face. The whole *rugged lumberjack* look suited him.

When I had greeted the others, I turned to Mickey and gave him a hug. "How are you holding up?" I asked quietly in his ear.

Mickey slid his arms around my middle. "Better now that you're here," he said, squeezing me tightly. He released me and gave me a tired look. "I can't wait for this whole thing to be over. At least now I know why I couldn't remember anything about what happened that night with Sid." He grimaced.

"Come on." I grabbed his hand and gave it a gentle squeeze. "I'll buy you a margarita." I tried to pull my hand back, but Mickey kept his own fingers laced through mine.

"Wait," he said in a hushed tone. Mickey held me back as the others followed Kat toward the restaurant's side entrance. "Did you find my pocketknife?" he asked, lowering the sunglasses from his eyes so he could meet my gaze.

My mouth crimped in a remorseful frown. "I'm afraid not," I said, that familiar feeling of guilt setting up shop in the pit of my stomach. Pretty soon I was going to have to start charging it rent. "It's my fault, Mickey. I should have done something about it when I had the chance—but when I went back for the knife, it was gone." I hung my head.

"Hey," Mickey said softly. His hand slid to my chin and tilted my head so that I was looking him in the eyes. "Don't beat yourself up. You've done more for me than I deserve. I just wish I knew who was trying to frame me."

"Well," I said, breaking free of his grasp to dig around in my purse. I retrieved my phone and pulled up the picture of Sid and Coral that I'd saved from ATL Night Beat. "Does she look familiar?" I asked.

Mickey took my phone in his hand and squinted at the screen. "I've never seen her before in my life." He winced. "At least, not that I remember." Mickey looked back to me, eyebrows drawn up in question. "You think this chick had something to do with what happened to Sid?"

"It's possible. This picture was taken the same night he was murdered, after he stormed out of Castle Rock."

Mickey shook his head, a smile burning at the ends of his lips. "See? You've already tracked down a lead. With you on the case, I'm liking my odds."

"Don't thank me yet," I told him, my cheeks turning pink.

Mickey noticed my blushing and chuckled. "You always were cute when you were embarrassed. Remember that time junior year when you spilled a vodka and cranberry juice all over your white top during our show at Smithe's Old Bar?"

A little gasp escaped my throat at the memory. "Oh my gosh! That was the worst. It looked like a vampire threw up on me."

Mickey's eyes twinkled. "Until I gave you my Radiohead tee—which you pulled off quite nicely as a T-shirt dress." He grinned. "The *In Rainbows* album cover never looked so sexy."

"Aww—er, thanks." My cheeks burned fiercely now. Mickey slid an arm around my waist. His gaze flitted to my lips, and his expression grew eager. I felt my own pang of sudden desire. His hands on me felt so natural, as if no time at all had passed since the last time he held me like this. It was a major workout for my self-restraint, but I managed to extract myself from his embrace before one of us did something *I* was going to regret.

"We should head inside," I said, moving quickly away from him. "The others are probably halfway through their first margaritas by now." I turned on my heel and awkwardly scurried toward the side entrance of the bright blue building. I heard a disappointed sigh behind me and then footsteps as Mickey followed.

Kat had reserved a secluded booth at the back of Taco Heaven's large patio, allowing the band to enjoy their meal without attracting too much attention from the rest of the restaurant's patrons. The table was already covered in a spread of chips, guacamole, salsa, and several margarita pitchers when Mickey and I slid into the two empty spaces at the far end. Bless Kat's heart—my bestie had already ordered a peach margarita for me and had it waiting on the table. I flashed her a look of gratitude and immediately downed a third of it. The sugary drink and alcohol mix was going to burn in my belly since I'd downed it so fast, but I didn't care. I needed the liquor to take the edge off my nerves, stat. Not only had my trip down memory lane with Mickey thrown me for a loop, but Dillon would be walking onto the patio stage any minute—and I'd sort of neglected to mention that he would be there. I hadn't even told Bronwyn.

"Ame, are you all right?" Reese asked from across the table, and nine pairs of eyes turned my way. "You look a little green."

"I'm fine," I insisted, ignoring the queasy feeling in my stomach. "Just thirsty." Our waitress dropped by then with a tray of waters. I grabbed a glass and chugged then gave a refreshed sigh as I set it down. "All better." I looked over at Ginger, who was seated between Zane and Suzie, swirling her straw around the fruit chunks in her white sangria. "How is everything going with rescheduling tour dates?" I asked her.

Ginger's delicate features became pinched. She tilted her drink to her lips before responding. "So far, we've had to cancel five shows," she said. "I won't know how many other venues to contact until this whole mess is resolved." She darted a disapproving glance toward Mickey, who grimaced and dropped his gaze to the bowl of chips in front of him.

"I don't know about you all," Jack said, giving Ginger a warning look. "But I'm enjoying a little time off. It's nice to be back in our hometown for a few days after so long." He smiled and slung his arm around Suzie, pulling her close. "Suz and I have finally been able to iron out some wedding details during the downtime. Right, babe?"

Suzie nodded, parting her lips in a shy smile. She tilted her face up to stare at Jack, her wide, doe eyes shining with adoration. "My biggest fan," Jack said, grinning. He leaned down and planted a kiss on the corner of her mouth. "I don't know what I'd do without you, baby." He raised his glass and looked around the table. "If I've learned anything over the past month, it's that life is short. So, live and let live, and be quick to forgive. Here's to Sid. Rest in peace, you crazy son of a bitch."

"To Sid," everyone echoed.

Suzie clinked her glass to Jack's and took a long sip. As she set it down, her diamond engagement ring slipped off her finger. "Shit!" she mumbled, leaning under the table to search for it. Jack and Chad ducked down to help her, with Chad recovering the sparkly bling.

"Damn," Jack said as Suzie placed the ring back on her finger. "That's the third time it's fallen off this month."

Suzie blushed and dropped her gaze to the table. "I guess I've lost a little weight since the accident," she said. "Maybe I should get it resized."

Chad took a swig of his own drink and then glanced toward the stage. His bushy, red eyebrows rose in surprise. "Hey, about that whole 'forgiving' part of your toast, Jack," he said coolly. "Look who just walked in."

I nervously bit my lip, my gaze darting to the patio stage where Tim Scott was strutting toward the microphone. *Ugh.* How had I missed that 95Rox was sponsoring the show? I rolled my eyes and then looked past the arrogant DJ. Dillon was standing right behind him.

"What the hell is *he* doing here?" Jack asked in a low, growling tone. His eyes narrowed, and his jaw clenched. Jack tightened his fist around the stem of his margarita glass, threatening to shatter it. Beside him, Chad and Zane both tensed, and even Suzie and Ginger looked uncomfortable.

Movement brought my attention several seats to my right where Bronwyn was jerking her head side to side, trying to catch my eye. "Nice!" she mouthed, giving me a thumbs up. Her green eyes danced with excitement. She was probably hoping for some action.

"No need to cause a scene, guys," Mickey said in a diplomatic tone. "Technically, we're on his turf. Let's just sit back, enjoy our dinner, and let him play."

"Great idea," I said. I held up my hand to signal the waitress, hoping a round of tacos and empanadas might diffuse some of the tension around the table.

Kat caught my eye and seemed to read my mind. "I'm starving," she said when our server approached. "Do you recommend the goat cheese quesadilla or the chorizo enchiladas?"

Up on stage, Tim and Dillon hadn't noticed our group. Tim adjusted the mic stand and smiled down at the crowd. "How're we all feeling tonight?" he called. He was met with tequila-fueled cheers—and a couple of boos, one of which came from Bronwyn—and applause from around the patio. "Welcome to 95Rox's first-ever Tune 'n' Taco Tuesday," Tim continued. "We'd like to thank our awesome hosts here at Taco Heaven for having us tonight." He paused for another round of applause, most of which came from the Taco Heaven staff.

Someone at a table near the stage threw a tortilla chip at Tim, and it caught in his goatee. Bronwyn and Kat snickered. Tim's expression soured, and he flicked it away. "*Anyway*," he said, ignoring the hoots and hollers from the table that had thrown the chip, "let's give a big welcome to tonight's first act, the Dillon Green Band!"

The other tables clapped and cheered as Dillon and two other men waved to the crowd and then picked up their instruments. To their credit, the members of Royal Flush didn't boo, and they didn't get up and walk out of the restaurant. If we could just make it through dinner, I could corner Dillon after his set and grill him about following Sid out of the strip club on the night he was murdered. Bringing the whole band along without warning them that he'd be here didn't top the list of *Amelia's Brightest Ideas*, but there was safety in numbers. Dill was potentially dangerous, and it helped to have five strong guys with me—plus I knew none of them would want to risk attracting more media attention by causing a scene. I just hoped everyone could keep their tempers in check. The night didn't have to end in more disaster.

Dillon's drummer, a skinny blond man with tattoos covering his arms, counted off the first song on his drumsticks. The trio launched into a fast-tempo rock number that reminded me a lot of Royal Flush's upbeat sound. It was actually quite good. I took a sip of my margarita and cast a nervous glance around the table. To my surprise, Jack, Mickey, and the other members of Royal Flush were leaning forward in their seats, staring attentively at the stage. Chad and Zane bobbed their heads to the beat, and Mickey tapped his index fingers on the table along to the drum rhythm. Even Jack seemed to be enjoying the music. Excitement flickered in his blue eyes, and he seemed energized by the song, bouncing slightly in his seat and nodding his approval. When the song was over, our whole table clapped and cheered enthusiastically.

"Wow," Kat breathed. "These guys are good!"

"Yeah. Dillon's really come a long way," Chad agreed. He gave Kat a high five and then slipped his arm around her.

Jack shook his head, his dirty blond hair swaying from side to side. "I have to admit, I didn't think Dill had it in him," he said. "But that was impressive."

The tension in my chest melted away. This was going much better than I'd hoped. Dillon and his band continued their set for the next twenty minutes with Dillon jumping from guitar to bass as he sang. At one point, he even sat down at a keyboard and plunked out a beautiful melody during one of the band's slower numbers. When their show was over, the three men stepped forward on the stage and bowed. They were met with a roar of applause (and a few more tortilla chip missiles) from around the patio. "Give it up for the Dillon Green Band!" Tim Scott called into his microphone from the side of the stage.

The members of Royal Flush removed their hats and glasses. They rose from their seats at our booth and clapped loudly, chanting "DGB! DGB!" over and over again in unison. It was kind of touching. Then again, it probably wasn't the smartest move. People all around the patio turned toward the source of the chants.

"Hey, aren't those the guys from Royal Flush?" someone called from a nearby table. *Uh oh. Cover blown.* People stood up from their chairs and peered at our table to get a better look at the rockers. Cell phones came out of pockets, and cameras flashed.

Back on the stage, Dillon gaped down at our booth, his dark eyes wide. The color drained from his narrow face. "Er, excuse me," he mumbled into the microphone. He handed his bass over to one of his band mates before leaping off the stage and bolting toward the parking lot.

CHAPTER THIRTEEN

———

Chairs scraped the floor as people either rushed to the edge of the patio to watch Dillon flee or approached our booth looking for an autograph or a photo opp. As the former head bouncer of Castle Rock, Reese's bodyguard-like instincts kicked in. He pulled himself up so that he was standing in his seat at the booth and then hauled himself over the side, coming around to stand in front of our table to block the advancing crowd. "Back up, people!" he barked in an authoritative voice. "Now!"

"Isn't he the best?" Bronwyn grinned and then followed suit, helping her honey hold back the over-eager fans. Despite her petite stature, Bronwyn was a force to be reckoned with. Several grown men even backed away from the table when she turned and gnashed her teeth at them.

I slid out of the booth and pushed my way past a couple of twenty-something women who were craning their necks to get a look at Jack. "Dillon, wait!" I called, sprinting toward the patio gate and hopping over the lowest bar. It was a good thing I'd gone with jeans and boots over the halter dress and heels. While Dillon had a good fifteen-second head start on me, he seemed to be running rather slow. I could hear him wheezing as he went. He'd smoked a pack of cigarettes a day in college, and I was willing to bet he hadn't yet kicked the habit.

Though I had the advantage of healthy, smoke-free lungs, there was still that pesky scar tissue from the stab wound in my calf that hadn't fully healed. I'd just closed the gap between Dillon and me down to about 10 yards when a horrible cramp tore through my leg. With a cry, I staggered forward and pitched over onto the ground. Bright pain seared my palms where they scraped the pavement.

"Ame!" Mickey cried from several feet behind me. I'd been so focused on catching up to Dill that I hadn't noticed anyone following. Mickey skittered to a halt next to me and dropped down on one knee, concern etched in his brown eyes.

"I'm fine," I said through clenched teeth. I jerked my head in the direction Dillon was headed. "Don't let him get away."

Mickey nodded and darted after him, with Jack streaking past me a few seconds later. The two of them easily caught up with the fleeing bass player. Dillon yelped in pain as they tackled him to the ground. I hauled myself up and gingerly dusted off my jeans, cringing at the bright red streaks that my bleeding palms left on the denim. I hobbled over to join Mickey and Jack, who still had Dillon pinned to the pavement.

"What the hell?" Dill cried. "Get off me!"

"They wouldn't have tackled you if you hadn't run away in the first place," I said, unable to keep the exasperation out of my tone. "Why did you bolt?"

"Because I didn't want to get my ass kicked," Dillon said through clenched teeth. His gaze flicked back and forth from Jack to Mickey. "You guys have always been way stronger than me, and you brought that gorilla from Castle Rock with you. He could crush me with one fist."

"If we promise to let you go, will you just talk to us?" Mickey asked. "Come on, man. For old times' sake."

"Fine." Dillon groaned when the two men released him. He rolled over onto his back and sat up slowly. "Ow," he muttered. Dillon looked up at Jack. "I'm sorry about what happened at that meet and greet the other night, really. I didn't think you'd show up to one of my gigs and kick the crap out of me as payback."

"We didn't know you were playing here tonight," Jack replied. "Not all of us, anyway." He shot me a knowing look, and my cheeks colored. *Busted.*

Jack turned back to Dillon. "But since you brought it up, that was a pretty rotten thing to do, picking a fight with Sid like that. You didn't just mess up our night—you ruined it for the fans. Not cool, man." He shook his head disdainfully. "Not cool."

Dillon's face flushed. "Look, it wasn't even my idea. I couldn't have cared less that you guys were back in town, to be honest. I've got a pretty good thing going right now with my own band. He stood up from the pavement and wiped a mixture of sweat and dirt off his dark brow. "I only did it because that DJ guy convinced me to. He promised to get my band's new single in rotation on the local rock station. Plus he threw in this gig." Dillon's lips quirked. "And the crowd loved us."

"You guys were really good," Mickey agreed. "Your bass solo on that funky third number? Dude, it was epic."

"Thanks." Dillon's smile widened. "I never stopped playing, even when things didn't work out with you guys." His expression pinched and his gaze slid to Jack. "Look," he said, quietly. "About what happened back in college, with Chrissy. I—I tried to kiss her once, man. I was drunk, and I felt terrible about it the next day. I'm sorry it tore our friendship apart."

Jack stared at him for a few long moments, his expression hard. Slowly, the lines in his face smoothed, and he reached out a hand to Dillon. "I forgive you. Water under the bridge." He shook Dill's hand and then clapped him on the back in a half-hug. "We've missed you, dude."

"I hate to break up the bromance," I said, stepping forward. "But if you didn't really mean to cause trouble, then why did you follow Sid Malone to the strip club after your fight?"

Dylan's brows lifted. "How'd you know about that?" he asked. Mickey and Jack exchanged surprised looks and then turned to stare at me.

I pulled my phone out of my pocket and was relieved to see the screen hadn't cracked when I landed on it. I located the saved image of Sid at the Saucy Minx and held it up for the three men to see. "What happened after this picture was taken?" I asked, narrowing my eyes at Dillon.

He blinked. "Look, Amelia," he said, his tone uncertain. "I don't know what you're getting at, but I didn't do anything wrong—aside from, you know, the whole incident at Castle Rock *before* I went to the strip club." He rubbed his hand over his face and pushed out a long, slow breath. "After I got booted from the venue, I needed to blow off some steam, so I took a cab to Saucy Minx. I didn't know Sid was gonna show up there. I'm glad he did, though. It gave me a chance to buy him a beer and a lap dance and apologize for stirring up trouble. I explained the deal I'd made with Mr. Scott and told him no hard feelings, ya know? I even wished him good luck with the rest of Royal Flush's tour." Dill shrugged. "We left at the same time and went our separate ways. The last time I saw Sid, he was trying to take that blonde chick home with him. I'm sorry he got killed, but if you're thinking I had something to do with it, you're wrong."

I licked my lips. Dillon didn't seem to be lying, and the evidence I'd found pointed towards a woman. "I'm sorry, Dill," I said guiltily. "Just trying to find out what happened. And when you ran, well—"

"Yeah, I know," he said. "Only guilty men run. That was my bad." He winced. "I just didn't want that Reese guy getting his paws on me."

"Aww, Reese is a total teddy bear," I said with a laugh.

Dillon scoffed. "Easy for you to say—he's never dragged you down two flights of stairs by your shirt collar." That won a chuckle from Mickey and Jack.

I turned back toward the restaurant patio, and my own smile evaporated. Tim Scott stood about fifteen feet away, a wolfish grin on his face. He gripped a short metal rod in his hands, and attached to the top was a digital camera. The little red video recording light was blinking.

"Bravo!" Tim pulled the camera down and turned it off. He tucked the camera and support stick between his arm and his side so he could clap with his now free hands. "That was great, you guys! I can't wait to see how many views this gets when I post it on the *Tune Talks* blog."

"What?" Mickey stared at him, mouth slightly open.

Tim walked over to us, his smile stretching from ear to ear. There might as well have been dollar signs in his eyes. "A chase scene, questioning a suspect, *and* the end of a long-standing rock 'n' roll feud. All in a five-minute video. You guys could have your own reality show."

"You're not posting that." Jack's jaw clenched, his blue eyes blazing with anger. He stepped forward and loomed threateningly over Tim. "Give me that camera, or I'm going to jam that selfie-stick down your throat."

Tim took one step back, but his smile remained. "The camera is my property. Same goes for anything I film with it. Sorry, Mr. Pearson. It's nothing personal, just good journalism." He gripped the camera tightly so that Jack couldn't snatch it away from him. "Ya know," he added, his expression smug. "A mention of the threat you just made against me will go nicely in the report that I post with this footage." He held a hand up in the air and swiped it from left to write, as if placing the headline. *"The Video Jack Pearson Doesn't Want You To See*—that's sure to go viral."

Anger burned in my gut. I'd love nothing more than to rip the jerk's stupid gray ponytail out. I was mad enough that I just might do it. Stalking forward, I brushed past Jack and stood with my face inches from Tim's. "You are nothing but a greedy, self-centered sack of crap, you know that?" I poked my finger hard against his chest. "First, you sensationalized a tragedy where I lost two friends last year, and then you bribed a normally decent guy—" I hiked a thumb back at Dillon— "to stir up trouble because your audience is bored with the lame stories about your glory days with a bunch of washed up rockers who probably don't even remember your name. You posted a video online of *me* getting punched in the face—that alone makes me want to knee you in the balls. And now, you've got the nerve to stalk my friends with a video camera in hopes of creating even *more* drama?" I spit in his face. "You're the Jerry Springer of rock radio, Tim. You're a joke, and everyone knows it."

Tim gritted his teeth and narrowed his eyes at me. "Sticks and stones, bitch," he said. "Call me whatever you want, but I'm still the king of music news. I'll post whatever I please."

To be honest, I'm not entirely sure he said that last part. I stopped listening after he called me a bitch. My blood boiled, and I swear I began to see red. Before I realized what I was doing, my fist connected with Tim Scott's jaw in a hard, painful blow.

"Ow!" we both cried, practically in unison. Tim staggered backward, dropping his camera and support rod to the pavement. I cradled my still-clenched fist in my good hand, cursing under my breath. That had hurt like a mother. Glancing down, I found that my knuckles were already swelling a little. *Worth it.*

"You hit me!" Tim cried, his voice a mixture of pain and disbelief. A few tears leaked from his left eye. "I can't believe you freakin' hit me."

"You had it coming," Mickey said. He stepped beside me and leaned down to inspect my hand. "Let's go get you some ice, Slugger."

"Wait." I gently pushed him away with my good hand and advanced on Tim again. "You're not going to post that video."

"Oh, I totally am," he replied, his face flushed with anger. I noted with some satisfaction that there was a bump forming along his jawline where I'd clocked him. "Right after I have you arrested for assault and battery."

"You won't do that," Dillon said coolly. All heads turned to face the bass guitarist, who was holding up his cell phone with the camera facing us. "Not if you don't want your precious audience to see a video of you getting the crap beat out of you by a woman half your size."

Tim blanched. "You wouldn't," he said, sounding more anxious than angry now. "Share that video with anyone, and you can forget ever hearing one of the Dillon Green Band's songs on 95Rox—or any other radio station in the Southeast. Your career will be over."

"Actually." Jack stooped to pick up Tim's fallen camera, his mouth stretching wide. "It's just beginning. Here's some breaking news for you, Scott: A Royal Flush reunion. Dillon's back in the band."

I'm pretty sure Dill, Mickey, and I all gaped at Jack with matching shocked expressions. "Wait—really?" Dillon asked softly. Uncertainty flickered behind his eyes.

Jack shrugged. "We need a bass guitarist. I was hoping maybe you'd wanna take the job. Of course, if you don't want to leave your band behind—"

"Done." Dillon's mouth quirked up. "Rick just plays drums to pick up chicks, and Oscar's been talking about quitting anyway. He'd rather act—next week, he's auditioning for that zombie show they're shooting just outside the city."

"Great." Jack fiddled with the panel on the back of Tim's camera and removed the small memory card. "Here," he said, handing the camera and selfie stick back to Tim. "Feel free to share the reunion news on your show if you're hard up for something to report. But as for your little movie from earlier," Jack snapped the memory card in half and shoved it in the pocket of his jeans. "That's off the record."

"And if you so much as threaten to bring charges against Amelia," Dillon added, holding up his phone, "I'll send this clip of her decking you to every one of your biggest competitors. The whole world will see you crying over being hit by a girl."

I'd normally be a little miffed at the sexist implications of that statement, but as it seemed to be working, I decided to let it slide. Tim looked from Dillon to me, his mouth opening and closing. Resignation spread slowly across his blotchy face. "Fine," he muttered. He held up his index finger. "But I get *exclusive* rights to break the story of Dillon's return to Royal Flush," he said.

"Deal." Jack offered Tim his hand. They shook on it, and Tim excused himself before slinking away to whatever dark place he crawled out of.

"Dill!" I exclaimed when the sleazy DJ was out of earshot. I high-fived him. "That was incredible. I can't believe you were quick enough to get that punch on film."

Dillon tucked his chin and dropped his gaze to the ground. When he looked up a moment later, he was grinning. "I didn't," he admitted. "I bluffed. Tim's so concerned with preserving his precious reputation that he bought it without question. Good thing, too." He swiveled his phone around so we could see the cracked screen. "I think it bit the dust when you guys tackled me."

"Aww, I'm sorry, man," Mickey said, clapping him on the back.

"I'll buy you a new one," Jack offered.

The four of us made our way back to Taco Heaven's patio. "I wonder how everyone else is faring with the fan stampede," I said.

"Oh, Chad is handling it," Jack replied, grinning. I arched a brow in question, but he waved me off. "You'll see. You know Egan's a sucker for attention."

Sure enough, as we returned to the patio, I spotted Chad and Zane standing on the stage, a long line of restaurant patrons winding around the tables. Bronwyn crouched at the edge of the stage. "Who's next?" she called down to the fans. "Who wants their picture with *the* Chad Egan and Zane Calloway of Royal Flush?" An excited middle-aged lady at the head of the line rushed forward to hand Bron her camera before slinging an arm around each of the rockers. Chad and Zane hammed it up for the photo, leaning in and puckering their lips against the lady's chubby cheeks and making kissing noises. The woman squealed with delight and planted her mouth on Chad's before he could protest. When the kiss ended, she happily jumped off stage to retrieve her camera phone from Bronwyn. Chad flicked a glance down to Kat, who was still seated at our reserved booth. He shrugged and made a face before turning to greet the next fan.

"The ladies love him," Kat said with a giggle as I slid into the booth next to her.

My lips quirked. "Jealous?"

"Nah." Kat took a bite of her goat cheese quesadilla then washed it down with a sip of her margarita. "It's kind of cute."

Mickey joined us at the table with a bag of ice he'd requested from the kitchen and gave it to me to treat my swollen knuckles and scraped palms. I gave him a grateful smile, but that nagging voice in my head reminded me that Emmett was the one who should be taking care of me right now. I hadn't heard from him since he'd left, and the little pit of worry in my stomach grew with each passing hour that he didn't check in. *He's out on assignment,* I reminded myself. *He'll call as soon as he can.* I forced Emmett out of my mind for the time being, hoping to enjoy the remainder of the evening free of stress. It was a tall order, but a girl can dream.

The server had brought our food to the table in our absence, and we quickly chowed down while Chad, Zane, and Bronwyn wrapped up their fan photo shoot on stage. In between bites, Jack, Mickey, and I filled in the rest of the crew on the reconciliation with Dillon, who had rejoined his band to pack up their gear. Mickey also told them about Tim's encounter with my right hook.

Kat nearly snorted margarita through her nose. "I have never been prouder of you," she said with a laugh. She clinked her glass to mine.

When the line of Royal Flush fans had died down, Chad, Zane, and Bronwyn returned to the table and scarfed down their food. "Thanks for handling the crowd," Jack said, high fiving Chad and then reaching across the booth to bump fists with Zane.

Chad shrugged. "Someone had to satisfy all the ladies in your absence." He winked.

Ginger finished her meal and pushed her plate away. "Well, I've certainly had enough excitement for one evening," she said, daintily wiping the corner of her mouth with her napkin. "We should probably pay the check and get back to Miss Taylor's house."

Bronwyn stood up quickly from the table. "You can't leave yet! I've got a surprise planned." All eyes turned curiously toward the pink-haired twenty-year-old. Bron pulled her keys out of her purse and waited for Reese to move so she could slide out of the booth. "I'll be right back," she called over her shoulder.

Kat looked from Reese to me, a confused frown creasing her lovely face. "What's going on?" she asked.

I shrugged. "I can honestly say that I have no idea what she's planned." That made me pretty nervous.

Reese just grinned and shook his head as the server stopped by to clear our table and deliver the check. "Sorry, but I'm not going to ruin it for her," he told Kat. "She's been excited about this all afternoon."

Bronwyn came bounding back onto the patio a few moments later, her arms wrapped around an overstuffed shopping bag from Party Land USA. I caught a glimpse of something glittery and covered in feathers sticking out of the top. *Oh, please, no.* My palms began to sweat, and I was overcome with the feeling that something horrible was about to happen.

CHAPTER FOURTEEN

———

"Surprise!" Bronwyn cried, tearing the bag open and spilling the contents onto the table. I was right—it *was* horrible. Tiaras, feather boas, and various phallic-shaped paraphernalia tumbled out. Chad picked up what looked like a fairy godmother wand with a glittering, golden penis attached to the end of it. "Um," he stammered, his bushy eyebrows reaching for his hairline. "Did a gay bar just explode on our table?"

"No, silly." Bronwyn giggled. I watched, mortified, as she rooted through the sparkly mound of novelty items and located a white veil and bright pink sash. "It's a surprise bachelorette party for Suzie."

"Me?" Suzie gasped, her brown eyes wide.

Bronwyn grinned. "Surprise." She scooped up the items and walked around the booth to stand behind Suzie. Before the poor young woman could protest, Bron slid the sash down over Suzie's shoulders and adjusted it so that the words *BRIDE TO BE* were displayed across her chest in zebra-print letters. Then she fashioned the veil above the girl's long, dark hair. Scurrying back around the table, Bronwyn grasped one of the plastic, silver tiaras and came back around to sit it on top of Suzie's head. "There." She stood back and placed her hands on her hips, admiring her handiwork. "Perfect."

Suzie glanced nervously around the table, her cheeks flaming. Clearly the poor girl wasn't used to being the center of attention. "I don't know—" she began, but Bronwyn cut her off.

"Come on, Suz," Bron coaxed, giving the girl's shoulder a gentle squeeze. "You're getting married! And being on the road all the time with the band, I imagine you don't get a lot of girl time. Let us take you out to celebrate. It'll be fun."

"Aww, Bron, what an awesome idea," Kat said. She reached across the table to grab a white feather boa and draped it across her shoulders. It made her look like a classic Hollywood starlet, with her low-cut blue sun dress and her light brown hair sleeked back. "Count me in." Kat locked eyes with me and grinned. "What do you say, Ame? Girls' night?"

I cast a nervous glance at Ginger and Suzie. I was almost positive Bronwyn's ulterior motive involved interrogating the dancer, "Coral", and this was her idea of a cover story. It was unfair to drag these women unknowingly into her little scheme. I did have to admit, though, it seemed that poor Suzie's car accident had left her traumatized—and being on the road with a group of guys and only one other woman to keep her company must be rough. Jack wouldn't let her out of his sight most of the time. A good night of female bonding would help us all blow off a little steam and might bring her out of her shell. "All right." I picked out a pink boa and a button that said *Bride's Official Entourage*. I gave Suzie an encouraging smile. "Let's do it."

Ginger blinked at Kat and me, disappointment written on her face. She must have expected us to put an end to Bron's plan so that she could retreat to Kat's house and get back to work. Seeing that she was outnumbered, she heaved a sigh of resignation and grabbed her own yellow feather boa, along with a handful of colorful beaded necklaces. "Fine," she said sulkily.

Jack placed a protective arm around Suzie's shoulders. "You won't let anything happen to her?" He looked directly at me, concern etched on his handsome face.

"She'll be fine," I promised.

"We'll have her home by one, sir," Bronwyn added in a goofy voice. She gave Jack a mock salute.

Jack tilted his face downward and kissed Suzie's forehead. "Have fun, baby," he said. "Just know I won't get a wink of sleep until you're home safe."

"Of course you won't, dude," Zane chimed in from across the booth. "If the ladies are going out, that means we can take you out for an impromptu bachelor party, too." Mickey, Reese, and Chad gave shouts of approval.

"I don't have to go," Suzie said in a half-whisper when the noise died down. Her eyes pleaded with Jack. I hoped her case of separation anxiety from her fiancé could be fixed with a few fruity cocktails.

"No, you should go. I know you miss your friends back in LA, so this is a good chance to make a few new ones." He smiled at Kat and me. "These girls will show you a good time. I'll see you back at Kat's place." He kissed Suzie and squeezed her hand.

Dusk had settled over Atlanta by the time we returned to the parking lot. Reese took the keys to the Escalade from Kat, and the men filed into the black SUV, leaving Ginger, Kat, Suzie, and me to ride with Bronwyn in her Fiesta. It was almost painful to look at Suzie without Jack by her side. She seemed so frail and timid, casting nervous glances around the parking lot and avoiding eye contact with the rest of us.

"You can ride shotgun, if you want," Bronwyn said to the shy woman, opening the passenger's side door for her.

"Thanks," Suzie said weakly. She folded herself into the front seat, and Ginger, Kat, and I climbed into the back. "I'm not really dressed for a night out," Suzie said, looking down at her plain black T-shirt and cropped pants.

"It doesn't matter," I insisted, gesturing to my own tee and jeans. "None of us are."

"You look fine, sweetie," Kat agreed.

"I could do your makeup really quick," Bronwyn offered. "I keep a few extra supplies in my car for emergencies." She caught my eye in the rearview mirror. "Ame, can you grab the little makeup bag under the back of my seat?"

I did as Bron instructed and pulled out a duffel bag that could easily fit a small dog inside. "A *few* extra supplies?" I asked as I lugged the bag onto the center console.

Bronwyn shrugged. "You should see the spread I've got at home. I own the whole Urban Decay and MAC lines. I'm an artist." She turned to Suzie, a sly grin curling her lips. "And your face is my canvas." Bron made quick work of applying a fresh layer of foundation, powder, and blush to Suzie. She deftly lined her eyes with dark black liner and blended light purple and gold eye shadow to her lids. After clumping about a month's worth of volumizing mascara onto the poor girl's lashes, Bron studied Suzie's face. "And now the lips," she said, rifling through her makeup bag. She came up empty-handed and frowned. "I must have left all my glosses at home." She leaned toward the backseat. "Anybody got lipstick?"

"No, that's okay" Suzie said quickly. "I think you've done enough." She gave Bronwyn a strained smile.

Bronwyn shrugged. "You're gonna look kinda weird with all that blush and no gloss, but suit yourself." She grasped Suzie's shoulders. "Turn around so everyone can admire your new look," she said, turning the woman slightly in her seat.

Admire was a strong word.

"Oh, wow," Kat breathed beside me. She gently poked my ribs with her elbow.

"Um," I stammered. "You look…" I trailed off, wracking my brain for something nice to say. The poor girl looked like she might spend the rest of the night on a street corner, propositioning passersby for a five-dollar 'handy.' "…very colorful," I finished, hoping it was ambiguous enough to be considered a compliment.

"You look *gorgeous*!" Ginger gushed. Kat and I whipped our heads toward the red-haired woman, our brows raised in surprise. Ginger reached over the back of Suzie's seat and squeezed her shoulder. "Simply stunning," she said. "Miss Sinclair is quite the cosmetologist."

"My true calling," Bronwyn said, beaming proudly. I met Kat's gaze and shrugged. Maybe clown cheeks, nude lips, and clumpy tarantula eyelashes were considered stylish in L.A.

"Thanks," Suzie said in her shy voice. I was relieved to see a smile touch her lips. Maybe now she'd finally loosen up.

It was fully dark out by the time Bronwyn pulled her little lime green car into the parking lot behind the Saucy Minx in the Little Five Points neighborhood. "A strip club? On a Tuesday night?" Ginger exclaimed, gawking at the flashing neon sign above the door. She turned to me, her face pinched. "I thought we'd be the ones doing the dancing—not paying to watch other people strut around half-naked."

"Relax," Bronwyn said as the car rolled to a stop. "This place is great. They have male and female dancers—plus it's eighteen and up, which means I can tag along instead of waiting out in the car all night while you ladies get your drink on."

Ginger cast another uncertain look at the dilapidated brick building. "If you say so," she muttered, climbing out of the car.

"I need a drink," Suzie said. She made a beeline for the entrance, and the rest of us had to hurry to keep up with her. The makeover seemed to have given her more confidence, at least. Either that or she needed liquid therapy to get through the next few hours without her rock star groom.

The heavy thump of bass all but swallowed us as we stepped past the bouncer at the front door. The main room of the club was dimly lit, illuminated only by rotating spotlights above the two raised dancing platforms on either side of the room. Each light blinked rapidly in a strobe pattern. A male dancer performed on the left stage, gyrating slowly as he showed off his, er, *assets*, while on the right side of the room, a red-haired woman swung from a pole, dressed in a green bra and panty combo covered in fake leaves. She looked like a slutty version of Poison Ivy.

"It's like I've died and gone to the set of *Magic Mike*," Bronwyn murmured near my ear. Her wide green eyes were transfixed on the blond beefcake in a fireman's hat that was strutting across the men's stage.

"I can't believe Reese was okay with you taking us here," I said.

"He said I can look all I want as long as I don't touch." Bronwyn grinned. "Best boyfriend ever."

I rolled my eyes and turned my attention back to the woman stripper's stage, scanning the area for Coral. "I don't see our girl," I said to Bron. "I'll ask the bartender if she's working." I turned to Ginger and Suzie. "You ladies want a drink? I'm buying."

"Sure." Ginger smiled at me. I was glad to see that she had loosened up a bit, too. She grabbed Suzie by the arm and led her toward the bar in the center of the room. Kat and I followed while Bronwyn staked out an open table for our group.

The bartender was a tall young brunette with her hair cut into a bob. She wore black leather shorts and a glittery purple tube top. Her gaze roved over Suzie's veil and sash, and a bright smile lit up her face. "A bachelorette party? How fun!" she exclaimed, turning to grab four shot glasses. "Congratulations. These first drinks are on the house." We thanked her and gave a quick toast to Suzie before tossing back the cinnamon-flavored whiskey shots. The liquor burned a path down my throat, pooling in my belly. *I'd better not have too many of those if I plan to make any progress with this investigation*, I thought, wiping my mouth with one of the bar napkins. I ordered a round of cocktails for the other ladies and discreetly asked the bartender to hand me a cranberry juice and Sprite, sans the alcohol.

"Is Coral working tonight?" I asked as I handed the young woman my credit card.

"Yep—you just missed her first set of the night, about twenty minutes ago. She'll be making rounds on the floor soon for lap dances, if you're into that." She gave me a sidelong glance.

A nervous giggle escaped my throat. "Hah! No, no. Happily hetero here. She's just a friend, and I was hoping to say hello—though the bride-to-be over there might get a kick out of a quick dance, if you wouldn't mind sending her our way." I slipped the woman a five-dollar bill.

The bartender nodded. "Sure thing."

I thanked her and joined the other ladies at the table Bronwyn had secured. Suzie and Kat were chatting amicably as they sipped their fruity beverages, and Ginger was asking Bronwyn for makeup tips. "In my opinion, the more eyeliner, the better," Bronwyn was saying. "Your eyes can never be *too* dramatic."

I turned my head to the side to hide my laughter, and I caught sight of Coral as she made her way toward our table. She was dressed in tight green shorts with sequins all over them, I assumed to resemble scales on a mermaid's fins. She wore a pink clamshell bra and had a matching shell pinning back one side of her golden hair. Her eyes lit up with recognition when she saw me. "Pepper Spray Girl!" she exclaimed as she sauntered toward our table. "I'm surprised to see you." She winked. "I didn't think you'd take me up on my offer for a dance."

I rose from the table to intercept her just out of earshot of the other women. "I actually needed to talk to you about something," I said. "I've got a few questions for you."

The stripper smirked. "Oh? Well, sorry honey, but I can only talk if I'm workin'." She looked past me to the table. "Twenty bucks for a three-minute lap dance or seventy-five for five minutes in a private room."

"Private room, please!" Bronwyn chirped from right behind me. I whirled and gave her a startled look. Bron ignored me and smiled pleasantly at Coral. "Here." She fished around in the pocket of her jeans and pulled out a one-hundred-dollar bill. "Take my friend in there and give her whatever she wants," Bron told her, slapping me on the back. "That's from Kat and me," she whispered in my ear. "I told her you'd explain everything later. We'll keep the others occupied, and you can pay us back." Bronwyn gave me a little shove toward Coral, who took my hand and led me toward a row of curtained booths along the back wall of the room. I glanced back at the table, blushing fiercely. Ginger whistled and cheered as I was led away, and Kat winked. Even Suzie was laughing.

Coral pulled back the red curtain to an empty booth and beckoned me inside. Swallowing hard, I stepped into the little room, glancing down in disdain at the black leather love seat. "Have a seat," Coral said in a sultry voice.

"No thanks, I prefer to stand." No offense to her, but I had a pretty good idea of the types of things that went on in these private rooms. They could scrub down and sterilize that furniture three times a night, and you still couldn't pay me to sit on it. *Ick.* "I'll make this quick," I said, stepping awkwardly aside so that she could perch on the love seat. "I was hoping you could tell me what happened when you left the club with Sid Malone the other night."

Coral's hazel eyes widened a fraction of an inch and then narrowed to thin slits. "I already talked to the police about that," she said, scowling. "I didn't kill him, dammit! He was alive when I left him, and the best I can tell, I was already on my way to lock-up by the time that douche bucket got what was comin' to 'im." She stood up and pulled Bronwyn's cash out of her seashell bra. "Get out," she said, handing it back to me. "I don't wanna talk about this anymore."

"Wait!" I pleaded. "I knew Sid." I placed the money back in her hand and pulled out another twenty from my purse.

"A good friend of mine is being framed for his murder. I'm just trying to find out what really happened that night. Anything you could tell me might help me keep someone I care about—an innocent someone—from behind bars. You know what it's like to spend time in one of those cells when you didn't do anything wrong. Please, Coral. Help me out, here."

The young woman shook her golden hair out of her face and settled back onto the little couch. She deposited the cash back into her bra. "Fine," she muttered. "What else you wanna know?"

"Just what happened when he left with you—where he went, where he was going when you last saw him—anything you can tell me will help."

Coral crossed her arms over her chest, a thoughtful look on her pretty face. "We left the club around two in the morning," she said. "I thought the fella was charming at first. I brought him back here, and he bought a couple of lap dances. He was a real sweet talker, too." Her expression darkened. "But after I agreed to leave with him, he got kinda rough. He was gripping my wrist too tight and half-dragged me to his cab. I started getting nervous that I'd made a mistake going home with him, but then I was saved by the bell—literally."

"What do you mean?"

"His cell phone went off. Someone texted him, I guess. He read whatever was on the screen, and then his whole attitude changed. He didn't want nothin' to do with me anymore. He said he had unfinished business with some other chick. Sid had the cab stop and drop me off two blocks from the club, and I walked back."

Some chick? I frowned. "How did Sid seem when he mentioned this other woman? Excited? Angry?"

"Eager. And kinda—I don't know—a little wicked, maybe? Something about that dude just seemed a little off." Coral pulled a tiny stopwatch out of her shorts. "Time's up, darlin'," she said, rising from the couch and pulling back the curtain to the private booth. "I hope that you find out who really killed him."

"Thank you," I said with sincerity. "I hope so, too." I stepped back into the main room and made a beeline for the table where Kat, Bronwyn, and Ginger were still seated.

"How'd it go?" Ginger asked, waggling her eyebrows at me as I collapsed into a chair next to her. There were three empty martini glasses in front of her, and she quickly drained the fourth. "Didya hav'a good time?" she slurred.

"It was, er, *different*," I replied, glancing at the empty chair where Jack's fiancée had previously been sitting. "Where's Suzie?"

"I bought her a private dance, too," Bronwyn said, proudly. "She was a little hesitant at first, but then I let her pick the dancer. She went with Five-Alarm Fred—the fireman from earlier." Bron nodded her approval. "Excellent choice." She pulled a stack of one-dollar bills out of her pocket and handed a few to Kat. "Wanna go stuff these in Gyrating Jerry's G-string?" She gestured to the walking six-pack with eyes that was grinding across the stage floor on the men's side of the room.

"Do I ever?" Kat grinned and snatched a few bills. She and Bron darted off in the direction of the humping hunk. That left me alone at the table with Ginger.

My mind wandered back to what Coral the dancer had told me about the *other woman* who was texting Sid. Whoever she was, if he left to meet her then she must have been in Atlanta. A groupie that followed him from another stop on the tour? An old girlfriend from the days before Royal Flush moved to California? I glanced over at Ginger. *Or a woman who's been close with him on the road all this time?*

I studied the red-haired tour manager with renewed interest as she bobbed her head along to the Lady Gaga song blasting from the club's speakers. She was in her early to mid-thirties—young enough to hold Sid's interest. Plus Ginger was pretty, and she had a nice figure. She'd also tried to chase after the spiky-haired bass player on the night he stormed out of Castle Rock. Maybe their relationship was more than just professional.

Ginger suddenly stood up from the table, teetering back and forth. "Those things'll go straight to yer head, huh?" she slurred, gesturing to her empty martini glasses. She hiccupped. "I need to hit the little girls' room. Wanna come with?"

I offered her a pleasant smile. "Sure. I could stand to freshen up a bit." I followed Ginger as she waddled past the bar toward the restrooms in the back corner of the building. She rushed into the only empty stall as I jockeyed for a position in front of the crowded restroom mirror. A few minutes later, the band manager reappeared and joined me at the counter. "So," I said casually as I touched up my mascara. "What's the scoop from the road? Any scandalous hookups or crazy backstage gossip?"

"Huh?" Ginger looked at me with droopy eyes.

I shrugged. "Just curious. I mean, I imagine it gets pretty lonely on the road with the band—unless you've got a playmate along for the ride." I gave her a conspiratorial wink. "You mean to tell me you haven't hooked up with one of the guys even once?"

Ginger's head swiveled from side to side. "They're not really my type," she drawled.

"I hear ya. They're a bunch of goofs," I admitted. "I just thought I picked up a vibe between you and Sid—"

"Sid?" she scoffed. "I wouldn't have even touched that jerk with someone else's lady bits." Her face tightened in anger. "He was a no-good, sleazy, arrogant..." Ginger's voice trailed off. Her expression deflated and sloppy tears streaked down her face, causing her makeup to run. "And he's dead. Here I am calling him names, and the stupid jerk is *dead!*" She dropped her purse, and its contents spilled onto the tiled floor. Several other girls who were standing in front of the mirror backed away quickly, not wanting to get involved in the poor woman's drunken meltdown.

"Oh, no. Ginger, don't cry," I begged, grabbing some paper towels to help wipe away her tears. "I didn't mean to upset you. I was just making conversation. Girl talk, that's all. I'm sorry." I helped her mop up her tears and then stooped to collect her fallen belongings.

Way to go, Ame, I scolded myself. *Making a drunk woman cry.* I reached for Ginger's fallen tube of lipstick, and I froze, my hand hovering over the container of pink gloss. *Unless those are really tears of guilt,* I thought, staring down at the little tube. I picked it up and examined the color more closely. It was a bright pink shade called *Devoted Diva.* I was almost positive it was the same hue that stained the cup I'd found from Royal Flush's tour bus—the one that had disappeared along with Mickey's knife. Maybe Ginger wasn't as innocent as she pretended to be.

"Here you go," I said, straightening to hand the crying woman her purse. I discreetly dropped the tube of lipstick into my own bag so that later I could compare it to the shade in the picture I'd taken of the cup. I smiled at Ginger. "All better?"

She nodded and gave my shoulder a grateful squeeze. "Yes, thank you," she said, sounding more lucid. It seemed the crying spell had helped to sober her up a little. "I've just been so stressed lately. There's so much pressure to keep this tour running smoothly, and things keep going wrong at every turn. I don't know how much more of it I can take. It's making me sick." Ginger's stomach made a gurgling noise. She met my gaze, and her complexion paled. "Oh, no," she moaned. "I think I'm actually gonna be sick." She dashed into the nearest stall.

I leaned against the sink counter and waited patiently to make sure that she was all right. When she hadn't emerged from the stall after a few minutes, I retrieved my phone from my purse, deciding that perhaps I had enough time to compare the photo to the tube of lipstick before she reappeared. No sooner had I located my cell than it chirped and began to vibrate in my hand. Kat's name glowed on the screen. "Did you run out of money to tip Gyrating Jerry?" I joked as I held the phone up to my ear.

There was no response on the other end of the line—or if there was, I couldn't hear it. The loud, distorted thrum of the club music boomed through my phone's tiny speaker, making it impossible to make out Kat's voice through all the noise. "Hello? Kat?" I called, jamming one finger in my other ear to try to block out the excess sound. "I can't hear you. Speak up." The flood of music and snatches of other loud conversations continued to pour through from Kat's end of the call.

"Ginger, I'm going to step outside," I called in the direction of her stall. I unplugged my ear and pushed open the door leading back out into the strip club. I glanced across the room toward our table and saw that it was empty. Kat and Bronwyn were no longer by the men's stage, either. "Kat, if you can hear me, stay on the line," I yelled over the loud music. "I'm going to find some place quieter." I turned from side to side, searching for a place that I might be able to block out some of the sound. My gaze landed on the door to the side exit of the club. *Perfect.* I'd be able to hear Kat better from outside. Once I figured out where she and Bron had run off to, I could check back in with the bouncer at the entrance to come back in. I shoved past a group of men coming out of one of the back VIP rooms and danced my way around three women staggering toward the bar. When I finally reached the side exit, I pushed out into the warm night air.

"That's better," I said into the phone. "Can you hear me now?" I walked several feet out into the parking lot to distance myself from the bass that was practically shaking the building. There was still no response from the other end of the line. I cast a glance around the parking lot and found that I was alone out there. An uneasy feeling crept over me. "Kat? I'm going to hang up and try calling you back." I ended the call and started to press redial, but the sudden echo of approaching footsteps froze me in place. The hair on the back of my neck stood on end. I began to turn around, but the feather boa draped over my shoulders was yanked backward, tightening around my windpipe.

I sputtered and coughed, one arm pin-wheeling backward to fend off my attacker while the other tugged wildly at the boa, trying to loosen it. Lucky for me, Bronwyn hadn't sprung for the highest quality costuming. The boa snapped in half, and I gasped, filling my lungs with air. My relief lasted only a fraction of a second. A cry of rage sounded behind me. I whirled to face my assailant, ready to deliver some serious payback for the near-asphyxiation. As I turned, there was a horrible crunching sound, and pain erupted in the crown of my head. My vision swam, disintegrating into shades of gray (not the sexy kind) before fading to black. As my eyelids tugged down, I hoped that the cracking noise wasn't my skull. Then the world fell away.

CHAPTER FIFTEEN

———

I awoke to an intense, throbbing pain—as if someone had stomped on my skull with a steel-toed boot, and they were still standing on my head. My breathing was shallow, and I felt incredibly thirsty and nauseous. Cracking one eye open and then the other, I was startled by bursts of double vision. *Oh, great,* I thought. *I'm actually seeing stars.* They swirled around my head in a circular blur like something out of a cartoon. As my sight gradually focused, I realized the whirring lights were actually coming from a revolving disco ball on the club's ceiling. Their movement worsened my queasiness. I slowly lolled my head to the side, focusing on the plush red carpet until the wave of nausea passed. I was in a small room, larger than the private booth where I'd questioned Coral, but more secluded than the main area. One of the Saucy Minx's special VIP rooms, maybe.

"I told you we shouldn't have moved her," said a woman. "She might have a broken neck—or a concussion. And all that blood..." Fear ran its icy fingers down my spine. I tried to swivel my head in the direction of her voice, but another sickening wave of pain surged through me. Dizzy, I closed my eyes again, thankful there wasn't any music playing in here. My head was already throbbing in time with the distant beat of the Lil Wayne song that blared from the main room's speakers.

"An ambulance is on the way," another woman replied. I sensed someone leaning over me and opened an eye to peer up at the brunette bartender I'd spoken to before. "You're gonna be all right, sugar," she said. "Can you talk?"

"Mrrph," I replied.

She pursed her lips, her expression grim. "I'll take that as a no." She placed a cool hand on my forehead, and it felt like pure heaven. I made another noise that I hoped conveyed my gratitude. "Hang in there, darlin'," she said.

"Stay with her, Jessa," said the other woman again, her voice sparking recognition. Though I couldn't see her, it sounded like Coral.

A door opened somewhere close by. "Hey," called a man's voice. "There are some ladies out here that said they know her." The music crescendoed (and with it, the angry swarm of bees buzzing around inside my head) as the door opened wider.

"They were with her when she ordered drinks from me at the bar," Jessa confirmed. A stampede of heels clattered toward me, each little click-clack against the floor driving through my brain like a railroad spike. I grunted my displeasure.

"Amelia!" Kat's piercing cry drove the spike deeper, making my vision swim again. "She's bleeding." Kat stooped beside me where I lay. Realizing I was on one of the icky black leather couches, my nausea doubled. "Are you all right?" Kat asked. I gave an involuntary shudder and rolled onto my side, yakking all over her shoes. Lucky for her that they were close-toed.

"Ew!" someone shrieked behind Kat. In the throes of my mind-crippling headache, I couldn't be positive who had screamed. It sounded like Ginger.

"Gross," Bronwyn murmured.

Kat and I had taken turns holding each other's hair back in college after late nights of parties and too many vodka Red Bulls, so she was unfazed by my digestive pyrotechnics. Or, at least, she was more upset about the blood. I yowled at the biting pain that came when she touched her fingertips to the top of my head. She drew her hand back and held it up so I could see the thick, dark blood coating her digits. "You're probably gonna need stitches," she said. Kat pulled a pack of tissues out of her purse and cleaned her hand. Then she wiped the spittle from my mouth before stooping to clean my puddle of sick off her shoes.

"Ohmigod! What happened to her?" came Suzie's voice in a high pitch bordering on hysteria.

"Someone whacked your friend on the head," said Jessa the Bartender. "I went out to the parkin' lot for my smoke break and found her on the ground covered in blood and yellow and pink feathers. It looked like someone had slaughtered Big Bird. One of the glass candleholders from our ladies' room was smashed next to her."

Yellow feathers? The restroom candleholder? I struggled to hold up my head and look around the room. My gaze landed on Ginger, who was still teetering slightly as she stared down at me. The yellow boa was no longer around her neck. "Her," I managed weakly.

Everyone turned to look at Ginger. Her eyes grew as round as saucers. "Me?" she protested. "I didn't do anything—I was tossing up my last martini in one of the bathroom stalls." Her cheeks flushed at the confession.

"Where's your boa?" Bronwyn asked her. "The yellow feather boa you were wearing before, when we got here."

"I-I don't know," Ginger stammered. "It must have slipped off in the restroom."

"Save it, lady." Lenny the Bouncer stepped forward and gripped her arms, wrenching them behind her back.

"Let go of me!" Ginger protested. "I didn't attack Amelia." She looking wildly around the room of accusing faces. Turning her head toward Suzie, she said, "You believe me, don't you, Suz?" Suzie's face pinched, and she dropped her gaze to the floor as she backed away from Ginger.

"I already called 9-1-1," Coral said. "An ambulance and the police should be here any minute."

Bronwyn sucked in a breath. She stooped down next to Kat and me. "If the Sarge finds out I was here, I'll be grounded till Nickelback wins a Grammy."

Kat snorted. "That'll never happen."

"Exactly." Bron grimaced. "Which means I'll be grounded forever."

EMTs burst through the door right then, and I was strapped to a gurney and carried off to the waiting ambulance. Because they couldn't tell the severity of my head trauma, the medics insisted on rushing me to the ER. Coral and Jessa followed us out, promising that Lenny would detain Ginger until the police arrived. Bronwyn called Reese to let the guys know what happened and that she was taking Suzie back to Kat's place. My bestie gave Bron her house key and accompanied me to the hospital, riding in the front of the ambulance.

Kat and I spent the next two hours at the Emory University Hospital. One CT scan, four stitches, and a hefty hospital bill later, I was cleared to be discharged. Though I didn't have a concussion, I was instructed to use a cold compress and take it easy for the next couple of days. "Don't stress yourself," the doctor said, his serious blue eyes boring into mine. "Get plenty of rest, and avoid stressful situations."

I blinked at him and then exchanged a look with Kat. Clearly he didn't know whom he was talking to. Asking me to "avoid stressful situations" was like asking the sky not to rain. I wasn't always blameless, but sometimes trouble just found me.

"You'll also need someone to stay with you for the next forty-eight hours, just to make sure your symptoms don't worsen," he continued. The doctor held out a bottle of prescription painkillers, and I eagerly grabbed for it. "One more thing," he said, pulling them out of my reach at the last second.

My hand closed around the empty air, and my face clouded. "What?" I groused.

The doctor gave me a pitying look. "Since you've been drinking alcohol, I'm afraid you'll have to wait at least another hour or two before you can take one of these." He handed the pills to Kat, who dropped them into her purse. "There is only one hydrocodone tablet in that bottle, which is enough to get you through tonight. You'll need to go by a pharmacy in the morning to fill the full prescription. I've also prescribed some antibiotic topical cream to keep your stitches from getting infected."

The man offered me a wheelchair, but I refused with an irritated shake of my head. Instead, I shambled down the hallway, cursing under my breath as Kat walked patiently beside me. I reached up to feel the top of my head. There was a two-inch patch where the doctor had shaved my head to apply the sutures. I ran my fingers over the tiny bristles of hair that remained and felt hot tears sting my eyes. Not only was my scalp still excruciatingly tender, but I had a bald spot. "I look like a freak," I muttered tearfully.

"Aww, it's not so bad." Kat slid an arm around me as we slowly made our way down the hall. "You can just part your hair differently and it'll cover it right up—or hell, why not just shave the whole right side of your hair and leave the left side long? It's what all the hipsters are doing nowadays." I gave Kat a dark look. "Aw, come on," she said, nudging me gently with her elbow. "Laughter is the best medicine, right?"

"Not nearly as effective as that painkiller is going to be." Detective Ben Dixon walked through the electric sliding doors just as we reached the lobby. I pulled away from Kat. "Can you find a ride home?" I asked. "I imagine I'm going to be here a while longer."

Kat put her hands on her hips. "I'll wait. You can't be alone for the next forty-eight hours, remember?"

I chewed my lip. "Right. Well, hang tight, then. I need to check out and then give Dixon my statement about what happened tonight. At least he's less likely to flip the interrogation switch on me this time around."

"Cool. I'm going to find a drink machine, then," Kat said. "Somewhere in this hospital, there's a Diet Coke with my name on it. I'll meet you back here." She turned and retraced her steps down the hall.

I caught Dixon's attention with a little wave of my hand and then motioned to the front counter. The detective came to stand beside me as I flipped through the small stack of medical paperwork, scribbling my signature at the bottom of each page. "We have got to stop meeting like this," he said, a playful smile touching his face. The humor quickly drained from his expression when he got a closer look at the sutures holding my scalp together. He swallowed hard, his Adam's apple bobbing in this throat. "That had to hurt."

"Understatement of the night."

The detective nodded, his expression sympathetic. "I know you're probably exhausted," he began. "But I'm going to need to get your statement while it's still fresh in your memory."

"As long as I can get some coffee first," I said. Between the cocktails and the near concussion, my eyelids felt like they were made of lead.

"Let's grab a cup in the cafeteria, then," Dixon suggested. When I'd completed my paperwork, he led me through a set of double doors and down another hallway. The hospital cafeteria was mostly empty at a quarter till two on a Wednesday morning. Our only company in the large room was two doctors huddled in a corner with their own cups of joe and a blonde nurse who appeared to be catching a quick nap, her eyes closed as she rested her head on the table. A thin stream of drool trickled down her bottom lip, and she was snoring softly.

"You know the drill," Dixon said as we sat down at an empty table in the opposite corner. He took a sip from his Styrofoam cup and then wiped droplets of coffee from his mustache with one hand. "Walk me through what happened tonight. Why were you at the Saucy Minx?"

"Bachelorette party for Jack's fiancée."

The detective pursed his lips. "Am I supposed to believe it's a coincidence that you picked the one strip club in town that employs a person of interest in my murder investigation?"

"Is Coral still a person of interest? Ginger's the one who just tried to split my head open." I sipped my own steaming cup of coffee and felt the blissfully hot liquid slide down my throat.

"Ginger Robbins has been taken into custody," Dixon said. "And I'll question her when I get back to the station. But I still have to explore every possibility. There were no witnesses, and from my understanding, you didn't see your attacker."

I shook my head, my stomach twisting in a knot worthy of a Girl Scout badge. "But her yellow feather boa was found outside with me—and so was a glass candleholder from the ladies' room. That's the last place I saw her."

Dixon nodded. "Circumstantial evidence." He set down his cup and stared, his expression calm but intense. "What I need to know is why she attacked you. I'm willing to bet it wasn't because you cut in front of her in line at the bar." The detective reached for the notepad in his shirt pocket. "I think you know something that she doesn't want anyone else to find out."

I shrugged, dropping my gaze to the table. "I don't have anything concrete," I said.

Dixon must not have believed me. He studied me for a few moments, eyes narrowed. Then his expression softened, and he leaned forward in his chair. "Work with me here, Amelia. Look, I'm not upset that you've been running your own little side investigation. I understand. I can tell you to stay out of this all day long, but your friends are involved, and you want to help. So I'm giving you the chance to do that."

I stared at him with one eyebrow cocked. "What do you mean?"

"You were an asset to us in tracking down your boss's killer last fall. I think you could help me find out what really happened to Sid Malone. So consider this your free pass—if there's something you've discovered that you haven't already told me, now's the time to spill."

I eyed him skeptically. "No consequences?"

"No consequences."

I sat back and drank my coffee as I weighed his offer. On the one hand, it'd be nice for the APD's Homicide Department to have my back. On the other, would telling him about finding—and losing—Mickey's pocketknife further incriminate my ex? Maybe not, considering he had a pretty air-tight alibi for the night that it disappeared from its hiding place—he was already in jail. I decided I had nothing to lose.

"All right," I agreed, straightening in my chair. I launched into my account of accidentally discovering Mickey's bloody pocketknife and the cup from Royal Flush's tour bus. Dixon's jaw muscle flexed, tightening in a frown of disapproval at my failure to call and report my findings. I ignored his sour expression and continued the story, telling him about the bum who claimed to have seen a woman in the bushes that might have been Ginger. I ended with my encounter with the tour manager in the strip club's restroom just minutes before I was attacked. "I know it's not much to go on," I said. "But I have her tube of pink lipstick. I'm almost positive it matches the gloss stains on the cup I found with Mickey's knife. I've got pictures." I pulled up the images of the knife and cup on my phone and passed it over to Dixon, along with Ginger's lip gloss.

Dixon studied the pictures intently, his gaze flicking back and forth from my phone screen to the lipstick. "I'm going to forward these images to my own phone," he said. The detective held up the tube of gloss. "And I'm going to hold on to this."

"Of course," I said. "Go right ahead."

Dixon pocketed the lipstick and tapped at my phone for a few moments. When he'd sent the pictures to his own cell, he slid mine back to me across the table. "You said you confronted Ginger about your suspicions tonight?"

"Kind of." My cheeks colored. "If by confronting her, you mean got her drunk and asked if she'd been secretly sleeping with Sid before he was killed."

An amused smile flickered across the detective's face. "I admire your methods," he said. "What was her reaction when you brought up Malone?"

"A meltdown," I replied. "Complete with ugly crying. She spewed some vitriol about Sid's character and then broke down into sobs. I was starting to feel bad for her until I found the lipstick that had fallen out of her purse. I swear it's a match." I finished my coffee and set the empty cup onto the table. "Ginger's been Royal Flush's manager for years, and she easily could've stolen Mickey's knife. Plus, she was the last person from their entourage to see Sid alive—she followed after him when he stormed out of Castle Rock Saturday night. Ginger claimed he was already rolling away in a cab by the time she reached him, but who knows? Maybe she caught up to him, and they had an argument."

Dixon considered this for a few moments, his expression thoughtful. "So you think that Miss Robbins realized you were onto her, and that's what provoked her to attack you tonight?" I nodded. The detective drained the coffee cup and crumpled the Styrofoam in his fist. "Thank you for cooperating, Amelia. All of this will help when I question her." His jaw clenched again, and I could tell he was fighting the urge to scold me. "Just do me a favor," he said, offering up a smile that didn't quite reach his eyes. "The next time you find a murder weapon, call me. Okay?"

* * *

Kat was waiting for me in the lobby when Dixon and I returned from the cafeteria. The detective offered to drive us home, but Kat had already called a cab. "I let Chad and the guys know that I'd be crashing at your place," she said as we walked out to the curb where our ride was waiting. "I figure things must be pretty chaotic at my house right now, and the cops will probably be dropping by to go through Ginger's things. Considering the doc's orders for you to avoid stress, it's probably best that we just put off dealing with all this until tomorrow."

"Thanks," I said. I glanced down at my Jimmy Eat World T-shirt. Some of the glass shards from the broken candleholder had torn little holes in the collar, and the front was stained with dried blood. "I could really stand to get out of these clothes." I frowned. "Damn. I loved this shirt."

"I'll order you a new one," Kat said. "Think of it as an early birthday present."

"How about giving me my pill instead?" I asked, wincing. My head was throbbing again. I gave her a pleading look through the pain. "I'm definitely sober enough now."

Kat shook her head. "Not yet." Her tone was full of apology. "As soon as we get to your apartment, though," she promised. "I don't know how strong these things are. If the painkiller knocks you out, I'm too beat to carry your butt all the way to the thirteenth floor of your complex."

"Fine." I sighed. The pain made the next ten minutes feel like ten hours, but we finally made it through my front door. I didn't even stop to turn on the lights as I dragged myself through the dark apartment. I heard Kat flip on the lamp in the living room and stoop to greet one of my curious kitties. A few minutes later, she padded into the bathroom to check on me.

I'd filled the tub and squirted nearly half a bottle of bubble bath into the hot water. I couldn't shower because of my stitches, and though the scrapes on my palms had begun to scab over, the soap still made them smart with pain. Kat graciously perched on the tub's edge and helped me wash my hair, careful to avoid my wounds. She ventured into my closet to find some pajamas to borrow as I dried off and threw on a tank top and pair of yoga pants. I tossed the wet towel into my laundry hamper and shuffled into the living room.

Kat was curled up on the couch watching a rerun of *Thirty Rock*. Two glasses of water sat on the coffee table in front of her. Her long hair was piled into a messy bun atop her head, and she was wearing my old Bobby Glitter T-shirt from high school and a pair of bleach-stained gray sweatpants. Even dressed in my rattiest pj's, she looked like a supermodel. "These pants are super comfy," Kat said, stretching one leg out in front her.

"Keep 'em." I sat down beside her and let Uno jump up onto my lap. "They look better on you anyway." I closed my eyes and absently stroked the cat's orange fur.

"Whatever," Kat said. "Sweatpants aren't flattering on *anyone*. These things make my ass look huge."

I cracked one eye open and grinned at her. "Maybe Chad likes a little junk in the trunk," I teased.

Kat's cheeks glowed. "Oh, hush." She leaned down to grab her purse from the floor. Kat pulled out the prescription bottle and dumped the lone pill into her hand. Then she offered me one of the glasses of water. "Maybe this'll shut you up," she said, though a little smile played at her lips.

I eagerly took the hydrocodone and popped it into my mouth, chasing it with a few gulps of the water. "You're a goddess," I said, my tone weary but grateful. I shooed Uno off my lap and curled my legs underneath me, settling back into the couch cushions. "You really do like Chad, huh?"

Kat grabbed her own glass of water and took a sip. When she met my gaze, her eyes gleamed with moisture. "Yeah. I do," she said. She blew out a breath, lifting several stray strands of her light hair from her forehead. "I'm just trying to take it slow. As soon as this mess blows over, Chad will be back on the road. We'll see what happens in a few months when Royal Flush wraps up the tour." Her expression turned thoughtful. "I wonder what they'll do now that they may not have a tour manager," she said. "If Ginger really attacked you, I mean." She met my gaze. "Do you really think she killed Sid?"

"Yes," I said after a few moments. "My guess is maybe he hooked up with her somewhere along the tour, and she felt scorned when he moved on to the next groupie that came along. Ginger probably didn't appreciate being just another check mark off his to-do list. She likes to be in charge of situations, and Sid wasn't the type to let someone else control him."

Kat nodded. "There's one thing I don't understand, though," she said, her face clouding. "Ginger could've just jumped you in the bathroom, but you went outside. What made you go to the parking lot?"

"Ginger wouldn't have attacked me in the restroom," I said, shaking my head. "There were too many witnesses. When I went outside to hear you better, she saw an opportunity."

"Huh?" Kat looked puzzled. "Hear me better?"

I yawned, beginning to feel the first effects of the medication. With any luck, the pain would dull to a tolerable degree within the next ten minutes or so. "When you called me," I reminded her. "It was too loud to hear you in the ladies' room, so I stepped outside to escape all the background noise." Kat stared at me as if I'd sprouted a horn. "What?" I asked, blinking sleepily at her.

"Honey, that painkiller must be messing with your memory," she said slowly. "I never called you."

It was my turn to stare. "Yes, you did."

"No, I didn't."

My face wrinkled. "Where's my purse?" I retraced my steps to the kitchen where I'd dropped it on the dining table when we walked through the door. I plucked my phone out from between my wallet and hairbrush and brought it back into the living room. Pulling up my recent call history, I held it up to show Kat. "See? You called me at 10:57 p.m."

Kat's blue eyes grew wide. "That's impossible." She fished her own phone out of her purse. Besides the call to the cab company about an hour ago, she hadn't dialed anyone since early Tuesday afternoon. "Your phone must be screwed up," she said.

"No." I shook my head again, a puzzled expression winding its way across my face as I tried to think through my medicated fog. I glanced back and forth from my cell to Kat's. Her name and number were on my caller ID, plain as day—but there was no outgoing call on her end. *Why does this feel strangely familiar?*

A light bulb went off in my brain. "Mickey!" I exclaimed.

Kat gave me an odd look. "What about him?"

I pointed to my phone again. "The same thing happened to Mickey on the night Sid was murdered. He said that Sid texted him and asked to meet him on the tour bus. Thing is, the cops looked through Sid's phone and couldn't find the text. They thought Mickey made it up."

"So what you think happened here is—"

"That Ginger set us both up," I said, cutting her off. "Other than you and Bron, she's the only person at the club tonight that knew both my number and yours. She somehow masked her number as Sid's when she texted Mickey Saturday night, and she did the same tonight when she wanted to get me alone outside to attack me." I pumped my fist in the air triumphantly. "We've done it, Kat—we've solved Sid's murder."

CHAPTER SIXTEEN

———

Not even mild head trauma could keep me away from Castle Rock on Wednesday. Sergeant Sinclair had finally given us clearance to reopen, and a local band called Jealousy Fetish was scheduled to play that evening. I pushed aside my mind-numbing exhaustion (Kat woke me up nearly every half hour the night before to be sure that I hadn't slipped into some kind of coma) and got dressed to head into the office. Despite the doctor's orders to take it easy, I desperately needed to catch up on paperwork and get the venue ready before the band showed up for their sound check.

Kat insisted on driving my car since it wasn't safe for me to drive on my medication. "You're constantly going out of your way to take care of your friends," she said, holding my car keys out of reach. "Let us take care of you for a change." With the little bit of sleep she'd had, I wasn't convinced she should be playing chauffeur either. I was too tired to argue though, so I poured myself into the passenger side and let Kat navigate, thankful when she took a detour to the nearest pharmacy to get my prescription filled.

My spirits were instantly lifted as I stepped through the employee entrance to Castle Rock around ten. There was something about the gray stone building and its velour red carpet that felt more like home than my apartment did. I hadn't realized just how much I'd missed the place in the few short days since Royal Flush's performance. Even the sour aroma of stale beer wafting down the hall from the Dungeon brought a smile to my lips.

My good mood lasted for approximately ten minutes—long enough for me to boot my computer and place a call to

Detective Dixon. His voice mailbox was full, so I made a mental note to try him again later. I was just about to check my email when the sound of knocking brought my attention to my office door. "Heya, boss lady." Bronwyn poked her head through the threshold, her expression sheepish. She stepped into the room and held up a to-go cup and white bag with the Java Joy logo printed across the front. "Nothing says, 'Sorry I bailed' like a dozen chocolate raspberry scones and a fresh coffee, right?" She set the drink and apology pastries on the desk and draped herself across my couch. "How are you feeling?"

My lips twisted in a sardonic smile. "Well, let's see— Ginger tried to choke me with a feather boa and then smashed a glass over my head. I've had practically no sleep, a migraine the size of Piedmont Park is pounding through my brain, and I've got a two-inch bald spot where staples are keeping my scalp from peeling open like a banana. So, I'm doing just peachy." I took a sip of the coffee. "Ooh, mocha!"

Bronwyn cringed. "Well, I hate to be the bearer of more bad news, but…" The words died in her throat when she caught my warning expression. "Er, nevermind."

I set the coffee down and peeked into the bag of chocolate raspberry scones before promptly pushing them across the desk. They would forever remind me of the morning I'd found Sid's corpse. I sighed. "Whatever it is, you might as well go ahead and tell me."

"It's something I'll have to show you, actually." She rose from the couch and came to stand beside me. "Pull up ATL Night Beat's latest photo gallery."

I did as she instructed and felt my stomach drop through the floor. "Oh, no," I breathed. The first picture featured yours truly. Someone had snapped a photo of Mickey and me standing outside Taco Heaven the night before, right at the moment where he'd leaned in to try to kiss me. The caption above the image said:

Sparks fly between Royal Flush drummer Mickey Ward and his former flame over dinner at Taco Heaven on Tuesday.

"I've got to call Emmett," I said, feeling sick. Of course the photographer hadn't posted a picture of what happened *after* the almost kiss—the moment when I'd pushed away from

Mickey and hurried into the restaurant. I scrambled for my phone and dialed Emmett's cell. It went straight to voice mail. My heart felt as if someone had reached in my chest and squeezed it to the brink of popping.

"It's going to be fine," Bronwyn assured me, giving my shoulder an awkward pat. "I mean, what are the chances that Emmett reads Atlanta's tabloids? Probably not very high."

I rubbed my eyes with the heels of my hands, not caring that I was smearing my makeup. "I hope you're right," I said. "The doctor told me to avoid stress, but at this rate I'll keel over by lunchtime."

"Anything I can do to help take the load off?" Bronwyn asked. "Contracts to file? Will call tickets to sort? Let me at 'em."

"Actually, I've got another project for you. Something not work-related."

"Ooh, more detective work?" she asked, eyes flickering with interest. She took a step closer, holding out her hands and wiggling her fingers. "Gimme!"

"Easy there, Veronica Mars." I wasn't keen on dragging her even further into this, but I needed her help. It *was* just some online investigating after all, and with Ginger already in police custody it wasn't likely that Bron would be in danger. I explained my conversation with Kat the night before about the call that had lured me out of the strip club, as well as the text Mickey received from Sid that mysteriously vanished from Sid's phone records. "I think Ginger found some way to mask her phone number as someone else's—maybe there's some sort of mobile app that does the trick," I said, showing Bron the fake call from Kat that I'd received the night before. "I haven't been able to get in touch with Detective Dixon to report it yet. Before I try calling him again, maybe we can do a little digging and find out how Ginger could've pulled it off. If we can verify that the call I received and the text to Mickey both came from the same number, we might be able to prove that Ginger set Mickey up."

Bronwyn grinned. "Done. My buddy Milo from school is a genius hacker. Get me Mickey's phone number and your billing password. Milo can decode the number-masking app, cross-reference your phone records to verify the real number that contacted you both, and then he can look up the name registered to that account. I heard the Sarge say Dixon was questioning Ginger this morning—but with Milo's help, we can have the case closed by the time doors open for tonight's show."

My lips quirked. "That's what I like to hear." I gave Bron the information she needed and waited for her to leave, but she just stood there. "Don't you have a call to make?" I asked.

Bronwyn shifted uncomfortably on her feet. "Kat told me not to let you out of my sight," she admitted. "According to her, you're supposed to have constant supervision through Friday to make sure you don't die, or something like that."

I pursed my lips. "Fine. You can work over there." I pointed to my couch.

Bronwyn nodded. "I'll just run and grab my laptop from the break room really quick—and I'll call Milo on the way." She disappeared down the hall and returned a few minutes later with her computer in tow. "Milo's on the case," she reported. "He said he'd hit me up as soon as he's got some answers for us."

"Great." I began flipping through the stack of performance contracts that needed reviewing. By noon I had barely made it through half the pile. My mind kept going back to the photo of Mickey and me, making it hard to concentrate on work. Every task was taking twice as long as it should. After updating our online concert calendar with several new shows, I caved and visited the gossip blog's image gallery again. The photo was taken from several yards away—some paparazzo must have been ballsy enough to creep within a few car lengths from where we stood. We'd been too focused on each other to notice.

Mickey's back was to the camera, his arms around my waist and his head bent low as he went in for a kiss. What bothered me the most had nothing to do with his body language. It was the look on my face. I was fully visible to the camera, and there was no mistaking the gleam of desire in my eyes.

I closed the website and looked away, guilt and longing swirling through me in a confused tangle. Mickey and I had an undeniable chemistry, but Emmett and I had a deep connection too. *At least, we used to.* The fact that he hadn't called even once since he left on Monday hadn't gone unnoticed. It was possible that he could be in the thick of an assignment—maybe he'd even caught Shawn Stone and would be calling soon to tell me the good news. But the more time passed without hearing from him, the more uneasy I felt.

I rose from my desk chair, slipping my phone in my pocket. Bronwyn looked up at me from her computer. "Where are you going?" she asked.

"Just the restroom," I lied. "No need to follow me there—you can continue your babysitting shift as soon as I get back. Five minutes, tops."

Bronwyn studied me for a moment, her eyes narrowed in suspicion. Finally she nodded and went back to working on her laptop.

I slipped out into the hallway and past Kat's closed office door, heading for the exit. Once outside, I made my way into Castle Rock's back courtyard. The area behind the venue was fenced in by a gray stone gate that matched the building's exterior. We'd recently begun using the large field for outdoor shows and summer festivals. It was my favorite spot in all of Castle Rock.

Climbing onto the raised platform that served as our outdoor stage, I retrieved my phone and dialed Emmett's cell again. I was hoping to catch him on his lunch break. I let my legs swing back and forth over the edge of the stage as I waited for him to answer. My heartbeat accelerated with each ring. One, two, three…voice mail. Had he ignored my call? *That's it,* I thought. I scrolled down my contact list and found the number of Emmett's partner, Special Agent Gavin Addison.

"Well, hey, Amelia," Gavin drawled in his thick Southern accent after the second ring. "Long time no see."

"No kidding." My mood brightened at the sound of his voice. Gavin had been a part of the undercover assignment that first brought Emmett into my life. Though he'd barely spoken a word during that first week that I knew him (Gav is apparently a terrible actor, and the Bureau ordered him to stay silent rather than risk blowing his cover), I'd grown fond of the guy.

"How're you doin', girl?" he asked, his voice warm.

"I'm fine, Gav," I lied. "Everything's great. I was just hoping you might be out on assignment with Emmett and could tell him to call me. I keep getting his voice mail, and I really need to talk to him."

"Oh." The change in Gavin's attitude was instant. "I'm not with Emmett," he replied in a guarded tone.

"Okay." My chest tightened. "Did you get taken off the Stone case? Or are you two just following up on separate leads?" I smacked my palm to my forehead. "I'm sorry—I know I shouldn't have asked that, with your work being top secret and all."

"Amelia." Gavin cleared his throat. "I don't know how to tell you this, but we're not following separate leads—in fact, Larson shouldn't be following any leads at all."

"What do you mean?" My voice trembled. He wasn't making any sense.

"Emmett hasn't worked a case for the Bureau in over a month. He resigned."

"He *what?*" Shock reverberated through me, and I began to feel dizzy. *Don't stress,* I reminded myself, taking several deep, calming breaths. I stopped swinging my legs and lay back onto the stage, staring up at the awning as I waited for my world to stop spinning.

"You really didn't know," Gavin said, and I could hear the pity in his voice. "Shit, Amelia. I didn't mean to drop this on you. I really thought he would've talked to you about it."

"What happened?" I asked, straining to keep my tone even.

"I'm afraid that's not for me to tell," he replied. "I can assure you that we're still on Stone's trail, though, so there's no need for you to worry."

"Right." My voice was flat. How could I not worry when I'd just learned that my boyfriend had been lying to me about leaving his job for over a month? Where was he right now? What was he doing? And, more importantly, why wasn't he being honest with me?

"Just talk to Emmett," Gavin was saying. "And if you do hear from him, can you please tell him to contact me? He's been dodging my calls for weeks, and I'm worried about him."

"You and me both," I murmured. After hanging up with Gavin, I set my phone beside me on the stage and remained in my prone position, my mind running through the possible scenarios where it would make sense for Emmett to lie to me about leaving the FBI. *Maybe he didn't quit and is so deep undercover that he had to make Gavin think that he resigned. Or maybe he's not really Emmett—he's a pod person. OR maybe this whole thing is one big prank and Ashton Kutcher is going to pop out and tell me I've been punk'd.*

"Ame?" Mickey's voice jarred me out of my thoughts, and I sat up quickly. Too quickly. Another bout of dizziness swept over me, and I teetered on the edge of the stage, beginning to slip. It wasn't far to fall, but it would still hurt like hell. Given my current condition and my streak of bad luck, I'd probably land back in the hospital, no pun intended. "Whoa!" Mickey called. A hand shot out from behind me and gripped my shoulder so that I wouldn't fall. "It's okay. I've got you." Mickey helped to steady me and then slowly sat down himself, slipping his arm around my middle.

"Where did you come from?" I asked, a confused frown pulling my mouth down at the corners.

"Chad told Kat he'd drive her rental car up here and bring a change of clothes," he said. "The rest of us decided to come along. Jack and Zane wanna get some practice in, and I wanted to make sure you were okay after what happened last night. I saw you sneaking out here when we pulled up, so I followed you." He gave me an appraising look, and his brow furrowed. "Have you been crying?"

"What? No," I said, remembering my smeared makeup. I wiped at the mascara under my eyes and self-consciously tugged at my hair, which Kat had helped me comb over to cover up my mini buzz cut. "I've just had a rough morning," I admitted.

"Wanna talk about it?"

Not really. I couldn't confide in the ex-love of my life that my current flame was fizzling out. "Did you see our picture on ATL Night Beat?" I asked instead, feeling my cheeks warm.

"Yeah." It was Mickey's turn to look embarrassed. "I'm so sorry. I had no idea that one of those stupid photo hounds was out there. I hope it didn't get you in trouble with Emmett."

"Screw him," I blurted.

Mickey's brows lifted in surprise. "You sure you're okay?"

I pulled my legs up onto the stage and turned so that I was facing him. Mickey still hadn't shaved, and the beard and shoulder-length hair made him look like a younger, hotter Dave Grohl. I lowered my gaze to his chest and felt a pang of bittersweet nostalgia. He was wearing the same navy blue Atlanta Braves shirt that Chad wore on Monday—the shirt he'd bought on one of our first dates. "I still have mine too," I said, placing my hand over the cursive *A* on his chest.

"Your heart?" His lips quirked.

I gave him a rueful smile. "No. That just got chucked in a coffee grinder. I meant my shirt from our first Braves game. I sleep in it sometimes." I looked away, feeling suddenly shy. "It reminds me of you."

Mickey put his hand over mine, lightly caressing my fingers. "What happened?" His voice was soft.

I just shook my head. "You've never lied to me," I said. "We had our ups and downs, but even when you left, you were honest."

"Of course. You should always be honest with someone you love, even if what you have to say isn't what they want to hear." His jaw muscle flexed. "Telling you that I was leaving Atlanta is one of the hardest things I've ever had to do."

My fingers curled, gently gripping the fabric of Mickey's shirt. I scooted a little closer to him. "You're not an FBI agent or a mafia hit man, are you?"

Mickey looked taken aback. "Kind of an odd question," he said. The corners of his mouth turned up in that same dimpled grin that used to drive me wild in college. "But no, the last time I checked, I was neither of those things. I'm just a drummer in some band." He winked.

"Good answer." Before I could talk myself out of it, I launched my lips toward Mickey's. The kiss set off a chemical explosion, sending sparks through me like an electric current. Mickey was caught off guard and toppled backward on the stage. I moved with him, swinging my right leg around so that I was straddling his waist. I couldn't tell if the dizziness was from my head wound or the rush of adrenaline that surged through me as the kiss deepened. My heart rate rocketed, and I moved against Mickey, pressing tightly against him as he grew hard beneath his jeans. *I've missed this,* I thought, feeling as though I might vibrate out of my skin.

Mickey moaned softly and reached up to run his hands through my hair. His fingers brushed against my stitches, and I cried out in pain. The spell broken, I tumbled off of him and lay on the stage, panting as the full gravity of what I'd just done pressed down on me. "I shouldn't have," I whispered, my chest still heaving.

"I'm glad you did," Mickey whispered back. He reached over and grabbed my hand, giving it a squeeze. "But I get it. You're still with Emmett, and you want to do right by him. I'll respect that."

"Thank you." I rolled over onto my side and met Mickey's gaze. "It's just...you broke my heart once," I said, my eyes growing misty.

A sad little smile stretched his lips. "You broke mine right back."

"I know. And I'm sorry. If I'd just taken some time to think things through, I might have gone off to L.A. with you and the band." My own lips quirked. "Who knows? We might still be together now."

"You were right not to just drop everything and run off with me, though. You had a life here, and it wasn't fair of me to expect you to put your own dreams on hold." Mickey brushed a lock of hair behind my ear. "I know that now."

I swallowed, forcing down the words that threatened to bubble out of my throat. Words that I couldn't tell Mickey when I was committed to someone else—even if that someone else had been lying to me for over a month and was currently MIA. A girl's got nothing if she doesn't have honor. "I should get back inside," I said instead. "Kat and Bronwyn will assume I'm comatose in a gutter somewhere if I'm not back in my office soon. I'm surprised they haven't already sent out a search party."

Mickey hauled himself to his feet and offered a hand to pull me up. "I don't know what's going on with you and Emmett right now, or what's going to happen tomorrow even," he said, leaning close and cupping my face in his hands. "But I've never stopped loving you, Amelia. I don't know that I ever will."

"Ditto." I stood on tiptoe and planted a chaste kiss on his cheek.

Mickey walked me back inside where we ran into Bronwyn pacing back and forth in front of the bathroom door. She halted mid step when she caught sight of me, her brows pinching together. "So, I guess you didn't fall into the toilet, then," she said, her tone impatient. "What were you doing outside?" Bron looked from Mickey to me, both of us red-faced and sweaty, and she held up her hand. "On second thought— don't tell me. I want plausible deniability if Secret Agent Man comes back to town. Anyway, come with me, both of you. Things just got cranked up to eleven on the weird scale."

Mickey and I exchanged a puzzled glance but followed Bronwyn without question. Back in my office, she pulled out her phone. "Milo called me back when I stepped away to help Reese, er, check the beer inventory." Her cheeks turned a shade of pink that was just a touch lighter than her hair. "Listen to the voice mail he left me." She turned on her speakerphone and played the message.

A young man's slightly nasal voice filled the room. "Yo, Bron, it's Milo. Check it—I did some digging on the two phone accounts you sent me. Looks like those questionable contacts both came from a number using Spoofer 2.0. It's an app that disguises your digits to display as any other number you want. That's why your pals thought they were hearing from someone else."

"See? I knew it!" I said, but Bronwyn held up a finger and made a loud shushing noise.

"Here's the real kicker, though," Milo's recorded voice continued. "This is some real Twilight Zone-level shit. The number that was calling and texting your friends is registered to a chick named Jessica Whitley out in Los Angeles. Home girl must've been pranking your buddies from the grave—she died a month ago."

CHAPTER SEVENTEEN

———

"He's joking, right?" I asked, feeling the blood leave my face. I looked from Bronwyn to Mickey and then back to the phone in Bron's hand. "That's impossible. That number called me *last night.*"

"Pretty creepy." Bronwyn shook her head. "But when it comes to hacking, Milo doesn't play. If he says this Jessica girl bit the bullet last month, then the chick is really six feet under."

"Maybe Ginger stole her phone," Mickey suggested. He ran a hand through his hair, his expression thoughtful. "We were in L.A. a month ago. The name doesn't ring a bell, but Ginger or Suzie might know her. Or one of the other guys."

I started for the door. "Let's ask 'em."

"They left," Bronwyn said, stopping me in my tracks. She gave me a pointed look. "I covered for you when Kat dropped by your office to see how you were feeling. I told her she'd just missed you and that you'd run to the restroom, like you *told* me you were."

"Thanks," I said, feeling sheepish. "Where'd they go?"

"They ran over to pick up pizza from Camila's for lunch. I told Kat to bring you back a pepperoni Super Slice and a Diet Coke."

I stepped over to Bronwyn and gave her a light pat on the head. "Best assistant ever."

"Keep that in mind the next time you're handing out raises," she said, a grin cracking through her stern expression.

"Hint taken." I glanced at Mickey. "We should research this Jessica Whitley and see what we can find out about her. Maybe we can uncover her connection to Ginger before everyone else gets back from lunch."

There was a knock at my office door, and the three of us turned our heads to see a tall, skinny young man in his late teens or early twenties. His spiky hair was bleached blond, and he was dressed in black leather pants and a white T-shirt with the words *You're Jealous* printed on the front in black block letters. A silver bar piercing sliced through the cartilage of his nose, and his eyebrows had each been shaved off and replaced by curved lines of silver studs. "Uh, we're here for sound check?" he said, the lilt in his voice making it sound more like a question than a statement.

I checked my watch. It was just after one in the afternoon. The band was early. "You're with Jealousy Fetish, right?"

"Duh." The kid didn't smile. "Didn't you read my T-shirt?" He shook his head disdainfully. "Where should we set up?"

"You're in the Dungeon," Bronwyn piped up, stepping forward. "Come on, I'll show you to the green room so you guys can get settled."

I shot her a grateful look as she left, and she held out her hand, rubbing her pointer and index finger against her thumb in the universal *show me the money* sign. "Raise," she mouthed before disappearing down the hall.

"That girl is something else," Mickey said, a smile playing at the corners of his lips. "You've got some pretty great friends here."

"The best." I crossed the room and sat down at my computer with my fingers poised over the keyboard, ready to enter Jessica Whitley's name in the search engine. My phone chose that moment to chirp from my pocket. A glance at the screen made my whole my body tense. It was a text from Emmett. *Just landed in Atlanta. Meet me at your apartment in an hour. We need to talk.*

At least now I knew why he wasn't answering my calls before—he'd been on an airplane, coming back to see me. A wide range of emotions flooded through me as I read the message and then reread it. Anger, hurt, suspicion…guilt. I flicked a brief glance back to Mickey and felt regret pool in my belly like sour milk. I'd been waiting for Emmett to return my calls, and yet suddenly I dreaded meeting him face-to-face. He'd lied to me, and I'd retaliated by running straight into Mickey's arms.

Mickey read the disconcerted look on my face and took a step toward the door. "You, er, need some privacy?"

I gave him a strained smile. "Actually, I need to head home for a bit."

The smell of pizza wafted through my doorway, announcing the group's return a few moments before Kat popped into the office. She'd traded my old T-shirt and sweats for a purple silk blouse and houndstooth-check capris. "How's my favorite head case?" she asked, holding out the cardboard pizza box and drink cup. "Hungry for a Super Slice?"

My stomach gave a hopeful grumble, but my heart wasn't having it. "No thanks."

Kat took one look at my somber expression, and her cheeriness evaporated. "Oh, God. Who died?"

Oh, just my relationship.

"Some girl named Jessica Whitley," Mickey said as Jack and Suzie stopped in the doorway behind Kat. Mickey glanced at Jack. "That name mean anything to you? She lived in L.A."

Jack was munching on a slice of pineapple and ham pizza. "Nope," he said once he'd swallowed. "Doesn't ring a bell. What about you, Suz?" he asked, looking down at his bride-to-be.

"No, I don't think so," she replied. Suzie flicked a glance at me and then to Mickey, her eyebrows raised in question. "Was she a friend of Ginger's?"

"That's what I'm trying to find out." I scooped up my purse and made my way over to Kat. "Look, I know you mean well with this whole caretaker bit, but I really need to get back to my apartment. Can I please have my car keys?" I gave her an imploring look.

Kat's forehead wrinkled. "I don't know if you should be driving just yet," she said, her tone uncertain. "When was the last time you took one of your painkillers?"

"About four hours ago, though I'm due for another. I've got a headache from hell." I dropped my voice. "Kat, please. It's Emmett."

Kat's blue eyes grew large. "Oh." She chewed her lip. "Honey, I just don't want something bad to happen to you. What if you pass out while driving? I'd never forgive myself."

"I could drive you." The offer came from Suzie. Kat and I both turned our heads toward the petite woman, mouths open in surprise. Suzie blushed. "Just trying to help," she said in her small voice.

Jack kissed the top of her head. "You're so thoughtful, babe." She smiled up at him and cupped his face with her hand.

"Yeah, that would actually be a big help, Suzie," Kat said. She turned to me. "Bronwyn, Reese, and I can handle day-of-show prep until Derek and the bartenders get here. Dillon is on his way up here too—I told Jack and Chad that the guys could have a rehearsal in High Court since there's no show up there tonight."

"Dill needs to learn our new songs for the tour," Jack chimed in. He gave Mickey a high five.

"Just promise me you'll take it easy for the rest of the day," Kat said, bringing my attention back to her. "I'll give Suzie your car keys so she can drive you home. As soon as Jealousy Fetish's show is underway, I'll send Bronwyn over for the next shift."

"You make it sound like y'all are guarding the crown jewels or something," I groused.

Kat winked. "You're just as precious," she teased. Jack snorted, and I cut him a dark look.

"Fine." I sighed. "Thanks for lunch." I took the pizza box and diet soda from Kat, deciding I'd save the grub for later. If the conversation with Emmett went any way like I imagined it would, I was going to need the comfort food.

Suzie gave Jack the type of good-bye kiss that should be reserved for X-rated movies. Kat, Mickey, and I averted our eyes. When she'd pried herself away from the rocker, Suzie took my car keys from Kat's outstretched hand and followed me out of Castle Rock. I ambled sullenly out to the parking lot and stood waiting next to the passenger seat, feeling like a petulant teen whose parents wouldn't let her drive the family car. Suzie gave me an apologetic look as she slid behind the wheel. "I know you don't want me to go with you," she said.

I blew out a breath and forced a polite smile. "It's not you," I said. "I'm just frustrated."

"I understand," she replied in her girlish voice. I gave her my address, and she pulled the Jetta out onto North Avenue. "I just wanted to be helpful," she said. "You and your friends have been so kind to me. And now Ginger's in jail for...*murder*." She whispered the last word as if she'd been afraid to say it out loud. She gave me a sidelong glance. "It's just all kind of crazy, ya know?"

I nodded absently. I was barely listening, my thoughts on the impending reality show-level fight that Emmett and I were about to have. And because the doctor told Kat that I needed a babysitter, Suzie was going to have a front row seat. I'd have to microwave her a bowl of popcorn first.

We reached my apartment a few minutes later. I set my purse and drink cup on the kitchen table and placed the Camila's pizza box in the fridge. "Home sweet home," I said, moving my arm in a sweeping gesture as Suzie walked through the kitchen.

"You have a lovely apartment," she remarked, taking a few steps into the living room and turning her head from side to side. "Wow. That view is to die for." She crossed the living room and slid open the glass door to my balcony. My thirteenth floor, one-bedroom apartment overlooked the gorgeous, sprawling green lawn of Piedmont Park. Kat and I often lounged out there during the summer, sipping cocktails while we watched people jog, do yoga, and play Frisbee out in the field.

"Yeah, it's great," I said. I cast a glance at the clock. It was nearly two-thirty; Emmett should be here within half an hour.

"Oh, hi there," Suzie cooed. I looked down to see Dos, my chubbiest cat, circling her ankles. He gave her an appraising sniff as she stooped to pet him. "Aren't you just the cutest—ow!" Dos hissed and batted a paw at her, claws extended. Suzie drew her arm back, tiny droplets of fresh blood welling on her hand. Dos rocketed across the floor in a streak of fur and disappeared into my bedroom.

"I'm so sorry!" I wet a paper towel and rushed forward to help Suzie clean her wound. "That's so weird—Dos is my friendliest cat. He's usually a total sweetheart." I cringed as the blood continued to flow from her hand. "He's never done that before. Here." I handed Suzie the paper towel so she could apply pressure to the wound and then turned in the direction of my bathroom. "I'll get you a Band-Aid."

I returned a few moments later to find Suzie seated at my kitchen table, still holding the paper towel against the scratch. "Thank you," she said when I gave her the bandage and some disinfectant.

The adrenaline spike from witnessing Dos's surprise attack ebbed, and I felt suddenly drained. My head throbbed its demand for my next dose of medicine. "I should probably take my meds," I said out loud, more to myself than to Suzie. Though I wanted to be alert when Emmett arrived, maybe the painkiller would also help dull the heartache.

Suzie saw the exhaustion in my face. "Why don't you go sit down and watch TV?" she suggested. "I'm supposed to be taking care of you, remember? Not the other way around." She smiled. "I'll bring your pills to you."

I dropped wearily onto the couch, a feeling of dread swelling in my chest. I needed a distraction to take my mind off of Emmett's betrayal—and my own. My gaze settled on my coffee table where my laptop lay open. I hadn't gotten the chance to research Jessica Whitley earlier—maybe I could look her up really quickly and send my findings over to Detective Dixon before Emmett arrived.

"Where are your pills?" Suzie called from the kitchen.

"They're in my purse. I can wash them down with the Diet Coke Kat brought from Camila's."

"Got it. I'll add some fresh ice—most of the cubes are probably melted by now."

I pulled the computer onto my lap and typed Jessica Whitley's name into Google. I scrolled past results for several Facebook and LinkedIn profiles matching the name, but the fifth entry on the page was the one that caught my attention. The link was for an article posted four weeks ago on the *L.A. Times* website. The headline read: *Local Girl Perishes in Automobile Fire.* I clicked the link and waited for the article to load.

The image above the story showed a badly burned sedan, nose down at the bottom of a small ravine. I grimaced. The car's frame was twisted and scorched, making it impossible to even identify the vehicle's make and model. Scrolling past the grizzly photo, I began to read the article.

A UCLA student was killed Sunday when her car veered down a steep ravine on a Southern California mountain road. According to a source at the Azusa Police Department, a call came in around 3:30 a.m., reporting the sighting of a vehicle fire off the edge of Highway 39. The car, belonging to twenty-three-year-old Jessica Ann Whitley, is said to have careened down the ravine, landing on its roof about 40 feet down. The vehicle was towed early Sunday morning, and Miss Whitley's body was found among the wreckage. The cause of the crash is unknown at this time.

I skimmed the rest of the article, but nothing jumped out at me—until I reached the bottom of the page. There was a photo of Jessica Whitley at the end of the article. I gaped at the girl smiling at the camera, feeling the air leave my lungs. The young woman had long, chestnut hair and a slightly rounder face, but the brown, almond-shaped eyes were the same. *If she dyed her hair black and thinned out her cheeks, she'd look just like...*

"Here's your drink," the girl pretending to be Suzie Omara said close to my ear, causing me to nearly jump out of my skin. I snapped the laptop shut and shoved it back onto the coffee table.

Suzie sat beside me on the couch, my cup of Diet Coke in her outstretched hand. The empty prescription bottle of hydrocodone was in her other hand, dangling upside-down with the top off. "It won't hurt," she said, the eerie calmness in her voice chilling me down to my core. "But I'm afraid it'll kill more than just your pain." Her pretty features were stretched wide in an unnerving smile, the scar on her cheek suddenly taking on a sinister quality.

"I'm not thirsty," I said, leaning away from her. My gaze flicked to my purse on the dining room table, about fifteen feet away. I had a good forty pounds on Suzie—I mean Jessica—but in my weakened state, she could easily take me in a fight. If I could just reach my purse and grab my phone, I could call for help. Or maybe Emmett would arrive in time to save me. I glanced toward the clock on the living room wall and saw that it was nearly three. He should be here any minute. *Unless he was never coming at all.* The realization struck me dumb. Jessica must have used the Spoofer app to disguise her number as Emmett's. That's why she volunteered to drive me back to the apartment—so she could get me alone and finish what she started last night in the parking lot.

Jessica followed my gaze to the clock. "In case you haven't figured it out by now, your lover boy didn't really text you." She stretched her arm farther, pushing the Diet Coke cup under my nose. "You need to hurry up and drink this," she said, her tone impatient. "I need the pills to take you before Bronwyn gets here."

"I'm not going to drink that," I said, a slight tremble in my voice.

Jessica smiled, showing her teeth. "Oh, I think you will." She reached into the pocket of her pink tunic. Fear spiked through me as she withdrew Mickey's pocketknife, the rust-colored stains of Sid's dried blood still on its blade. "Either you drink this, or I start stabbing."

My whole body quivered, and my mind slipped back to the last time I'd been stabbed. I remembered the searing pain of the knife biting into my flesh with agonizing clarity. I reluctantly took the cup from Jessica's hand. *You've got to fight!* screamed a voice in my head. *But how?*

A desperate idea struck me. Jessica leaned forward, gripping the knife firmly with the blade pointed toward my gut. I slowly lifted the Diet Coke to my lips. At the last second, I tipped the cup away from my mouth and flung it in Jessica's face.

The small woman gave a startled squeal as the sticky drink splashed in her eyes. She lunged forward with the knife. I dived off of the couch just in time. The blade missed me by mere inches and tore through the cushion where my chest had been. I lay on the floor in a state of fear-induced paralysis. My legs just wouldn't cooperate. Jessica mopped the soda from her face with the front of her tunic and glared down at me, gnashing her teeth. "You bitch!" she cried. She gripped the handle of Mickey's pocketknife and yanked it out of the couch cushion, tearing the hole in the fabric even wider. Seeing the sharp blade again galvanized me. I scrambled to my feet as Jessica leaped from the couch.

I was too far away from the dining room table now—she'd turn me into Ame-kabobs before I reached my phone. Instead I skittered through my bedroom and into the bathroom, locking myself in. Less than two seconds later, Jessica rammed the door with surprising force. It shuddered on its hinges, and I skittered away from it, nearly tripping backwards into the bathtub. My quick movement was greeted with a hissing sound. I whirled around to find Uno and Tres curled up in the tub, something they normally only did during lightning storms. My furry pals must have sensed something was wrong the moment Jessica and I had stepped through the apartment door. *No wonder Dos was so freaked out,* I thought. My blood ran cold in my veins as I looked back and forth from the tub to the door. Only two of my three kitties were safe in here with me. Dos was still out there with that slightly crazier version of Yoko Ono.

An angry yowl sounded on the other side of the door, seizing my heart in a vice. She'd found him. "Amelia, I hope you like Chinese food," Jessica called through the door. "Because if you don't open that door in the next ten seconds, I'm turning this little jerk into sesame seed kitten." Dos gave another yelp, and a surge of anger crashed through me like a tidal wave. It was one thing to mess with me—but you did *not* mess with a poor, defenseless animal.

"I'm coming out," I said. "Don't hurt him." I swiveled my head from side to side, looking for something I could use as a weapon. I was fairly sure she'd have sliced and diced me long before I managed to nick her to death with my dull razor. Jessica began to count slowly to ten, and I grabbed the closest thing I could reach: it looked like I'd be bringing a toilet plunger to a knife fight. I suppose there's a first time for everything.

"Okay, here I come," I said, unlocking the door and slowly turning the handle.

I pushed the door open and peered through the threshold. My bedroom appeared dark and empty, with no sign of Jessica or her feline hostage. As silently as I could, I grabbed the spare roll of toilet paper off the rack and tossed it through the doorway at eye level. Jessica leaped out of the shadows, her expression murderous. She buried the blade in the bundle of white tissue, not registering right away that it was only a decoy and not my pasty white face. I was relieved to see Dos blur by, seemingly unharmed as he darted under the bed to hide.

Jessica toppled to the ground with the toilet paper roll. She sat up quickly, her brows knit in confusion. Understanding dawned a moment too late, and her jaw went slack just as I sprinted forward, ramming the plunger suction-side first into her face. I'm not sure what I was expecting, really; maybe that I would let go of the plunger and it would stick to her like something out of a cartoon. Unfortunately, real life isn't nearly as hilarious.

Jessica knocked the plunger out of my grasp and reached for the knife again. "Why couldn't you just leave it alone?" she shrieked, hopefully loud enough that my neighbors could hear. With nowhere to go, I retreated toward the bathroom, Jessica blocking my only route of escape. She had me cornered, and the blade trembled in her hand. "If you had just minded your own damn business, I wouldn't have to do this." She almost sounded sorry. "Jack and I could've been happy. He'd have gone his whole life believing I was his precious Suzie."

"He would've figured it out eventually. We all would have." The words didn't come from me. Jessica whirled toward the newcomer's voice just as Mickey wrenched her arms behind her back. The knife slipped from her grasp and landed with a thud on my bedroom carpet. "I've been looking all over for that," Mickey said through clenched teeth.

"Suzie?" Another voice flitted through the open bedroom door. Jack stood in the threshold, pure anguish written on his face. "I don't understand," he said, his voice quavering.

With all eyes on Jack, Jessica sprang into action. She struggled in Mickey's grasp, twisting around to face him. Her knee came up fast and connected with his groin. Mickey grunted in pain as he doubled over on my bedroom floor.

"Mickey!" I screamed. I dashed toward the knife, but Jessica dove onto the carpet and beat me to it. I rolled away and backed toward Mickey before she could strike. Instead of lunging after me again, she took a menacing step toward Jack.

"I love you," she snarled, glaring at him. "Way more than that snotty bitch Suzie ever did. She was cheating on you with your own band mate!" Jessica took a ragged breath, her face straining. When she spoke again, her voice was soft. "Someone like her could never really deserve you, Jackie."

"You're lying," Jack said, his words dripping with emotion. "Suzie wouldn't betray me. She was my everything."

"And you're *my* everything," Jessica said. Her own voice was trembling. "I changed my whole life to be with you. My name, my hair, even my face." She lightly touched the scar on her cheek, and her expression twisted into something wicked. "But if I can't be with you, then nobody can." Jessica stalked toward Jack with the knife raised.

Jack stood motionless, his own face a mixture of pain, fear, and confusion. Why wasn't he stopping her? I scrambled to my feet, but Jessica was too far away. I wouldn't reach her in time.

A deafening explosion reverberated through my bedroom. I clapped my hands over my ears, my vision nearly doubling from the pain the noise set off in my injured head. Jessica halted in her tracks, her body jerking backward as if some invisible force had slammed into her chest. "Jackie?" she called weakly. She crumpled to the floor and didn't move again.

CHAPTER EIGHTEEN

———

There's no doubt in my mind that Detective Ben Dixon saved Jack Pearson's life that night. His quick thinking and accurate aim stopped Jessica Whitley dead in her tracks. Well, not *really* dead, though the pain from the beanbag round to her chest probably made her wish she was. When she'd been cuffed and read her rights, Jessica was taken to the hospital to make sure the impact hadn't cracked any of her ribs (though, after she threatened my sweet baby, Dos, I secretly hoped that it did). At the least, the hit shattered her nerves, and she gave the detective a full confession.

Like most teenage girls in the mid-2000's, Jessica was a huge fan of Royal Flush. Over the years, her appreciation for their music developed into an unhealthy obsession with Jack. After high school, she moved from Idaho to Los Angeles just to be closer to the band. When the disillusioned fan met the real Suzie Omara on campus at UCLA, she saw a morbid opportunity. Not only was Suzie engaged to the man of Jessica's dreams, but she was practically her twin. Convinced that she and Jack were really meant to be together, Jessica devised a plan to take over Suzie's life. She spent several months befriending Jack's unassuming fiancée and learning everything she could about their relationship. Over her last spring break, Jess blew the rest of her college fund from her grandparents on a trip to Germany where plastic surgery was cheap and discreet.

When Jessica returned stateside, she bought a bottle of Rohypnol from a drug-dealing friend and put her plan into action. She drugged Suzie and sent the poor woman crashing down a ravine to her death. When the police found Jessica's car, identification, and a badly burned body that matched her description, she was assumed dead. Free to take over Suzie's life, Jessica contacted Jack while Royal Flush was away on tour in Japan. She pretended to be a nurse at a local hospital, calling to inform Jack that his fiancée had been in a car accident and suffered head trauma, resulting in some memory loss. This helped Jessica account for things that *Suzie* couldn't remember when she assumed the dead woman's identity.

Jessica slipped easily into Suzie's life for the first week. Then Sid started making passes at her when Jack wasn't around. Unaware of Suzie's fling with the bass guitarist, she ignored his advances. Sid made one final pass at Jessica on the night she killed him. Angry that Jack and the guys hadn't backed him up in his fight with Dillon, Sid threatened to tell Jack all about their little tryst. That was when Jessica put two and two together and realized that the real Suzie had been cheating on Jack with the sleazeball bass player. She'd worked too hard to let Sid ruin her plans to marry Jack—especially over someone else's infidelity.

After Jack fell asleep that night, Jessica sneaked out of the hotel and asked Sid to meet her on the tour bus. She needed someone to take the fall and didn't have a lot of time. Jessica remembered recently seeing Mickey sharpening his pocketknife, and it gave her an idea. She'd been unable to part with her old cell phone since her voicemails and pictures were all she had left to remember her family. Jessica pulled the phone out of its hiding place and downloaded the number-spoofing app, which she used to lure Mickey onto the tour bus. She poured the two men a drink and dropped in the roofies. As soon as they were passed out, Jessica stabbed Sid and left Mickey behind, assuming the drugs would erase any memory he had of seeing her there. Unfortunately for Mickey, she'd been right.

Jessica may have been bitten by the lunacy bug, but crazy doesn't equal smart. Instead of leaving the knife on Mickey for the cops to find, she took it with her. In a panic, she ditched it in the bushes down the road from Castle Rock, along with the plastic cup she'd been sipping from when she tricked Sid and Mickey into drinking the drugged liquor. Jessica later realized that if the knife and cup were found, they'd have her prints all over them. She returned the next night to retrieve them, which was when she saw me leaving the same bushes where she'd hidden the evidence.

When Jessica realized that I was on her trail, she starting looking for ways to take me out of the picture. Her first opportunity came when she was in a bathroom stall at the strip club. She overheard Ginger talking to me and used the phone-spoofing app to trick me into going outside. Jessica set Ginger up to take the fall for my attack and even slipped her lipstick in the woman's purse earlier that evening. She'd hoped that putting the suspicion on the red-haired tour manager would buy some more time before the police turned their attention her way.

Jessica hadn't expected me to continue my search for the truth after she put me in the hospital. While they were at Camila's the next evening, Kat mentioned my discovery of the spoofed phone call. Jessica realized that I hadn't given up after all. She couldn't let me find out her true identity, so she decided she had no choice but to finish me off.

My friends were tipped off that something was wrong when Emmett called shortly after I left Castle Rock with *Suzie*. He'd apparently tried my cell and couldn't get through, so he rang my office phone, which Kat answered. Not only had he not sent a text message asking to meet me at my apartment—he was nowhere near Atlanta. Meanwhile, Bronwyn looked up Jessica Whitley and stumbled upon the same *L.A. Times* article that I had been reading. The girls called Detective Dixon to tell him they thought I was in danger, but Mickey insisted on coming to my rescue. Jack came with Mickey, unable to accept that the woman who'd driven me home really wasn't his fiancée. Luckily for me, they showed up in time to stop Jessica from carving me up like a Thanksgiving turkey.

Emmett caught the red eye from Vegas to Atlanta and called me as soon as he landed Thursday morning. Kat had insisted I stay at her house since I couldn't bear to return to my apartment after Jessica's attack. I gave Emmett Kat's address and slipped onto her front porch to wait for him, not wanting to wake my sleeping friends. He arrived a short time later, looking as tired as I felt, with dark circles under his eyes and his short, black hair sticking out at odd angles. He was dressed in green khakis and a camouflage T-shirt that was covered in a light dusting of dirt. Emmett halted mid-stride in Kat's driveway when he saw me, taking in my new bruises and cuts with a look of horror. "What happened?" he asked once he found his voice.

"That's what I want to know." I couldn't keep the edge from my tone. "Where have you been since Monday?" I held up a hand to stop him before he could launch into some fabricated explanation. "Don't tell me you've been on assignment," I warned. "I talked to Gavin yesterday, Emmett. I know you're not working with the Bureau anymore."

Emmett's back went rigid, and the color drained from his face. He stood stock-still for a few moments, his expression strained. Finally, he exhaled. "I knew we'd have to have this conversation sooner or later," he said with resignation. He glanced past me, up the steps to Kat's front door. "Mind if we go somewhere private?"

I narrowed my eyes at him. "I don't know if that's such a great idea," I said coolly. "I'm not sure I feel safe with you anymore."

My words must have stung him. Emmett's eyes grew misty. "I guess I deserve that," he said quietly. "But I need you to believe me. I never meant to hurt you. In fact, all I did was to try to protect you."

"If you wanted to protect me, you would've been here," I snapped, rising from Kat's front steps. Emmett reached out and laid a gentle hand on my arm, but I bristled at his touch. Ever since Jessica's attack, I'd wanted nothing more than to see Emmett, to have him fold his arms around me and tell me that everything between us was okay. Now that we were face to face, I couldn't fight the hurt and frustration welling inside me. "You told me you loved me." Words fell out of my mouth in short, angry bursts. "But you've been lying to me. For over a month." My face burned. "Why?"

Guilt crept across Emmett's face, and he hung his head. He sat down on the steps and patted the spot next to him. I grudgingly reclaimed my perch on the stairs and glared up at him. "I didn't want to worry you," Emmett began, fixing me with sad, green eyes. "I know you still have nightmares about Shawn Stone. I figured as long as you thought I was still on the case, you'd feel safe."

"Why *aren't* you on the case?" I asked, the anger slowly draining out of me.

"Ame, I didn't resign by choice." Shame was evident in his tone. "I was forced to—after Montana."

"What happened in Montana?" An uneasy feeling knotted in my chest. "You mentioned that the Bureau tracked Stone there, right?"

"We thought we did." He blew out a breath and ran a hand through his short, black hair. "I should start at the beginning, back when Gavin and I first came to Atlanta last fall." He wouldn't meet my gaze. "When I blew my cover to protect you, it got me in hot water with the Bureau."

"So this is my fault?"

"No, I didn't say that." Emmett held up a hand. "Gavin reported me—I don't blame him. He didn't really have a choice. Our operation fell apart, and Stone got away. Our superiors had questions. Gav was just doing his job. If the roles had been reversed…" He shrugged. "Anyway, that was my first strike. Then the sting in Montana happened, and everything fell to shit."

I looked down to see that Emmett's hands were trembling. "It's okay," I said softly, reaching out to steady him. "You can tell me."

Emmett grabbed my hand and squeezed tightly, as if he were afraid that if he let go, he'd be swept away. "I wanted to close this case so badly that I would've done anything." His jaw muscle flexed. "I let my emotions cloud my judgment. I made a huge mistake."

My throat felt dry. "What did you do?" I asked, though I was suddenly afraid to hear the answer.

Emmett turned and looked at me, his green eyes swimming. As I watched, a lone tear rolled down his cheek and splashed onto the porch steps. "I shot a civilian." Emmett seemed to cave in on himself. He slumped over, gripping me around the middle. I held him, gently stroking his hair as he cried in my lap. I felt oddly empty, as if someone had hollowed me out and set me on Kat's porch like a jack-o'-lantern. I'd spent all this time being suspicious and angry when Emmett was going through something soul-crushingly awful. The guilt had been eating at him for a month now. It was a wonder he'd kept it together for as long as he did.

"Our intel was no good," Emmett said when he could finally speak again. He sat up and wiped his eyes with the heels of his hands. "Stone was never in Montana. It was just some eccentric old hermit living in a cabin out in the woods. He looked so much like Shawn that I couldn't tell the difference." Emmett swallowed, averting his eyes. "Maybe I wanted it to be him so badly that I couldn't see anyone else." His voice grew thick with tears again. "Maybe I'm crazy."

"You're not crazy." I reached for his hand, but he drew it away. "What happened to the man you shot?" I asked, hearing my own voice quake. "Did he…?" My words caught in my throat.

"No. He's alive." Emmett replied, and relief washed through me in a cool wave. "But I put him in the hospital. An innocent man." He sighed. "I had to go before the board for a disciplinary hearing. They gave me a choice: resign or be fired. You know the rest."

"Oh, Emmett." I slid my arms around him again, wishing there was something I could do or say to take away some of his pain. "Why didn't you tell me before? You could've come down to Atlanta when it happened. You could have stayed with me."

"I was too ashamed," he admitted. "I've spent the last month trying to track down Stone on my own."

I stiffened. "Em, that's dangerous. Without the FBI and their resources, things could go horribly wrong."

"Things can't get any worse than they already are," he replied. "And as long as he's still out there, I can't guarantee your safety." His jaw tightened. "Another reason why I wish you'd agree to join Witness Protection."

"We're not having this argument again," I said, trying not to sound irritated. "I already told you that I'm not giving up my life and my friends to go into hiding. If I do, then Shawn wins, whether he finds me or not. Plus his mob family disowned him when the whole scandal hit the newsstands last year. The only threat to my safety is Shawn himself, and he has yet to show his face in Atlanta again."

"Well, you know how I feel about it," Emmett grumbled. "I think it's stupid not to take every possible precaution. Stone is dangerous."

I narrowed my eyes at him. "Did you just call me stupid?"

Emmett's jaw went slack. "What? No—that's not what I meant." He pushed out a breath. "I just think you're being irrational, putting yourself through unnecessary risk. You're a sitting duck down here, Ame."

"If I leave the city, it's going to be on my own terms," I said, feeling my face grow hot. "Not because of anything you or some washed up mobster dictates."

"Fine." Emmett stood up, his mouth set in a firm line. "Be stubborn." He took a few steps toward his rented red Corolla.

"Where are you going?" I started down the stairs. I caught up to Emmett and grabbed his arm. "You just got here."

"I'm sorry." The anger drained out of Emmett's voice. He turned back to face me, a pained look on his face. "I'm screwed up right now, all right? I need to get my life sorted out."

"So, what are you saying?" My voice was small. I swallowed hard. "You flew all this way just to…what? Break up with me?"

"I didn't plan any of this." Emmett gently gripped my shoulders, leaning down so that our heads were touching. "As long as Stone is still out there, we're both always going to be on edge. I care too much about you to keep fighting with you all the time. Good-bye, Amelia. I love you." He pressed his lips to my forehead and turned away.

I watched, stunned, as Emmett climbed into the red Corolla and drove off. He never looked back. "I love you, too," I whispered to his disappearing taillights. Then I returned to the porch steps, held my head in my hands, and had a nice, long cry.

* * *

"You wanna talk about it?" Kat asked me later that afternoon. She and the guys had woken up by the time I came back inside the house, my eyes swollen and my face streaked with tears. Being the amazing friend that she is, Kat diverted everyone's attention with an offering of fresh cinnamon rolls and coffee. Then she'd waited until we were alone in my office to ask for the lowdown on the reality show drama that is my life. She listened attentively as I filled her in on my conversation with Emmett and his hasty exit. "Didn't see that coming," she murmured. "I kind of expected you to be the one to end things."

I lay my head down on my desk. "I really do care about him," I said miserably. "I just don't understand. He's been through some really hard stuff in the past month. I could've been there for him if he'd only told me."

"Give the guy a break," Kat said, though her voice was gentle. "Like he said, he's screwed up right now. He didn't want to drag you down with him because he loves you."

"He wants me to leave town." My face pinched. "He brought up the whole Witness Protection thing again." I swallowed. "Maybe he's right, Kat."

She furrowed her brow. "Do you really wanna end up working on some farm in Iowa with a name like Ellie Sue? Or as Alexandra the Accountant in Poughkeepsie?" Her frown deepened. "I might never see you again."

I chuckled. "Come on—that'll never happen. You're stuck with me, kid." My smile faded. "What I meant was maybe I really should consider getting away, at least for a little while. After last night, I don't even feel safe in my own apartment. There are just too many bad memories around here lately."

"You're preaching to the choir, sister."

"Oh, man. I'm sorry." Guilt colored my cheeks. "I shouldn't be saying stuff like this to you, after everything that happened to you last year—"

"Hush," Kat said, holding up a hand. "What kind of BFF am I if you can't tell me how you really feel?" She unfolded her legs and rose from my office couch. "I totally understand, and I think getting out of town for a while would do you some good. But what's best for you isn't always best for me, ya know? I mean, yeah, a vacation sounds nice. I just couldn't bring myself to leave Castle Rock long-term. This place is all that's left of Parker. Even with Chad back in my life, I'm always going to hold on to that." Kat crossed the room, headed for the door.

"You've got to do what's right for you, Amelia," she said, pausing in the threshold to give me a meaningful look. "If you need a place to stay, my home is always open. But if you do need to get away for a bit, your job at Castle Rock will be waiting for you when you come back. Just remember that."

I smiled. "I will. Thanks, girl."

"Love you, chick," she replied with a little wink. Kat turned back toward the threshold and almost bumped into Mickey on his way into my office. "Whoops, sorry!" she said, scooting passed him.

"Hey," Mickey said softly as he closed the door behind him. He grabbed the chair in front of my desk and flipped it backwards, straddling it with his legs and draping his arms over the back. "How are you feeling?"

"Like I wish people would stop asking me how I'm feeling," I answered in a sarcastic tone. "I'm fine, really." I pointed to my head. "Doesn't hurt right now, even without the painkillers."

"Good." Mickey gave me his signature boyish grin. His smile faltered a little as another emotion passed behind his eyes, something I couldn't quite identify. "Listen," he said, dropping his voice low. "I didn't mean to eavesdrop, but I heard you talking to Kat about leaving town."

"Oh, it was nothing." I gave a dismissive wave. "I was just telling her that maybe it would do me some good to get away from Atlanta for a few days, maybe a week. I just need to recharge."

"What about two months?" He looked at me, his expression serious.

I squinted at him. "What are you getting at?"

"Ginger quit this morning." Mickey's lips quirked. "She said we weren't paying her enough for what we put her through. Apparently getting thrown in jail and accused of murder and assault wasn't in her job description." He shrugged. "To be honest, she's been a bit high-strung for a while now. I think the tour was too much for her. Some people just aren't cut out for life on the road."

I blinked at him. "And you think *I* am? Mickey, we had this same conversation five years ago, and it only ended in heartache for both of us."

"But you said yourself just the other day that you've always wondered where we would be if you *had* gone to L.A. with me," he said. Mickey leaned so far forward that the chair was practically tipping over. "Look, our bags are all packed, and Dillon's on board to join the tour. We're flying to Orlando this afternoon for tomorrow night's show, but we'll be back on Saturday when the tour bus is ready to be picked up from the crime lab." He flinched, dropping his gaze to my desk. "They're, er, stripping the carpeting and cleaning up the mess…Detective Dixon promised it would be like a whole new bus. No trace of…what happened." Mickey swallowed hard then looked back up at me. "Just take a few days and consider it, okay? You have until Saturday morning."

He rose from the chair and reached for something in his back pocket. Mickey laid it down on my desk: a black lanyard with a laminated badge attached. Royal Flush's burning card logo was on one side; the other had the word *STAFF* printed across it in all capital letters. "Think about it," he said, walking around my desk to lean down and plant a kiss on my cheek. Then he walked out of my office.

I watched him go, a feeling of longing tugging at my heart. Not longing for Mickey—I was still reeling from my breakup with Emmett, and despite the chemistry I still shared with my once almost- fiancé, I wasn't ready to jump into another relationship. But I was ready for a change. The question was, would I find what I was looking for out on the road with Royal Flush?

* * *

"Flight Seven-Thirty-Five from Orlando to Atlanta is on time," Kat read off the monitor in the baggage claim area. It was nearly noon on Saturday, and we were waiting for the members of Royal Flush to arrive at Hartsfield-Jackson Airport. The tour bus had been gassed up and dropped off at Castle Rock earlier that morning. The cleanup crew did an excellent job—there wasn't a speck of blood on the new carpet or furniture. It was almost as if they'd brought over a brand new bus.

My suitcase was already on board.

"Are you sure you're ready for this?" Kat asked, slipping her arm around my waist and giving me a half-hug. "I'm going to miss the hell outta you, ya know. I don't think we've been apart for two whole months, like, ever." She blinked back tears.

"Hey, don't get all mushy on me. Bronwyn already hit me with the waterworks this morning, which was kind of disturbing. Although, I'm pretty sure hers were happy tears since I'd just handed her a key to my apartment." Bronwyn was staying at my place and cat-sitting while I was away, which got her out of her parents' house for the two months before her dorm reopened at Georgia State. I had also asked her to fill in as Castle Rock's official booking agent for the rest of the summer, and Kat had given her a hefty bonus for taking the job.

"The tour will be over before you know it," I continued. "Plus you already have tickets to two Royal Flush shows in Asheville and Charleston. Not to mention the VIP passes to come hang with us backstage at the Jamisphere Festival in Tennessee next month. You'll be seeing plenty of me and your lover boy."

"Don't call Chad that," she said, scrunching up her nose. Kat's lips quirked in a scandalous grin. "I call him—"

"I don't wanna know your sexy nicknames for each other. That's TMI territory." I backed away from her, holding my arms out with my index fingers forming a cross. My smile faded. "I'm gonna miss you too."

"Here come the guys." Kat pointed, and I turned in time to see Chad and Zane striding toward us through the crowd. Jack wasn't far behind them, though it was hard to spot him through the cloud of college-aged girls that engulfed him. I hoped the attention eased his heartache at least a little bit. Dillon followed after Jack, and Mickey brought up the rear.

I suppressed the feeling of excitement at the sight of Mickey, reminding myself that I wasn't in the market for another boyfriend right now. His honey-brown eyes glowed as he spotted me too, and he quickened his pace. As he drew closer, Mickey searched my face, no doubt trying to read my decision in my expression. I took a deep breath and then reached underneath the collar of my T-shirt. I pulled out the Royal Flush *STAFF* lanyard that I wore around my neck and waved it at him.

Mickey's smile was radiant as he rushed forward to scoop me in his arms for hug. It was going to be hard not to fall in love with that smile again over the next two months, but I was up for the challenge. There was no turning back now. No matter what happened, it was going to be an interesting summer.

ABOUT THE AUTHOR

Anne Marie used to work in radio, and it rocked! After studying Music Business at the University of Georgia, Anne Marie worked for several music venues, radio stations, and large festivals before trading in her backstage pass for a pen and paper. (Okay, so she might have kept the pass…) Her debut novel, *Murder at Castle Rock*, was the winner of the 2012 AJC Decatur Book Festival & BookLogix Publishing Services, Inc. Writing Contest, and the 2013 Book Junkie's Choice Award Winner for Best Debut Fiction Novel. It was also a finalist for Best Mystery/Thriller in the 2014 RONE Awards.

Aside from all things music and books, Anne Marie loves college football, Starbucks iced coffee, red wine, and anything pumpkin-flavored. She is a member of Sisters in Crime and the Sisters in Crime Guppies chapter.

To learn more about Anne Marie Stoddard, visit her online at www.amstoddardbooks.com

Enjoyed this book? Check out these other novels
available in print now from Gemma Halliday Publishing:

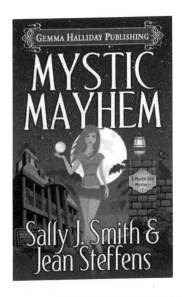

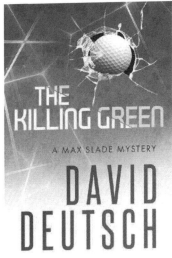

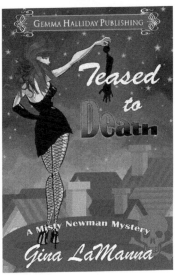

www.GemmaHallidayPublishing.com

Printed in Great Britain
by Amazon